rawhead
in love

Also by David Bowker

The Death Prayer

The Secret Sexist

The Butcher of Glastonbury

From Stockport with Love

Rawhead

rawhead
in love
DAVID BOWKER

MACMILLAN

First published 2004 by Macmillan
an imprint of Pan Macmillan Ltd
Pan Macmillan, 20 New Wharf Road, London N1 9RR
Basingstoke and Oxford
Associated companies throughout the world
www.panmacmillan.com

ISBN 1 4050 3291 X

1 3 5 7 9 8 6 4 2

A CIP catalogue record for this book is available from
the British Library.

Typeset by SetSystems Ltd, Saffron Walden, Essex
Printed and bound in Great Britain by
Mackays of Chatham plc, Chatham, Kent

For Rod Mackintosh

1

'O, where have you been, my long, long love,
This long seven years and more?'
'O, I've come to seek my former vows
Ye granted me before.'

'The Daemon Lover', Anon.

On the eve of his wedding, Billy Dye received a warning from a dead man. It was a message scrawled in blood.

Billy recognized the writing.

He recognized the blood.

When Billy came down to breakfast, the card was waiting for him, propped up against the toast rack. It was early. The hotel restaurant was half empty. There was a package beside the card, which Billy opened first. The package contained two advance copies of the US version of *Dances with Werewolves* by William Dye. The book's jacket, which Billy had never seen before, showed a wolf's green eye with a miniature Fred and Ginger reflected in its centre.

Billy smiled at the book and the legend on the back: 'his American debut'. This was a lie. His first novel, *Unholier Than Thou*, had been published by a tiny Boston company six years before, when it had sold precisely five copies.

Billy turned his attention to the card. He took his time, studying the envelope to see if he could guess who it was from. The address was neatly typed: William Dye, The Bridal Suite, The Skene Castle Hotel, Argyllshire, Scotland. There was a

Manchester postmark. The card within was home-made, its corners trimmed with lace in the Victorian style. On the cover, a heart-shaped window looked onto a fetching little collage of snakes, skulls and tombstones.

Billy was the first member of his party to surface, so no one saw the look on his face when he opened the card and looked inside. The effect that the message within had on Billy was remarkable. He turned lime pale and held his hand to his mouth, as if to stifle a curse or a flood of vomit. Then he picked up the card, ignoring the waitress who had arrived to take his order, and strode out of the restaurant.

At the foot of the stairs he almost collided with his bride-to-be and their young daughter. They were coming out of the lift, but Nikki was carrying the baby in her left arm while her right hand forced back the heavy old-fashioned lift gate and she failed to notice him.

When Billy reached their room, he was trembling. He studied the card again, not wishing to believe what he'd seen the first time.

I Shall Be With You On Your Wedding Night.

The message was a quotation from *Frankenstein* by Mary Shelley. In the novel, Frankenstein starts to construct a female companion for his monster, then decides against it. The monster retaliates by murdering Frankenstein's wife after the ceremony.

Frankenstein was one of Billy's favourite novels. It was also loved by Rawhead.

From anyone else such a promise would be meaningless. But Rawhead tended to carry out his threats. Wherever he walked, he brought death and destruction. He was the most frightening man alive. Billy had tried to kill him. It was now apparent that he had failed. The monster had returned.

It was alive, alive.

And it wanted blood.

Billy was shaking.

He walked over to the minibar, a tiny fridge stocked as usual with overpriced miniatures and second-rate soft drinks in slim cans. Without thinking, he emptied a bottle of gin into a glass and gulped it down.

Then he walked to his sock drawer and took out the gun that was hidden there. It was a Smith & Wesson 360 PD. A short-range firearm, but that didn't matter. Billy was a short-range marksman. He had purchased the gun months ago from a lunatic in a pub. At home, he liked to stand before the mirror, aiming the gun at his reflection. *So. You think you're a match for the big boys?*

There was a time when Billy had despised guns. But now he sympathized with Chuck Heston, who thought that every decent, law-abiding citizen should have a gun to deter mother-fuckers. Particularly those motherfuckers who wanted to raise their children in a safe, non-violent world. (How dare they?)

If the police had caught Billy in possession of the Smith & Wesson, he would probably have faced a prison sentence. Billy didn't care for the police. As far as he was concerned, the police were the root cause of all criminal activity. When Rawhead came looking for him, where would the police be? Swapping porn, dealing drugs, getting pissed, arresting penniless old ladies for stealing tins of beans.

Carefully, Billy set fire to the card, carried it into the bathroom and dropped it into the washbasin. When it was charcoal, he broke it into pieces, turned on the tap and flushed the black mess away.

*

Billy put on his overcoat and slipped the gun into his right-hand pocket. He left the room, smiling at a pretty chambermaid on his way out. Underneath the tall Christmas tree in the hotel lobby lay a mound of parcels in tartan wrapping paper. Billy walked past the tree, nodded to the stony-faced receptionist (*You don't have to be charmless to work here but it helps*) and stepped out into the freezing Highland air. Outside the hotel – formerly a fake castle built by an English factory owner – he crossed the car park and took the steps down to the beach.

It was a cold, dark morning. The North Sea bucked and crashed.

Great white rollers exploded on the rocks and their spray was borne outwards and upwards on the wind.

Billy was inadequately dressed, but he was too upset to feel the cold. He glanced back at the hotel on the cliff with its four symmetrical towers and conical turrets. The light burned in his room, high in the left-hand tower. Behind him, the trail of his footprints was the only blemish on the soft brown sand.

Billy couldn't stop thinking of Rawhead and the fear he brought with him.

The bright eyes staring.

The fragrance of the pit.

There was no one on the shore, not even the customary twat with a dangerous dog. As Billy walked, the sea hissed and begged at his feet.

Billy was afraid for his family. He was afraid for his child. But mostly, crucially, he was afraid to lose the only period of real happiness he had known. Since he and Nikki had been reunited, all the doors that had once been closed to Billy had mysteriously opened.

He had written a TV series called *Gangchester*, which was about to go into production. An American film studio had optioned *Unholier Than Thou* for a generous sum. George Leica was on board to direct.

Strangest of all, Billy's bank manager had written him a

personal letter, hinting that if he wished to take out a loan, the bank would guarantee him a very generous rate of interest – a kindness that was never offered when Billy actually needed it.

The British press, having heard about the Hollywood dollars, was suddenly eager to interview Billy. Nothing excites British journalists more than American money. Magazine editors who had once despised Billy for being so cynical and nasty now wanted him to write nasty, cynical little articles for large fees on subjects he knew nothing about.

Billy was invited onto a TV arts programme, where he talked shit with three other shitheads. When he and Nikki were in London for the recording, Billy phoned the Ivy restaurant and actually managed to secure a table for that very evening. This was a miracle in itself. But what astonished Billy more was that the woman who took his booking had actually *heard* of him.

The only thing that wasn't perfect was his relationship with Nikki. That was why he had asked her to marry him. He wanted it to be a new beginning.

And now, out of the blue – or, rather, the howling void – Rawhead, the demon of desolation, had re-entered his life.

Billy tapped his pockets and located his menthol cigarettes. Apart from the odd spliff, he hadn't smoked since his teens. But yesterday, feeling the urge to commune with his boyhood self, he had bought a packet of menthol cigarettes and a box of matches. He opened the packet and, like his boyhood self lit six matches before he succeeded in igniting the cigarette.

The tobacco was unimpressive. There was no Proustian rush, just a weary sensation of bad luck returning. Billy's guts clenched in protest, wondering why they were being offered minty fumes instead of tea and toast. He exhaled a cloud of blue smoke and the sea wind blew it back in his face.

Unlike Billy, Rawhead was fast and strong. He'd wish you good morning then lunge like a barracuda. A man who would attack without fear or restraint. Before you knew it, you were bleeding. Then you were pleading. Then you were dead. Instinctively, Billy clutched at his heart to ensure it hadn't happened already.

He couldn't go to the police. By the time the investigating officer had peddled round on his bicycle, Billy, his family, the wedding guests would be dead, their hotel burned to the ground.

He couldn't even tell Nikki. She had a tendency toward depression, so Billy had shielded her from the truth of his recent past. She knew that Steve Ellis, Billy's boyhood friend, had been sent to a juvenile offender's institution. She was not aware that Steve had reappeared in Billy's life as a fully grown murderer called Rawhead.

Remembering Nikki and their daughter Maddy, knowing they needed his protection, Billy turned and started walking back to the hotel. It was what Charlton Heston would have wanted.

The long beach stretched for miles. Sheer, crumbling cliffs leered down at him. He turned slowly, treading parallel with his own winding footprints. He coughed, spat and flung his half-finished cigarette into the foam, wondering how smoking could ever have caught on.

The wind hurled a gull off the cliff and it spiralled above his head, out of control and shrieking, not finding its wings until it was out over the sea. Billy watched it for a while, then glanced back.

A solitary figure stood on the shore far behind him.

At this distance it was impossible to see whether it was a man or a woman, or whether the stranger was standing still or approaching. But something about the shape of the figure made Billy uneasy.

He turned back and carried on walking.

Billy knew what he must do. There could be no wedding. They had to leave now, immediately. Nikki wouldn't like it, but nor would she enjoy seeing her friends and family butchered. Any minor considerations such as losing money, disappointing guests and alienating friends and family forever would have to be put aside. The only important consideration was to keep his family safe. They had to keep moving. A long trip abroad seemed like a very good idea.

Again he looked back. The figure on the sand appeared no closer than before. Yet Billy sensed it had stopped moving at the very moment he had turned, like a child playing a game of statues.

The light was changing for the worse. Grey clouds were drifting inland, drawing a curtain of darkness over the water.

Billy stole another backward glance. The stranger had gained on him. It now looked like a tall man, in a long, dark, flowing coat. So what? He told himself. Lots of people wear long coats. *Like who?* Billy could only think of one man. He caressed the gun in his pocket and quickened his step. The only thing that prevented him from fleeing for his life was a very English fear of looking foolish.

The towers of the Skene Castle Hotel appeared over the rim of the cliffs. Above them, the clouds raced darkly. Almost safe. Billy looked over his shoulder. His pursuer was even closer now, a mere twenty paces away. Billy stopped and stared. It was him. Unmistakably. There were the lean face, the dark eyes, the long stride and straight back that he remembered so clearly.

Rawhead.

With one hand on the gun in his pocket, Billy started running. So did Rawhead.

Salt spray blew into Billy's face as he lunged forward, feet sliding in the sand. When he realized that it was hopeless, that Rawhead would always be stronger and faster, Billy stopped and pulled the gun. But before he could turn and take aim, Rawhead barged into him, knocking him off his feet. The gun skidded across the beach. The two men scrambled on the ground, kicking up sand.

Before Billy had time to retaliate, Rawhead gripped his shoulders and spun him round. Now he was flat on his back with Rawhead sitting on his chest. It was an exact replay of the way their first ever fight had ended, back at Manchester Grammar School two decades before. 'Are you ready for eternity?' said Rawhead.

'By Calvin Klein?'

Rawhead laughed and got to his feet.

Billy just lay there, staring, chest heaving.

Rawhead picked up the Smith & Wesson and opened the cylinder. 'Nice piece. Pity it isn't loaded.'

'What? The guy who sold it me swore it was loaded.'

Rawhead laughed. 'You mean you didn't look?'

Billy looked sheepish. 'I didn't know how to work it.'

Billy remained horizontal, looking up at Rawhead.

'What're you doing down there?' said Rawhead.

'If you're going to kill me,' said Billy, 'you might as well do it while I'm lying down. Saves me the trouble of falling over.'

'Kill you? Why would I want to do that?'

'Because you're a murderer?'

'I wouldn't kill you.'

Unconvinced, Billy stood up and brushed the sand off his clothes.

Rawhead looked fit and tanned, as if he'd just returned from holiday. His eyes shone with that strange light that Billy associated with junkies and visionaries. His head was shaved – the only evidence of hair was a dark shadow covering his scalp. And everything about him, from the jutting bones of his face to his brutal, neatly polished shoes, promised broken teeth and bereavement.

'Sorry I haven't been in touch, Bill. Dead bodies kept getting in the way.'

Billy stood and stared, wondering if he was being mocked.

Rawhead turned away, staring far out to sea. 'I suppose you went back to writing books?'

Billy nodded. His heart was throwing itself against his ribcage like a deranged prisoner. He was afraid to speak in case his heart came bursting out through his open mouth.

Rawhead picked up a pebble and skimmed it over the waves. It bounced four times before sinking. 'Tell me something. If you're still an author, how come you can afford to get married here?'

'I had a bit of luck,' said Billy. His voice, strangled by nerves, came out sounding thick and slurred. 'A movie director wants to film one of my books.'

Rawhead skimmed another stone. 'Which one?'

'George Leica. He made *Feeding Frenzy*.'

Rawhead turned his head slowly to give Billy a faint, sardonic smile. 'I meant which book.'

'The first,' answered Billy.

'That's my favourite.' Rawhead spat on the sand. 'This director, is he American?'

'As American as the electric chair.'

'They must be true, then. These rumours I hear about you.'

'What rumours?' said Billy. His mouth was so dry that he could barely swallow.

'That you've given up on horror. That you've turned into a whore. '

Billy coughed in an attempt to mask his fear, but only succeeded in looking like a scared man with a cough. 'The bit about being a whore is true,' he said. 'But I haven't given up on horror.'

'I hope not. Because that'd be like betraying your soul. Graveyards, monsters and death. That's our world. That's what you should be writing about.'

'Listen. I've been fuck-poor, so poor that I only had fifty pence left in the world and didn't know whether to buy a tin of beans or a loaf of bread. Because if I bought the bread, I couldn't have any butter on it. And if I bought the beans, there'd be no fucking toast with it. What's fucking more, I will not be lectured on whoring by a man who kills people for money.'

'It was never the money, my friend. Thought you understood that.'

'I understand more than you might think.'

Rawhead scratched his nose and saw Billy flinch. 'Is something wrong?'

'No.'

'Only you don't seem very pleased to see me. You're sweating and you've gone a strange colour. '

Billy said nothing.

'I've been taking life a little easier.' Rawhead held out his left arm. The back of his hand was a shiny pink mound of scar tissue. 'I had a close encounter with the dark angel, Billy. Almost got burned alive. Remember my caravan? I must have left a spliff burning, because I went to sleep and when I woke my bed was on fire.' He made a noise between a snort and a grunt. 'Would have been ironic, wouldn't it? Half the hard men in Manchester fail to take me out, but a fag-end shows me no mercy.'

Billy kept staring, unable to believe his luck. Was it possible that Rawhead didn't realize Billy had started the fire? Either that or he was the most stunning actor Billy had ever seen.

'Of course, you knew nothing about it. You'd already fucked

off by then. Run back to that precious life you seemed to like so much. Knew you would. Always knew you'd be off, first chance you got.'

Billy pretended to look abashed. Rawhead put his arm around Billy's shoulder. 'I do understand, you know. You'd never make the grade as a criminal. You talk too much.'

Rawhead glanced at Billy's right hand. 'Where's your ring?'

When the boys were teenagers, they'd both bought tacky skull rings as a symbol of their friendship. Billy had thrown his ring away shortly after discovering Rawhead was a mass murderer. Now, with Rawhead's eyes upon him, Billy shrugged.

Rawhead reached into his pocket and withdrew a small box, lined with black velvet. He passed it to Billy. 'Here.'

'What's this?'

'Call it a wedding present.'

'Wedding presents are supposed to be for the bride as well as the groom.'

'Why would I buy a present for your wife? I don't even know her.'

Billy opened the box. It was a brand new ring, an exact replica of the cheap original. 'Twenty-four-carat gold. See the eyes? Rubies.'

'I don't know what to say,' said Billy.

'Don't say anything,' said Rawhead. 'Just try it on.'

Billy slipped the gift onto his ring finger where it glittered coldly. Rawhead held out his right hand, which bore an identical ring. 'It's a sign of the vows we've taken, Billy.'

'What vows?'

'The vows we swore when we mingled blood. Don't tell me you've forgotten?'

Billy shook his head gloomily.

Rawhead glared at him coldly, then smiled as he handed back the Smith & Wesson. There was studied contempt in the gesture, as if Rawhead doubted Billy's ability to pull the trigger, let alone hit anything.

'Where are you staying?' said Billy, trying to sound casual.

Rawhead yawned and stretched. 'Nearby.'

'Great. Fantastic.' Billy swallowed noisily. 'I hope . . .'

'You hope what?'

'Nothing.' Then came a lie so enormous that Billy could scarcely give it utterance. 'Just that you'll be around for the wedding?'

'Oh, I'll be around, Billy.' The waves crashed. The dark morning grew darker. Rawhead placed a hand on Billy's shoulder and looked directly into his eyes. 'I'll always be around.'

*

Billy and Nikki were having a quiet nightcap in the hotel bar when Rawhead walked in. He was dressed conservatively, in a dark suit with a white linen shirt open at the neck. He nodded and smiled at them, ordered a drink and remained at the bar.

Billy had already told Nikki that an old friend from school had turned up, neglecting to mention that he was a professional murderer who despatched people he didn't know for money and killed people he didn't like free of charge.

'Why don't you call him over? He looks OK,' said Nikki.

'Oh, he's a real barrel of laughs,' said Billy darkly.

Nikki wasn't listening. She was slightly drunk. She walked over to Rawhead, shook his hand, linked her arm through his and brought him over to their table.

'I don't understand,' said Rawhead innocently. 'It's your wedding tomorrow. I thought you'd both be having girl and boy parties.'

'As if I'd have a party and not invite you,' said Billy sarcastically.

'We don't go in for that kind of crap,' said Nikki. 'Tomorrow's going to be long and noisy. Tonight we just want to be peaceful.'

'Fine. As soon as you want me to go, just say the word,' said Rawhead.

She reached out and touched his sleeve. 'No. You must stay. I want to know all about you. I don't even know who you are.'

Rawhead told her.

Nikki was astounded. 'Steve Ellis? Steve the best friend?'

'That's me.'

'Billy, this is amazing. Why didn't you tell me he was coming?' She turned to Rawhead. 'You won't believe how often he's talked about you.'

'Nothing bad, I hope,' sneered Rawhead.

'Well, I know you went to prison. But that was a long time ago.'

'Drugs were my downfall,' lied Rawhead smoothly. 'And when I came out of prison, I saw I had a clear choice. Either I could continue along the path of crime and substance abuse, or I could do something positive. So I studied hard and went to medical school.'

'Wow,' enthused Nikki. She turned to Billy, whose face was in his hands. 'Billy, why didn't you tell me any of this?'

'I didn't know,' said Billy sourly.

'As soon as I qualified as a doctor, I decided to specialize in the treatment of drug addiction. I opened my own clinic, which I still run. The rest of the time I work as a travelling ambassador for the World Health Organization.'

'That's an incredible story.'

'I just wanted to put something back.' Rawhead raised his glass to Nikki and smiled. 'So tell me: do you think you'll feel differently when you're married?'

'No,' said Billy and Nikki simultaneously.

'Then why do it?'

'We wouldn't have bothered,' explained Nikki. Her eyes suddenly turned dark and hard. 'But then Billy started making money, we bought a house, and if our relationship goes down the pan, I want to make sure I get my share.'

Rawhead laughed.

'Isn't that the most romantic thing you've ever heard?' said Billy.

Rawhead regarded Nikki appraisingly. She was a handsome woman, with dark, knowing eyes. 'If that's your attitude, why get married in a castle?'

'That was William's idea,' she said. 'He wanted us to be like Guy Ritchie and Madonna.'

'Except they got married in a real castle,' said Billy.

'You may as well live while you can,' said Rawhead, raising his glass to them both but looking only at Billy.

*

It snowed that night. The woods beyond the hotel glowed white in the darkness. When Billy and Nikki were in bed with the lights out, the room was filled with silence and a blue icy glow. They lay in each other's arms, huddled together because of the cold. When Billy was drifting off to sleep, Nikki asked him a question.

'Tell me the truth. He's nothing to do with the World Health Organization, is he?'

Billy sighed. 'No.'

'Did you invite him to the wedding?'

'God, no.'

'So how did he know where to find you?'

'It's a long, long story and I really don't feel like telling it now.'

'Just tell me this: have you and him been having a gay relationship?'

14

'No!'

'Well, why does he look at you that way?'

'What way?'

'As if he owns you.'

'Do you mind if we have this conversation tomorrow?'

'This isn't a conversation, Billy. We don't *have* conversations. Because you won't talk about anything.'

'Why are we getting married then?

'It beats me.'

Billy said nothing. But in his head, he thought, *Fuck off, I'm leaving you. The first offer I get from an ugly woman and I'm out the door.*

He could hear Maddy snoring softly in the next room of their suite. Billy lay still for a long time until Nikki's breathing became regular. When she was obviously asleep, he relaxed enough to doze. It was now almost one o'clock. All the creaks, footfalls and lavatory flushes of a large hotel gradually died away. The silence grew profound, as if the blizzard had moved indoors.

Then he thought of Maddy and wondered if she was warm enough.

Billy got out of bed and walked into the next room. As he stood over the cot and his sleeping daughter, he glanced to his right and saw Rawhead sitting in a chair by the balcony window. He was wearing his overcoat and there was a shotgun across his knee. The curtains were open, bathing him in the blizzard's pale glow.

'Jesus Christ,' said Billy. Then he realized he was naked. With one hand covering his privates, he turned on his daughter's night light.

Rawhead held a finger to his lips. Then he got to his feet and opened the balcony doors. Icy air blasted into the room, rattling the doors. He nodded to Billy and stepped onto the balcony.

Seconds passed. Billy got curious and stuck his head out of the French windows. There was no one out there. They were four floors up, there was nowhere else to go. But Rawhead had vanished.

Billy sat by Maddy's cot all night, too jangled to go back to bed. He felt physically sick. He couldn't believe his bad luck. Rawhead was back. It was only a matter of time before people started dying.

*

On the following afternoon William Edwin Dye finally lived up to his initials by marrying Nicola May Bourne. Just before the ceremony Billy had taken an artificial additive to see him through the ordeal and jolly himself up after his sleepless night. He felt so happy, that the solemn nature of his vows was lost on him. He was glad to be marrying a woman, but it didn't particularly matter which one.

Billy and Nikki were married by Patricia Izzard, a Justice of the Peace. She was patient, elegant and kind – not at all the podgy civil servant with halitosis that Billy had expected. The witnesses were Lorna Bourne, sister to the above, and Roger Alton, Billy's brother-in-law. Billy and his brother-in-law had never struck up any kind of relationship, but Billy thought he'd make as good a witness as anyone.

Billy had decided against having a best man. His only real friend, Tony the corrupt policeman, had mysteriously disappeared while Billy had been staying with Rawhead. It would have seemed callous to elect another best man just because his real best man was missing, presumed dead.

Billy wore a suit – his first ever – and Nikki looked resplendent in a dress of black satin, her long dark hair scraped back to show her fine cheekbones. Everyone said the bride looked stunning and that the groom looked as if he'd actually taken the trouble to have a bath. After the ceremony and the photographs, they went in to dinner.

Many guests had used the bad weather as an excuse for not coming. The room was half empty. Billy and Nikki sat at a long table with their immediate family. Their daughter Maddy sat between them, imprisoned in a high chair.

Roger, to everyone's surprise, insisted on giving a speech. 'I've known William – Billy – since he was seventeen. I can easily say, without fear of contradiction, that marrying Nikki is the only sensible thing he's done in all that time . . .'

Laughter and applause.

For reasons known only to himself, Roger was wearing a kilt in the colours of the Campbell clan. Billy found this a little strange. Roger wasn't a Campbell, although he had possibly eaten the occassional tin of Campbell's soup. But he *was* a scoutmaster, and spent a great deal of his life wearing shorts, showing off his hairy legs.

Billy wondered if Roger's legs were the link. Maybe he was a bit of a perv. He'd have to be a perve to sleep with Billy's sister Carole, who always wore frilly, patterned dresses. Today her hair was piled high on her head in the manner of Princess Margaret. She reminded Billy of a Stepford Wife that had gone horribly wrong.

Yet he loved his sister. He even loved her husband. Mostly he loved their teenage sons, Mark and Chris, who unlike their parents were still recognizable as living organisms. His heart went out to the boys, who had been made to wear matching suits and looked profoundly embarrassed by their father's out-pourings.

'When I first knew this young man,' Roger continued, 'he liked to think of himself as something of a rebel. He would never have entertained the very idea of marriage, such was his horror of conforming. What he didn't appreciate – and has now, perhaps, come to understand – is that conformity can actually be quite pleasant. We may have said goodbye – and some of us would say "good riddance" – to William the rebel. But I think you'll all join me in bidding a hearty hello to William the polite, responsible husband.'

At one time Billy might have shouted, 'Fuck off! I'm still a rebel. I'm just a married rebel. And you're a white-haired cunt!' But today Roger's platitudes had no effect on him.

He was too busy thinking of Rawhead, the harbinger of death.

The man who thought killing people was a merciful act.

As the Ecstasy wore off, Billy started seeing flashing pictures in his mind. He knew these fleeting visions were connected to Rawhead and the night ahead. Billy tried to blank out the images, but they kept on coming. All he could see was the hotel dance floor piled high with massacred bodies.

*

Nikki's cousin, a music teacher in Iceland, had brought a band of jazz rock musicians from Reykjavik over for the wedding. Billy guessed that in Iceland, jazz rock was still considered vaguely dangerous. The music was loud and difficult to dance to. This made no difference to Billy. By six o'clock he was too pissed to dance.

He contented himself with circulating among the guests. Billy's uncle Bert was already bad-mouthing his wife, Olive. 'See this burn on my collar?' he was saying. 'Olive did that. Forgot to turn the iron off. A perfectly brand-new second-hand shirt . . .'

Nikki's father, Kev the slob, was carrying on the fine tradition of wedding stupidity by pretending to dance with a child. The child was Maddy. Kev was so ugly that people regularly mistook him for Nick Hornby. His wife, Marian, was even worse.

As hideous as they both were, they hadn't been able to resist having sex with each other. And the result, miraculously, had been Nikki and Lorna, who were both beautiful. It almost gave you faith in the benign will of the universe.

Maddy, who had her mother's face and Billy's frown, was staring, goggle-eyed, over Kev's shoulder. Kev didn't know it, but Maddy had dropped a mouthful of drool onto his jacket, leaving a long, glistening trail. It looked as if a slug had crawled down his back.

Marian, hardly Billy's greatest fan, came over to smear lipstick on his cheeks. She was wearing a hat that resembled a back-street abortion. There were tears in her eyes. 'Now, I know we've had our little differences, but I hope that's all over and done with. I hope I'm not gaining a daughter, I'm losing a son.'

'Don't you mean that the other way round?' said Billy.

Fatty Potts, Billy's agent, had turned up. Fatty had established an alarming rapport with Billy's brother-in-law.

'Thanks for coming,' said Billy to Potts.

'I wasn't aware that I had!' said Potts and laughed up-roariously.

Roger shouted something that sounded like 'Bare backside!'

'Where?' said Billy, looking round.

Roger got to his feet to repeat his enquiry, this time bellowing directly into Billy's ear. 'Where's the bride?'

Billy was forced to admit he had no idea. Roger told Fatty Potts this was a great omen for the couple's marriage. Fatty almost pissed himself.

*

The roof of the hotel was surrounded by a narrow battlement. A notice on the fire door leading to the roof claimed it was out of bounds to guests and that opening the door would automatically trigger a security alarm in the lobby. This was a lie. Billy and Nikki had already visited the roof several times without incident.

Now Nikki, still wearing her wedding dress, stood alone looking out to sea. It was snowing again. The wind had messed up her hair and she was crying. For some time now, Nikki felt she'd been living the wrong life. Not a bad life, just someone else's. She had a new home, which she'd decorated herself. She had a huge garden, planted and cared for, all ready to blossom in the spring. But in her heart she felt dead and unfulfilled.

It wasn't that Nikki didn't love Billy or their daughter – just that whatever she had hoped her life might be, this wasn't it. Now that she was married to Billy, that feeling of wrongness was stronger than it had ever been.

'Hey,' said a voice behind her.

It was a man's voice. Nikki was so cold, drunk and dazed that she felt no surprise, only mild curiosity. She turned to see who it was. It was Steve, Billy's friend. He was standing behind her, wearing the clothes he'd worn the night before. His face was grave and thoughtful. His head and shoulders, like hers, were speckled with snow.

Rawhead looked at her. He hesitated, reached out and wiped away a tear with his forefinger. With a little sob, she nodded and fell into his arms. It was below zero, but his body felt perfectly warm to her. He took off his jacket and draped it around her shoulders. 'You'd better go down.' he said. 'It isn't safe up here.'

She looked at him. He was staring fixedly towards the sea, as if he sensed something out there. Something in his voice frightened her. 'Go down,' he repeated.

He turned to her. There was no reassurance in his cold, dark eyes. She gave him back his jacket and walked towards the fire door, glancing back at him several times to see if he was following. Rawhead remained where he was with his back to her, jacket in one hand, gun in the other, eyes staring over the roof at the ground below.

*

Billy noticed she'd been crying, but didn't ask her why. He had a feeling he wouldn't like the answer.

A little later, as Billy was dancing with his new bride, Rawhead entered the ballroom and sat in a corner. Billy was trying to dance like John Travolta in *Pulp Fiction* – a mistake many people have made. Then he saw Rawhead over in the corner, watching him like a cat stalking a mouse. Billy felt cold, as if someone was pressing a slab of ice against the back of his neck. The look on Rawhead's face was murderous. Billy knew his dancing was shit, but he didn't think it was *that* bad.

First Billy and Nikki stopped dancing, then everyone else followed. The party atmosphere died, as if someone had rolled a diseased heart into the exact centre of the dance floor. The waves of hatred drifting through the ballroom were toxic. Few could absorb them and live.

Billy's sister and her family retired first, joined by Fatty Potts. Their exit gave the more distant relations courage. Feeling they didn't know Nikki or Billy well enough to risk evisceration at the hands of a gaunt psychopath, the great-uncles and maiden aunts, the friends and neighbours, all started trooping out in threes and fours.

Billy went to the gents for a piss. The lavatory was empty. He was very drunk. He stood over the urinal, forehead resting on the cold tiles, listening to the pipes dripping. When the door to the gents creaked open, Billy turned, expecting to see Rawhead. But it was one of Billy's cousins, a guy he hardly knew. The two men exchanged shy nods, embarrassed to be standing side by side in public with their dicks out.

When Billy returned to the ballroom, it seemed even emptier. Rawhead was still sitting in the same place, emanating pure hatred.

An uncle of Nikki's approached Billy to ask who the scowling maniac in the corner was and should they call hotel security. Billy confessed that the man in the corner was not an escaped lunatic, but a friend of his. Besides, he wasn't threatening anyone. There is no law against the evil eye.

The band played on valiantly for another few numbers, until they too succumbed to the pestilence of fear. The lead singer lost heart in the middle of *Mustang Sally*, simply stopped singing and sat down on an amp. Then the musicians put down their instruments. It made no difference that they were being paid until midnight and had only twenty minutes to go. The atmosphere in the ballroom had become too oppressive to endure.

They'd had enough. They didn't even offer a last dance, because no one was dancing. They packed their equipment away hurriedly, anxious to leave the venue before something terrible happened. Finally even Nikki deserted Billy, mumbling something vague about checking up on Maddy.

An overzealous waiter turned out half the lights. Then it was only Billy and Rawhead. Rawhead got up and walked over to Billy, two men standing alone in the darkened ballroom. When they were face to face, both were silent for a few moments.

'I need you to come with me,' said Rawhead.

He turned and walked out of the ballroom. Billy followed a few paces behind him. The two men climbed the stairs to the hotel lobby and nodded to the sleepy night porter, who opened the doors to a white wilderness.

They walked through the car park, their feet sinking deep into clean, untrodden snow. A calm had descended upon Billy. He hadn't left a will. But now that he was married, all his

wordly goods, all future royalties from his books, would automatically pass to his wife and heir.

Huge crystals spun down from a dark grey sky. Billy raised his face to them, wondering why only one snowflake in six seemed to feel wet against the skin. There was a stone wall at the back of the hotel, separating the hotel grounds from a track and the woods that rose in the west. When Rawhead clambered over the wall, Billy considered running back to the hotel and raising the alarm. But he felt this would merely sentence his wife and daughter to death.

The snow was deep on the slopes leading to the woods. The water flooded Billy's thin leather shoes. He kept slipping. Rawhead kept hauling him upright, more like an alpine guide than an executioner. Then they walked into the shade of the pine trees, and the eerie white carpet at their roots.

They walked on, brushing past branches, growing wetter and colder. Billy saw a stout fallen branch on the ground. He contemplated picking it up and using it as a club. But he doubted he could kill Rawhead this way. More likely it would just make him angrier.

They came to a large clearing, out of the shadow of the trees. Snow hurtled down vertically, blocking out the sky. The pines towered around them on all sides. Billy peered through the dense blizzard. About a hundred yards away, a grim little tableau awaited him. It was as if a lunatic had designed a child's snowstorm, imprisoning an abomination under the glass rather than Father Christmas or a fairy cottage.

In the centre of the clearing stood a young fir tree, no more than twelve feet tall. From its branches, like a macabre Christmas decoration, hung a dead man. He was upside down, his left leg caught in a noose, his hands trailing on the ground. He was dressed like a trapper in a thick parka, sturdy boots, leather mittens and a woolly hat. His throat had been cut. The blood that filled his eyes and mouth resembled treacle threaded with ice.

Billy didn't want to look. But he couldn't help himself. The corpse's mouth gaped. Its eyeballs were sugar-coated. Snowflakes fell on the extended tongue. Billy had seen two dead people in his life. This was the second. On both occasions he'd been in the company of Rawhead.

'Who is he?' said Billy.

'I don't know,' said Rawhead. 'I was hoping you'd tell me.'

In a single, fluid movement, Rawhead drew a huge, broad-bladed knife.

Billy looked at the knife and looked at Rawhead. 'Now it's my turn?' he said.

Rawhead gave a solemn nod.

A snow-laden breeze spun around Billy Dye's head and ears. All he could think of at that moment was his daughter. He regretted that he'd never see her grow up, or even live to see her second birthday. But mingled with the sadness was an unmistakable sense of relief.

He'd never have to brush his teeth again or comb his hair. Never have to get up in the morning or worry about money, or desire the unattainable or regret anything ever again. He'd never grow old or sick.

Death definitely had its good points.

Rawhead, eyes sunk in shadow, cheekbones protruding savagely, gazed down at Billy.

Then the moment passed.

Rawhead turned away, grabbed the corpse's head and lifted it. The hat fell off, showing sparse, tangled hair. Rawhead's right arm began to move in a rapid sawing motion.

At first, Billy felt drunk with relief. Then he edged closer and realized that Rawhead was cutting off the corpse's head. 'Aw, Jesus,' said Billy.

Ignoring protests, Rawhead continued to slice through muscles and tendons.

'What're you doing that for?'

'I want to know who this is. Normally, I'd take a snapshot. But I don't happen to have a camera on me.'

There was a crack as the head came free. Rawhead put the knife away, took out a pocket torch and shone it into the dead man's face. An undistinguished face, fat, coarse and bearded. He looked extremely surprised.

'You're sure you don't know him?' said Rawhead.

'Positive.' Billy jumped back as the head swung close to his leg. 'Keep that fucking thing away from me.'

'OK. But would you do me a favour? Would you have a closer look?'

'No way.'

'I'm not going to do anything.'

Reluctantly, Billy leant closer. Rawhead thrust the disembodied head into Billy's face. Their mouths touched in a frozen kiss. Billy jerked his head back far enough to scream, then Rawhead grabbed his neck and repeated the exercise.

'Billy, meet Nobody. Nobody, meet Billy.'

Billy fought and punched himself free, then sprawled on the floor, gagging and rubbing his lips with snow to take away the taste of the dead, gaping mouth.

'You are such a horrible bastard,' said Billy, when he'd got his breath back. 'Just kill me and get it over with. At least I won't have to look at you again.'

'What's all this shit about me killing you?' said Rawhead.

He turned away and stormed back through the woods. Billy followed reluctantly, snow-laden branches flicking back against his face and body.

'So we're just going to carry on like we did before, are we?' shouted Billy. 'How many people are going to die this time?'

'I can't tell you, Bill. That'd ruin the surprise.'

'What gives you the *right* to fuck up my life?' screamed Billy.

'You're the one who fucks up lives, Billy. At least twenty people have died already because of your big mouth!'

'Yeah. And who fucking killed them?'

They were on the rim of the woods. Rawhead stopped abruptly and extended his left leg. Billy fell over the leg and skidded downhill, head first. He came to rest against a tree trunk, groaning and holding his head. Rawhead stopped, lit an elegant spliff and knelt down beside him, resting the startled corpse-head against the trunk of the tree. Rawhead seemed relaxed, even amused. 'So you really don't know who this poor, plain-faced bastard was?'

'No,' said Billy.

Rawhead passed the joint to Billy, who took a deep drag, then coughed. Rawhead gave a short, dry laugh.

'What's so fucking funny?' said Billy.

'Your face. When you saw me on the beach. Talk about shock.'

'I wasn't shocked. I knew you were coming.'

'Bollocks.'

'Course I fucking knew. You sent me a card, remember.'

'What card?'

'Don't give me that. The fucking Frankenstein wedding card.'

'I don't send cards,' said Rawhead. 'I've never sent a card to anyone in my life.'

'You are such a fucking liar.'

'I didn't send any card.'

Billy was stunned.

Rawhead persisted. 'What card? Let me see it.'

'I haven't got it. I burned it.'

'Same old fucking idiot,' said Rawhead dismissively.

He snatched the spliff from Billy, picked up the dead man's

head and started walking. Billy got to his feet and scrambled to the foot of the slope. Rawhead had taken the track and was walking parallel to the wall, away from the hotel. A tall, purposeful figure, head bowed against the wind, a human head dangling from his right hand.

'So that's that, is it?' shouted Billy. 'You come back, ruin my fucking wedding, scare the fuck out of me, then just walk away?'

Rawhead kept walking. He didn't look back.

'Psycho,' said Billy under his breath.

Billy looked down and saw a large rock, half covered by snow. He leaned over and prised the rock out of the frozen earth. With a quick, dark thrill, Billy decided to end the nighmare. To get right what he'd tried and failed to do before.

Rawhead was now lost to view, but his fresh footprints trailed away into the white night. All Billy had to do was follow the tracks. He rushed forward. The snow was unexpectedly deep, as high as his calves. The sweet, freezing air filled his lungs as he ran.

Rawhead's trail carried on and on, clear and deep. Long footprints made by huge, sturdy boots.

A minute passed. All Billy could hear was his own breathing. He was panting like a schoolboy on a cross-country run.

Dense snow flew into his eyes, so that he could only see a few inches in any direction. His feet burned with the wet and cold. He couldn't feel his right hand. The fingers clutching the rock had turned bright pink.

Any second now, Billy expected to see that gaunt, unmistakable frame, swinging its grisly burden. He saw only the deep footprints and the white veil descending. He stopped and listened, standing so still he could hear the snowflakes landing on his clothes.

And up ahead, there was another sound. The distinctive trudge of boots in the snow.

He was close now. Very close.

One determined sprint. That was all it would take. Billy quickened his step, stumbling and sliding in the snow, face aglow from the heat of his exertions.

But Rawhead always remained ahead of him.

Always just out of sight.

2

Oh, turn away those cruel eyes,
The stars of my undoing!

'The Relapse', Thomas Stanley (1625–1678)

Ever since Rawhead had pointed a gun at him, Lol Shepherd had been ill with his nerves. Not that his nerves had been in good shape prior to that event. As a young man, Lol had been infamous for his tendency to jump at the slightest sound. He was incapable of raising a cup and saucer without an accompanying rattle or carrying a drink across a room without spilling it, and as for unfastening a bra strap – well, forget it.

Lol had once worked for Malcolm Priest. Until his death, Priest had been the formidable leader of the Priesthood, the gang that ruled Manchester. Most gangsters have a sentimental streak and Priest was no exception. Finding Lol's tremulousness oddly endearing, Priest had hired him as a chauffeur, dog-walker and trusty retainer. It had been easy money – should have been a lot easier after Rawhead shot the dog.

But Lol was a gentle soul who had never stolen or intentionally hurt anyone, and meeting a hooded assassin on a dark night had wrecked him. It made no difference that Rawhead, apparently on a whim, had spared Lol's life. Lol's trust in life had always been fragile. Now it had been shattered.

Lol was afraid to leave his home. He was afraid of the dark. Mostly he was afraid of going to sleep. Yet, oddly, he wasn't isolated. He had many visitors. People sought his advice, valuing his long memory and his encyclopedic knowledge of Mancunian low-life.

A week before, Chef himself had paid a visit, bringing oranges. Lol guessed that Chef had chosen oranges because Don Corleone buys oranges in *The Godfather*. Chef had asked Lol's advice. Little Malc sometimes called to do the same. Lol was careful not to repeat to one visitor what another had said. As they used to say in the War, careless talk costs lives.

Every Wednesday morning Lol's eldest daughter, Julie, came to take him shopping and to the cemetery to change the flowers on Violet's grave. Violet, his second wife, had died suddenly a few years ago. Not as suddenly as Rawhead's victims, but suddenly enough. The coroner said it was an embolism. To this day, Lol had no idea what an embolism was.

Violet was buried in Norbury churchyard. Julie waited in the car while Lol walked to the grave. Today the noise and bustle of the supermarket had proved too much for him – Lol had been obliged to sit in the cafe, shaking over a cup of chicken soup, while Julie rushed round the aisles, loading his groceries into a trolley and ticking them off on a list.

Lol was swaddled in a brown Abercrombie coat. On his head he wore a trilby. Both the hat and the coat were at least thirty years old. Lol drew comfort from old things.

He felt safe in the cemetery. The people that lay here were not about to jostle him or make demands. The morning was cold but bright. The winter sun shone, warm and comforting.

But the sun could not penetrate the bleakest corners of the graveyard. Patches of unmelted snow clung to the base of the churchyard wall, and the gravel over Violet's plot wore a thin veil of ice. Lol took off his hat as a mark of respect.

The inscription on her headstone read:

rawhead in love

VIOLET SHEPHERD
1932–1999
Beloved wife of Lawrence (Lol),
Sadly missed mother to JULIE and Suzanne.

'If Tears Could Build A Runway
And Love could make a Plane
I'd fly all the way to heaven
And Bring you back again'

And at the foot of the stone:

headstone kindly donated by Malcolm Priest

Lol's daughters had queried the taste of having Priest's name on their mother's memorial. But Lol had insisted. Priest had paid for the funeral, as well as the headstone. No one else had offered, and Lol was not a wealthy man. Malcolm's only stipulation was that his generosity should be immortalized in stone. And who was Lol to refuse?

He took the dead chysanthemums out of the vase on the grave and replaced them with fresh blooms. It was funny how he missed her. She'd been a bitch to live with. When Lol's age and his drinking caught up with him, giving him a nose like a crimson light bulb, she'd drawn attention to the defect in public. 'Look at his nose,' she'd complain to her friends. 'I can't even dress him up any more.'

Yet, strangely, her absence was not the pleasure he'd anticipated.

Lol got up to leave. It was cold here in the shade, and he was not the kind to make Jimmy Stewart-like speeches to the dead. As he straightened his legs, his knees cracked. He sighed, and turned.

31

To see Rawhead standing behind him.

Lol made a sound like a little dog begging at a door.

Rawhead was wearing the same hangman's hood and long dark coat that he'd worn on the night of the massacre. Five people had died that night – all had worked for Malcolm Priest; some had been Lol's friends.

'Remember me?' said the man in the hood, as cold and implacable as the crosses and the graves. He was holding a Sainsbury's carrier bag.

Lol could only nod. He noticed a very bad smell, like rotten cabbage and shit. 'Excuse me, I need . . .'

'What?'

'I need to take a tablet,' said Lol hoarsely, pointing to his heart.

Lol took a small white vial of heart pills out of his coat and tried to open the lid. But his hands were trembling too violently. Rawhead placed the carrier bag on the ground, took the vial, twisted off the lid and handed one of the small white pills to Lol. Lol popped it under his tongue. His eyes were watering. Whether it was through cold, or fear, or the strain of trying to breathe, Rawhead couldn't tell.

'Better now?' asked Rawhead.

'Yes, thank you.' Lol had to stop himself from adding 'sir'.

'OK,' said the hooded man.

He tipped up the cheap carrier bag and a white football rolled onto the ground, nudging Lol's shoe. It looked like a crude papier-mâché dummy of a human head. The skin was too pale, the eyes too glassy to be real. Then Lol realized that the foul smell was coming from the head, and that the hair and stubble framing the startled face were real.

'Do you know who this belongs to?'

'No,' said Lol. 'Oh, my God.'

'Look at the face.'

'Please. I need to go home now—'

'Look at it.'

Squinting sideways, Lol forced himself to study the bloated features. 'It's no one I've ever seen.'

'Not a member of the Priesthood?'

'No. I know them all.'

'Even the new guys?'

'I'm still in touch with Chef. Oh, my God . . . excuse me.' Lol released a deafening belch. 'I don't know who this fella is.'

'Is Chef still looking for me? said Rawhead.

'No. He was afraid to. He wanted the killing to stop . . .'

'But?'

'But a lot of people are. Looking for you, I mean. Fifty thousand is a lot of money.'

'I think you'd better start again. From the beginning.'

Lol waited. His long face turned ashen, his body shuddered. With a despairing groan, he bent double and clutched his chest. When he raised his head, Rawhead was gone. He looked to the cemetery gate and saw his daughter rushing towards him as fast as her fat legs would carry her.

*

That night Lol's nerves were in uproar. He couldn't concentrate on a TV programme without jumping at the slightest noise. Each tick or creak launched him into a bloody fantasy that always ended the same way.

First he was kneeling on the floor, pleading for his life.

A gun to the back of his head.

Then blood and brains fountained out of his forehead.

The temptation to phone Chef was powerful, but Lol clung to one indelible fact. Twice he had crossed Rawhead's path. Twice his life had been spared.

In the Priesthood, Lol had only ever been the driver. Not a

getaway driver, or the man who drove people to Rawhead. Just a chauffeur to Malcolm Priest, his mother and the poodle. And perhaps this was why he'd survived. He was no soldier. He was a civilian.

But if Lol were to tell Chef that Rawhead was back, he would become an informer. And informers, regardless of their civilian status, usually died.

Lol went to bed at ten o'clock, hoping to wipe out the bad memories of the day with sleep. But he did not sleep. He lay in his bed in the darkened flat, alert to every sound in the night. Every time a car passed in the street outside, a comet of light shot across his bedroom wall.

He could hear the TV in the flat next door, the solemn self-important drone of some journalist reporting from a war zone.

Outside, a front door opened. Milk bottles clinked. Someone called to a cat.

A plane passed overhead.

A train rattled over the distant railway bridge.

It sounded as if everyone in the world was wide awake except him.

Lol lay on his back, sweating and fretting and shaking.

Finally the neighbourhood went quiet. Lol dozed. He was awoken by a soft jolt. He half opened his eyes and raised his head from the pillow. He could see the outline of a head. Someone was sitting on the bed.

A man's voice said, 'We didn't finish our conversation.'

Please, Lord, let this be a dream.

He spoke again. 'You mentioned fifty thousand.'

Then Lol knew it was real. That Rawhead had returned, along with the stench of death and decay.

'The reward money.' said Lol.

'What reward money?'

'Malcolm Priest Junior put a price on your head. Fifty thousand for information leading to your death or capture.'

'Why?'

'He thinks you killed his father.'

'I didn't touch his father.'

'I know. He thinks you did. I'm surprised you don't know this. I thought it was common knowledge.'

'I've been away. I've got a lot of catching up to do.' There was a silence. 'So the face you saw today. You think that could have been some kind of bounty hunter?'

'Yes.'

'Who does my job now? Do you know?'

'Pardon?'

'Don't play games with me or I'll get very angry.'

Lol started to cough. 'Chef doesn't tell me things like that.'

'I didn't ask you what Chef had told you,' said the voice in the dark. 'I asked you what you know.'

Lol swallowed hard. 'All I can tell you is what I've heard. It's just a name. That's all I've got.'

'Go on.'

'The Spirit. Short for "The Spirit of Darkness".'

'What does that mean?'

'I don't know,' said Lol. *If it came to that, what does 'Rawhead' mean?*

'It means that people who upset me tend to die.' Lol started in surprise. Now the monster was reading his mind. 'If you tell anyone you've seen me,' said Rawhead gently, 'I'll kill you and all your family. Do you doubt that?'

'Not . . . not at all.'

With infinite slowness, the shadow by the bed backed away, inch by inch, until it appeared to melt into the wall. Lol heard no footsteps. No doors opening and closing. Yet the bad smell lingered. It was a long time before he found the courage to sit up in bed and fumble for the switch of his bedside lamp.

When the light came on, the first thing Lol saw was the white, decomposing head with its blind, protruding eyes. The head was perched on the mattress at the foot of the bed. It was wearing his trilby hat.

3

Then stay, dear love, for, tho' thou run from me,
Run ne'er so fast, run ne'er so fast, yet I will follow thee.

Anon.

In daylight, Rawhead rolled down his window and inched slowly past the club where Little Malc held court. He was driving a Black BMW, not a conspicuous car in this part of the city.

It was late morning. Somebody nearby was frying garlic with onions. The snow in the street was turning to grey slush in the mild sunlight. Little Malc's club was a huge converted warehouse near the river with a lot of opaque glass around the entrance and the word DIVA in lights on the wall above. A large delivery van was parked outside the door. A fat man with curly hair was helping the van driver to unload cardboard boxes.

Rawhead drove round the block and came back, still cruising, peering around with a furrowed brow like he was lost. This time he glimpsed a round-faced guy of about forty, wearing jeans and a conservative short-sleeved shirt. Rawhead recognized him immediately as Malcolm Priest Junior, known to friends and associates as Little Malc. Rawhead had never met Little Malc in person. But he had seen him on TV recently, raising money for the Malcolm Priest Sunny Bunny Trust, a holiday fund for sick children that Little Malc had started in his father's memory.

Little Malc was chatting amiably to the van driver, who

passed him a clipboard and a pen. The fat guy with the curly hair was nowhere in sight. Little Malc looked up, noticed Rawhead. There was absolutely no interest in the glance. A split-second later Little Malc returned his attention to the form, slamming a full stop after his signature as if he was hurling a spear.

As a broker might say, it was a wonderful opportunity. The street was empty. In another twenty seconds the situation would have changed. The van driver would be sitting in his cab, lazily consulting his itinerary or sending his wife an urgent text message: 'I am sitting in a van.' Little Malc would be back inside the dark club.

The Ruger Super Blackhawk tucked into Rawhead's belt held six .44 magnum rounds. Two for Little Malc, one for the driver. Rawhead estimated that it would have taken ten seconds to stride across the road, kill both men, gun down the first idiots to come running and drive away.

But something didn't feel right. Rawhead worked alone, outside the law, and he relied upon instinct at all times. That was how he managed to pass through doors unseen, to sense when it was possible to take a life easily, alone and unobserved. His instinct, his finely tuned killer instinct, told him to retreat.

He parked the BMW near the Science Museum and walked down to Mick Hucknall's bar. The winter sun was still shining, failing completely to penetrate the damp shade by the canal. But he ordered some coffee and pizza and waited at an outside table, the collar of his overcoat high around his ears.

Rawhead had come to know Manchester without loving it. He knew its churches, its graveyards and its dripping arches.

It was a dark city, darker than the circles around Myra Hindley's eyes.

Its paving stones were spattered with the gore of many beatings. Once you accepted this – that Manchester was a vile goddess who demanded sacrifice – you could kill and run. And the city would hide you, fold and conceal you in her stinking black skirts while the sirens howled for your blood.

Manchester was getting fancier, but all the designer stores and little cosmopolitan coffee-shops in the world couldn't erase the stench of a place that had grown rich on blood and child labour.

It was true that infants no longer worked in its factories – not officially. Now they robbed, shot up junk and traded their arses in the slums of Ardwick, Moss Side and Hulme. The centre of the city, with its galleries, theatres and windows full of baubles, was like a pacemaker attached to a failing, diseased heart, a middle-class oasis in a centuries-old desert of darkness, ignorance and want.

The coffee and food arrived, delivered by a charming blonde woman who gave him a full twenty-eight-tooth smile. 'It's turned into quite a nice day, really,' she said. 'Enjoy your meal.'

Rawhead nodded sullenly, making her flustered, so that she spilt his coffee. While she went back to get him a replacement, two men sat down at a neighbouring table. They were studying the menu. Rawhead stared at them for a few seconds before realizing that one of them was Little Malc, now wearing a thick jacket. The other guy was a little, nervous type with steel-rimmed glasses.

Rawhead had been asking around. Little Malc had indeed put a price on his head, fifty thousand for information leading to his capture or death. This singular act of foolishness had created something of a rift between Little Malc and Chef. Having experienced at first hand the carnage inflicted by Rawhead, Chef had no wish to visit further damage upon the Priesthood by antagonizing a madman. That was the story and Rawhead believed it.

During his years as the Priesthood's number-one hitman, Rawhead had come to know Chef as cautious and thoughtful.

As for Little Malc – Rawhead knew next to nothing about him.

The little man with the glasses went into the bar to order. Little Malc was now sitting alone at his table, a faint smile on his mouth as he watched a squabble between a squirrel and a pigeon. Rawhead couldn't believe it. Little Malc was either incredibly brave or naive to the point of madness. After offering a reward for information leading to the capture of Manchester's most prolific killer, he was sitting in a public place in broad daylight without any protection or any apparent sense of danger.

Rawhead took out the Ruger and flicked off the safety catch. Then he raised the gun over the level of the table and pointed it calmly at Little Malc's head. He felt absolutely no emotion as his finger closed around the trigger. A man this stupid would be fortunate to die so humanely. You cannot put a price on the head of the Lord High Executioner and expect to live.

In Rawhead's mind, it was already done. He could already hear the shattering roar of the magnum, always louder than expected. He could see Little Malc's head bursting like a melon, and the bright cascade of blood and brains springing high into the air. One for Little Malc. One for Malc's friend as he came running out to see what had happened. One for the waitress who had seen the killer's face.

Yet still Rawhead hesitated.

The squirrel leapt at the pigeon, snatched the bread from its mouth and darted away. Little Malc threw back his head and laughed. Little Malc's friend walked out of the bar and Rawhead thrust the gun out of sight, just as Little Malc turned to Rawhead and grinned. 'Did you see that? Did you see that fucking squirrel? He'd been after that bread for the last five minutes . . .'

Rawhead smiled back. Little Malc looked like a milder, less vicious version of his father. He was in his early forties. His teeth were nicely capped, his thinning hair was combed forward unconvincingly. Although Little Malc was built like his hatchet-wielding father, his face was softer and somehow innocent. He turned his attention to the man with glasses, who had brought two beers in tall glasses. Little Malc chinked glasses and drank.

Rawhead slipped his gun back into his belt. He ate his food slowly and in silence, already planning his next move.

*

Rawhead was living where no one would think to look for him, lodging with a nice old lady in a leafy suburban street in Sale. His landlady's name was Mrs Mary Munley. She was slightly deaf and, because she was arthritic, she never went upstairs. Rawhead had the first floor to himself.

Mrs Munley liked company, so Rawhead would play cards with her. He called her Mrs Munley and she called him Victor. The names Rawhead invented for himself always had a horror connection – Victor was Frankenstein's Christian name. With Mrs Munley's permission, Rawhead used the tools in her late husband's workshop. He repaid her by driving her to the doctor every Tuesday for her physiotherapy. Afterwards he took her to the supermarket for her weekly shop.

Mrs Munley was under the impression that Rawhead worked for a security firm, guarding buildings and people at short notice, hence the odd, unpredictable hours he worked. Some-times he stayed out all night. She was a good sleeper and was rarely aware of his nocturnal arrivals and departures. She and the neighbours found Victor to be quiet, even mysterious, but pleasant enough.

If he was home, she liked to cook him a meal. Something warming and simple, like shepherd's pie. That was what she cooked him tonight, when he came home from not shooting Little Malc. They ate together, Rawhead and the nice old lady, sitting at a table in the tiny dining room. Rawhead had a huge plate of food, Mrs Munley had a child's portion on a saucer. On a bookcase by the window stood framed photographs of the grandchildren she never saw. Her son and daughter lived in Australia.

'You should get yourself a young lady, Victor,' said Mrs Munley. 'You're nice looking enough. How old are you now?'

Rawhead looked at her coldly, but she didn't seem to notice. 'Thirty-four,' he said finally. She read his lips.

'Thirty-four? That's not old. But it's not young either. You should have settled down by now.'

'I've never been able to find the right woman,' confessed Rawhead.

The kettle had boiled. She wandered off into the kitchen. 'What kind of girl are you looking for?'

'A woman who knows when to lie down and when to shut her mouth,' he replied, knowing she couldn't hear him.

'What was that?' she said from the kitchen.

'An honest woman, who will never pretend that she knows better than me. A wise woman, who, when I'm tired of her, will have the good grace to leave before I'm forced to hit her with a shovel and bury her in a lonely place.'

'It's no good, Victor,' shouted back Mrs Munley. 'I can't hear a word.'

*

That night at eleven, Rawhead drove into Manchester. He parked the car at the far end of Water Street and squirted shaving foam over his registration plates. Then he slipped on a woolly hat and ski goggles and walked back to Little Malc's club. Two bouncers stood on the door. From behind them came the repetitive boom of dance music. One of the doormen was the fat guy with the curly hair Rawhead had seen earlier. The other was a little Scottish guy with swollen knuckles and a horribly flattened face.

'Where do you think you're going?' said the Scot, holding his hand out so that Rawhead walked into it.

'In there,' said Rawhead.

'Not dressed like that,' said the fat guy, glancing rapidly up and down the street.

'But these goggles cost more than your suit,' protested Rawhead.

The Scot pointed to a sign on the wall. 'See that? "Dress code: smart casual". No way are you smart. Now fuck off before I smack your legs. '

'But I'm a special guest of Little Mike's,' said Rawhead.

The bouncers exchanged smirking glances.

'Little "Mike", eh? You're no special guest of nobody,' said the Scot. 'Now do what the man says while you've still got teeth.'

'Did you realize you're supposed to call me sir?'

'You fucking what?' said Fats.

'I'm a member of the public. And even if you refuse me admission, you're still meant to call me sir.'

'Do you know what I love most about knuckledusters?' said the Scot to no one in particular. 'The way you can hear the crack as they split open a fella's jaw.'

'Mmm, yummy,' agreed Fats.

'That's a bit unfair,' said Rawhead, addressing the Scot. 'I'll have you know I give a lot of money to your charity.'

'What fucking charity?'

'The Jimmy Krankie Benevolent Society for Little Scottish Spastics.'

Before Rawhead had finished speaking, the Scot took a direct swipe at his face. Rawhead stepped back, caught his wrist and yanked him down the step. While the Scot was still struggling,

Rawhead hit him once in the mouth. The Scot went down, shaking his head as if in repeated denial.

The fat man charged, and caught Rawhead off guard with a surprisingly fast right to the gut. Rawhead blocked the follow-through and butted the fat man in the exact centre of his angry red face. The fat man lost his balance, slipped and landed on his back, gasping for breath.

Rawhead started to walk away. Spluttering threats and fragments of teeth, the little Celt ran after him. Rawhead glanced back, saw something flashing in the Scot's right hand. Rawhead never found out what it was. Unhurriedly, ignoring an approaching taxi, Rawhead unfastened his jacket, withdrew the Ruger Blackhawk, aimed at the ground in front of him and fired. The Scot ran right into the bullet, which penetrated the instep of his right foot.

Roaring in pain and fury, the diminutive doorman hopped sideways, fell off the kerb and landed in the path of the taxi. He bounced off the bonnet and landed in the road. The taxi driver braked and swerved and ran over him again.

A woman in the taxi screamed. Rawhead walked on briskly, stepping aside so as not to collide with two teenage boys who came sprinting past him in their eagerness to inspect the damage. The way they were running, you'd think they'd never seen an acccident before.

4

But if you want me, if you do need me,
Who waits, at the terrible door, but I?

'The Terrible Door', Harold Monro (1879–1932)

At two minutes past eight, the big man with the long, melancholy face opened his heavy-lidded eyes. Every night, in his dreams, he was John Stavri, a little Greek immigrant boy. But when he awoke he was always Chef, leader of the Priesthood, the most powerful gang in Manchester.

He was in Malcolm Priest's bedroom, in Malcolm Priest's large, comfortable house in Knutsford. As usual, he had slept alone, his long, large-boned frame filling the queen-sized bed. There was a knock on the door. Then the door opened and in walked the Philosopher, one of Chef's most loyal men. The Philosopher bore Chef's breakfast on a tray; orange juice, porridge, a pot of tea, butter and toast. Normally, the Philosopher would have left the tray on the bedside table.

Today he hovered.

'Fireworks at the club last night.' For a big man, the Philosopher had an unlikely voice. It was like a jockey's voice, high and nasal. 'Someone got shot.'

'Who?' The hope in Chef's eyes was unmistakable.

'Not Little Malc. Scotch Harry.'

'Is he dead?'

'No. But he'll never dance the Highland fling again.'

The Philosopher laughed at his own joke. Chef eyed him sternly. 'Did they get the gunman?'

'He fucking legged it.'

'Nothing to do with Little Malc, then.'

'Possibly not. More likely just another drunk twat who's cracked out for the weekend.'

Chef smiled as he stirred his tea. He liked the way the Philosopher talked. The way he said 'Possibly not' when he meant 'Fuck knows'. It created the impression, at least in Chef's imagination, that he had quality people around him.

'It's only a matter of time,' said Chef. 'Someday soon, someone's going to box the guy. He's trouble.'

The Philosopher scratched his arse reflectively. 'Confucius say, "Sooner or later, man who mixes with wankers will get spunk in eye."' He waited for a laugh that never came. Then added, 'It's a shame, really.'

Chef glanced at him sharply. 'What's a shame?'

The Philosopher shrugged. 'Nothing. Just that whenever me and the girlfriend go to the club, Malc always makes us welcome. Not in a crawling, arse-licky sorta way. I think the guy means it. '

Chef nodded. 'Now you know how I feel. I've known him all his life. He used to play dirty doctors with my own daughters.'

'I'll tell you what, though. He's no fucking Tom Jones.'

Chef agreed. 'But you can't box a guy for singing out of tune.'

'Everyone I know says he's a nice bloke.'

'Fuck nice,' snarled Chef. 'Nice doesn't build a business. Especially our kind of business. I mean, he won't even let us stash knock-off at the club. They've got this massive loft down there, just lying empty. But he thinks that if he's found with stolen goods on the premises, Madonna won't agree to play a gig there.'

'Madonna wouldn't play a fucking gig there anyway.'

'Try telling Little Malc that.'

'Someone's gonna box him. I can see it coming.'

'Yeah. I just don't want it to be me. I owe his father that much.'

The Philosopher gave a slight nod. Secretly, he was thinking, *But you killed Little Malc's father, boss. It's common knowledge. You set him on fire. Then you fucking shot him.*

*

Malcolm Priest's house had always been the centre of operations for the Priesthood. Priest's sudden disappearance had not altered that fact. Although Chef had a house of his own in Hyde, where his resentful wife and work-shy son resided, he rarely went there. Now that he was the undisputed leader of the Priesthood, it felt right to sleep in Malcolm Priest's bed. Just as a cannibal devours his enemy in the hope of possessing his enemy's spirit, so Chef believed that sleeping in Priest's bed and eating at Priest's table would give him Priest's authority and power.

So far, that was how it had worked out. Chef had assembled a new inner circle of disciples to replace those butchered by Rawhead. Profits were up. Because he was less headstrong than his predecessor, he enjoyed a more cordial relationship with the Greater Manchester Police. In exchange for a small percentage Clive Bosworth, the new chief constable, let Chef run all the drugs, porn and whores he wanted. The only thing Bosworth didn't like was guns, so Chef didn't sell them. It was a nice, civilized arrangement.

The only turd in Chef's swimming pool was Little Malc.

The only shark, the one human being he feared, was Rawhead.

But Chef hadn't thought about Rawhead in a while. Not until that morning, when Bryan Edwards brought a heavy-duty brown paper envelope into Chef's study.

Bryan, a charming but dishonest young man from Rusholme, had once been on Malcolm Priest's hit list. But when Priest died, Chef declared a general amnesty. Partly because killing is bad for business, but mainly because Rawhead had murdered all of his best men.

This was good news for Bryan, who found himself promoted overnight from hanger-on to the inner circle, the seventy pounds he'd stolen from Malcolm Priest's house a distant memory. Chef was careful to warn Bryan that any further pilfering would result in the loss of his bollocks. And Bryan struggled to justify the faith Chef had shown in him. His trainers and Man City shirts were a thing of the past. Now he wore bespoke suits and creamy silk shirts from King Street.

'I've found something out, boss.'

Chef, who'd been checking his offshore bank account online, was irritated by the interruption. He tossed his head backwards, silently inviting Bryan to surprise him. Bryan opened the envelope and took out a bound A4 manuscript.

On the top sheet was typed the word:

Gangchester

'What's this?' Chef gave the manuscript a shove, to show that whatever it was, it was obviously a pile of contemptible shit.

'It's a fucking whadyacallit . . . a TV script.'

'I can see that. What's it got to do with me?'

'Use your fucking eyes.'

'*What?*'

'Sorry, boss. It just slipped out. But look. Just look who fucking wrote it.'

Warily, as if he was afraid that a jet of sulphuric acid might leap up from the typeface and hit him in the eye, Chef peered at the name under the title.

rawhead in love

William Dye

It took Chef a few seconds to work out that William Dye was Billy Dye. Then a shudder of disgust pulsed through him, as if he'd inadvertently bitten into a dog-shit sandwich. Billy Dye was the big-mouthed little bastard who had started all the trouble two years back.

'TV?' said Chef. 'I thought he wrote books. Books that nobody reads.'

'The guy's branching out,' said Bryan. 'Now he's going to write TV shows that no one'll fucking watch.'

'Is someone actually going to make this?'

'Looks that way.'

'Who?'

'Larry Crème, no less.'

'Who's Larry Crème?'

'I don't fucking know,' admitted Bryan. 'But Shonagh reckons he's very important in tellyland.'

'Who the hell's Shonagh?'

'This actress I'm fucking. She's juice. She plays Dorita Green in *Coronation Street*. You know, Dorita who works behind the bar. It was Shonagh who gave me this script to read.'

'Bryan.' Chef leaned back in his chair to survey the scrawny young rogue in front of him.

'Yeah?'

'I'm not in the least bit interested in who you're shagging or why. I wouldn't give a toss if you were a stud or a virgin. You can spend the rest of your life wanking into a bucket for all I care.'

Bryan half laughed, half gasped in surprise.

'All that matters to me is that you're loyal. So why are you wasting my time with this shit?'

'For a very good reason, boss,' said Bryan confidently. 'This thing Billy Dye's written, it's about gangsters from Manny. About *us*. Don't know about you, but I think it's a bit of a fucking cheek to make a series about us and not ask us to be in it.'

Chef pondered the point. The fingers of his hands were interlocked over his chest. His thumbs caressed each other like women in prison.

'They should have consulted us,' he admitted. 'No doubt about that. They haven't shown respect.'

Bryan suppressed a smirk. Chef was a strong leader and few would have dared to cross him. But his obsession with Sicilian honour was a constant source of amusement to his men, all of whom were aware that Chef's parents were Greek immigrants, greasy cafe owners from Hazel Grove, near Stockport. Not even a decent greasy cafe, but the kind that serves your tea lukewarm with dandruff whirling on the surface.

'How did it happen?' said Chef, frowning. 'That's what I don't get. One minute he's writing spacko books, suddenly he's in TV.'

'Way I heard it, Dye writes this gangster book that no one wants to publish. His agent sends it to fucking Granada, who think it might make good telly. That's what Shonagh told me, anyway.'

'Will you fucking shut up about this fucking Shonagh?'

'Sorry. Anyway, what do you want to do?' said Bryan. 'Do you want Dye saddened?'

'No.'

'Should I cut off a horse's head and stick it in his bed?'

'Does he keep horses?'

'Shouldn't think so.'

'Well, there wouldn't be much point then, would there?'

'I was just joking, boss.' Bryan smiled expansively to demonstrate the correct reponse to a joke.

'Forget about Dye. He's already being taken care of. It's this Larry Crème guy we need to be talking to.'

'What about?'

'About whether he wants to do business with us or spend the rest of his life in a wheelchair.' Chef picked up the manuscript and leafed through it idly. 'What's the script about?'

Bryan looked startled. 'How the fuck should I know?'

Chef flung it across the table. 'Read it.'

'That's easy for you to say. This thing's seventy fucking pages long.'

'I take it you *can* read?'

'Course I can fucking read. I just happen to hate fucking reading. Give it to the Philosopher. He reads real books. I've caught him at it.'

'Bryan, you're a lazy bastard. Take it home. Now.'

'Aw, fuck. Don't be cruel to me, boss. In me whole fucking life I've never read anything longer than the label on a beer bottle.'

Chef said. 'Exactly. You're virtually illiterate.'

'You saying I'm a bastard?'

'I want intelligence around me. Culture. Understand? I want this organization to go upmarket.'

'OK. But will you do us a favour, boss? Will you lend us some feed 'til payday? I'm skewed out.'

Grumbling to himself, Chef slapped forty quid into Bryan's outstretched hand. *Upmarket?* Fat fucking chance.

*

The next morning there was no one on the door of the club. Rawhead, dressed in the suit he'd worn for Billy Dye's wedding, walked through the entrance and into the club itself. On a blackboard outside, someone had written 'Tonite for one nite only: Koo La Grace.' Koo La Grace was a famous Mancunian drag artiste. Little Malc was on stage, microphone in hand, rehearsing some crap patter. 'Ladies and gentlemen . . . all the way from Little Lever, near Bolton . . . the sensational, the unprintable, Manchester's first lady . . . did I say lady? . . . Ladies and gents, let's hear it please for the inimitable Koo La Grace.'

A cleaner, somebody's worn-out mum from Levenshulme, was wiping the bar for the minimum wage. A bored old twat sitting behind a drum kit gave his cymbal a clout. Little Malc grimaced. 'What the fuck was that, Peter?'

Rawhead sat down on a stool, not in a hurry, taking his time.

The drummer shrugged. 'I thought it sounded all right.'

'It sounded like a very old man breaking wind,' said Little Malc. 'Start again . . . Let's hear it for Koo La Grace.'

Little Malc waited. So did the drummer.

'What are you waiting for?' demanded Little Malc.

'I don't know.'

'I just gave you your fucking cue.'

'When?'

'When I said "Let's hear it for Koo La Grace".'

This time the drummer provided four bars of hi-hat.

'What the fuck's that?'

'It was meant to sound like a train.'

'What's a fucking train got to do with a drag queen from Bolton?'

'Yes.'

'What do you mean, yes?' said Little Malc. 'Did I ask you a fucking question?'

'No.'

'Well, why did you say yes?'

'It seemed appropriate,' said the drummer.

'Appropriate to fucking what?' Little Malc covered his face in his hands. 'Look. All I want is a drum roll, You can do a drum roll, can't you?'

The drummer provided a perfect drum roll.

'Good. Right,' said Little Malc. 'Now try doing it when I say, "Let's hear it for Koo La Grace".'

Another drum roll.

'What was that drum roll for?' said Little Malc.

'You said I should do it when you said "Koo La Grace".'

'No! No!' Little Malc kicked the stage. 'That wasn't your cue! That was me *telling* you about your cue!'

'Well, how the fuck was I supposed to know?' complained the drummer.

'Jesus Christ. Take fucking five,' said Little Malc, attaching his mike to the stand and walking off.

Rawhead got up from the stool and waited for Little Malc to pass. 'Mr Priest?'

Little Malc turned to look at him. 'Who are you?'

'Er, excuse me, Mr Priest, I heard that you might need a doorman.'

'Did you really.' Little Malc looked Rawhead up and down. 'You opportunistic bastard. Yes, we fucking do. Are you any good?'

'I used to work for Tommy Dean in Leeds.' Rawhead passed Little Malc a forged reference. Little Malc peered at it.

'"Abraham Stoker". Is that your name?'

'Yes, Mr Priest.'

'Are you clean, Abraham? Reason I ask, see, is I can't use anyone with a criminal record. I'll get closed down if I do things like that.'

'I haven't been in trouble since I was a kid.'

'Er, no. Sorry.' Little Malc handed back the letter. 'When I say clean I mean fucking clean.' He started to walk away.

'Your dad would have given me a chance,' said Rawhead.

Little Malc turned round, his eyes narrowing with venom. 'What? What did you say?'

'I met your dad once. At Maine Road. When I was a kid, a guy I washed cars for lent me his pass to the director's box. That's where I met your dad. He was really a great guy. Bought me drinks all afternoon, really looked after me. He could see I was a little bastard but he treated me with kindness. So, yeah. I think he would have given me this chance.'

'Oh. You do, do you?'

'Yes, sir.'

Little Malc took out a packet of Rothmans, put one in his mouth and fumbled around for a light. Rawhead produced a silver Harley Davidson lighter and offered a flame to Little Malc. Little Malc gave a small nod of thanks, inhaled smoke and stared into a corner. 'You're a slick twat, I'll give you that.' Little Malc stepped back and looked sideways at Rawhead. 'And you really want a job, do you?'

'Yes, sir.'

Little Malc nodded sceptically. 'Standing on a door, arguing with drunken pricks who want to know why they can't come in wearing their underpants over their fucking heads?'

'That's right.'

'You realize it's only five quid an hour? No sick pay, health insurance or paid holidays?'

'I don't care. I want to work, Mr Priest.'

'OK. Tonight at eight. But only because I'm fucking desperate. Understand? You're on trial. If you're late, you're sacked. If someone lays you out, you're sacked. If you start any trouble or try bad-mouthing difficult customers, you're out.'

'Thanks, Mr Priest.'

'And no weapons. If I ever catch you carrying a gun or a knife, you're also fucking out. Is that clear, *Abra-fucking-ham*?'

'Absolutely, Mr Priest.'

*

Rawhead's first night passed without serious incident. He worked the door with a young black kid called Brando, a sullen body-builder with a bad attitude. A coachload of Liverpudlians arrived. Two of them, both men in their twenties, didn't have tickets. Calmly, speaking softly and politely, Brando refused them entry. Rawhead stood back and watched, interested to see how the kid performed. One of the Scousers claimed that Brando's refusal to admit them owed nothing to their lack of tickets and everything to the fact that they came from Merseyside.

'You think we couldn't buy a couple of poxy tickets if we wanted to?'

'Well, why didn't you?'

'You Manchester cunts think you're better than us.'

Brando aped astonishment. 'What do you mean, I said you sleep in a dustbin?'

'You fucking what?'

'I never said anything about you eating cockroaches off the floor.'

The Scouser drew back his arm to launch a long-distance idiot swipe. While his arm was fully extended, Brando hit him. It didn't look like an especially hard blow, but the effect was impressive. The stricken man froze, his eyes rolled, he opened and closed his mouth like a goldfish, then tottered around in concentric circles until he fell over. His friend helped him up, spitting threats. 'Youse bastards are gonna regret this. We've got mates in high places.'

'Yeah. High-rise tower blocks with shit down the walls.'

When things were quiet again, Rawhead asked Brando where he'd learned to fight.

'I got corrupted by television.'

'Me too.'

'TV is destroying our culture. It always has done. All those

medieval torturors that caused unspeakable agony to millions –
do you think they were self-taught? No way. They got all their
ideas off the TV. Same with Hitler, same with Genghis Khan.
None of these guys would have hurt a living soul if it weren't
for television.'

'I agree. So why are you working as a doorman?'

'I'm a complete fuck-up,' said Brando. He unwrapped a stick
of gum and chewed it thoughtfully. 'What's your excuse?'

Rawhead just looked at him.

'Actually,' said Brando. 'I just got out of the sadhouse. Six
months for burglary. Can you believe that?'

'Easily.'

'But don't tell Malc. He doesn't employ criminals.'

'You don't find him a little, well, simple?'

'Listen. Where I've been, someone like Malc would be classed
as a fucking genius. You ever been inside?'

'Once.'

'There are guys in there who could have been great world
leaders if they'd only had a stable home-life.'

'Yeah?'

'No. But there are guys in there who could definitely open a
can of beans after seven months' intensive training.'

'You haven't got much heart,' observed Rawhead. 'I like that.'

Brando looked Rawhead up and down as if he'd made up his
mind to like him. 'Abraham. That's your name, right?'

Rawhead nodded. 'But you can call me Stoker.'

'Abraham was a prophet. You believe in God?'

'Yeah, I believe in God,' said Rawhead. 'What about you?'

Brando shrugged. 'Man, I sleep in a fucking car. I've got no
money, no woman. I'm near rock-bottom. But I'm not so far
down that I'll start praying to a fucking pancake in the sky.'

'Have you considered going back to burglary?'

'I can't pretend it hasn't crossed my mind.'

'Would you like to work for me?'

'What as? Your butler?'

A great roar of laughter rose up behind them. Koo La Grace had just told a joke about asylum seekers.

Rawhead never got round to answering Brando's question. A taxi pulled up outside the club. Two drunken men staggered out, accompanied by two giggling women. On closer inspection the two drunks turned out to be weasel-faced bruisers in their thirties. They had similar red faces, nasty little eyes and worryingly low foreheads. 'Evening, gentlemen,' said Brando, waving them through.

'What a polite little nigger,' said the leading weasel. His brother guffawed. One of the women laughed. The other was embarrassed, but not embarrassed enough to walk away.

'Why'd you let them in?' said Rawhead, watching the party laughing and farting their way through the entrance hall.

'The Medina brothers. Friends of Chef's,' said Brando.

'Did you hear what he said to you?'

'Don't act so surprised, man. That's nothing. Try six months in Strangeways. In there, even the prison chaplain calls you nigger. '

Rawhead was quiet for a long time. Then he said: 'Are you working tomorrow night?'

Brando nodded. 'No rest for the poverty-stricken.'

'Something might happen. I want you to stay at home.'

'Yeah, great idea.' Brando thought it was a joke.

'I'll see you get your money, even if I have to pay you myself.'

Rawhead smiled calmly. But as Brando looked, the man at his side underwent a subtle transfiguration. His eyes darkened and he seemed to grow in stature. The face, which until that moment had looked mild and friendly, became a mask of primitive evil.

And there was something else. A sweet, sickening smell. It was the perfume of murder, like a fragrant breeze blowing through the hole in a man's skull. Inexplicably, Brando tasted blood in his mouth and for a few seconds he forgot to breathe.

'Did you hear what I said?' asked Rawhead.

Brando stared.

'Skip work tomorrow night,' said Rawhead slowly and deliberately, making absolutely sure he was understood. 'There's going to be trouble.'

5

With how sad steps, O Moone, thou climbst the skies!
How silently, and with how wanne a face!

'Astrophel and Stella', Sir Philip Sidney (1554–1586)

The Old Cow, a small, squalid establishment in Glossop, was renowned for its beer, its curries and its gangland shootings.

The yellow-toothed landlord, Snowy Rains, had a habit of standing at the bar and interrupting the conversations of his customers. Rumour had it that Snowy watered down the beer with his own piss. He didn't. It just tasted that way.

Snowy liked to think of himself as a face and quietly enjoyed the fact that small-time hoods came in to drink and occasionally kill each other on the premises. As long as the customers didn't start on him, he felt the pub's ominous reputation reflected favourably on his manhood.

It was no exaggeration to say that Snowy's worthless life consisted of butting in, boasting, drinking, sleeping and farting. He liked to claim that he had rampant sex with young women whenever his wife Sheila's back was turned, but this was untrue. The pub opened every day from eleven to three, and seven to midnight. There was a lock-in every night, which meant the last stragglers would not be leaving before 2 a.m. This left little time for fornication.

'We've had members of the Priesthood drinking here,' announced Snowy.

Until then, the pub had been silent. It was a Sunday lunchtime after Christmas. There were only four customers. In the snug, an old man and his son were watching televised darts.

Two thugs at the bar, Pest and Jammer, were working their way through a wad of stolen scratch cards to see if they'd won anything.

Irritated by the lack of response, Snowy tried again. 'The Beast used to come in.'

'I knew him,' said Pest, without bothering to look up.

Pest was a little hook-nosed scumbag. When he was stoned, which was most of the time, he had a habit of threatening anyone in earshot. His companion, Jammer, was a tall, angular man who said little and, to his shame, hadn't had a fight since he was thirteen, when he'd been soundly thrashed during a dispute about a packet of Jaffa cakes.

Pest and Jammer were both grammar-school boys from the seventies who had deliberately dumbed down in the hope of being accepted into the criminal fraternity. It hadn't worked. Now they were middle-aged, bitter and unemployed.

'That's right,' said Snowy, cig hanging from his mouth, pint of bitter in his hand. 'Big bloke, quiet voice, horrible ginger hair.'

'My wife's ginger,' said Jammer.

'Oh, sorry,' said Snowy. 'Didn't mean anything by it. Sometimes you can get very attractive red-haired people.'

'Not my wife,' said Jammer.

Pest nodded and smirked.

'He knows,' said Jammer, nodding to Pest. 'He's fucked her.'

'Several times,' said Pest, shaking his head to dispel the memory.

Another customer came in, tall, wearing sportswear, ski goggles and a woolly hat. Snowy glanced at him dismissively and continued his story.

'Anyway, the Beast comes in, has a couple of pints. Nice chap, we have a chat about football. Next thing I hear, he's dead. Apparently, he parked his car at the lights on Glossop High Street, up comes some little prick biker on a 125 and bang, shoots him fucking dead.'

'I heard it was the public bogs in Stockport,' said Pest. 'He's having a piss, then the guy pissing next to him leans over and sticks a meat skewer through his neck.'

'I've just won fifty quid,' said Jammer.

'Half that money's mine,' said Pest, peering at the card covetously. He looked up at Snowy.

'The Beast wasn't shot,' said Jammer. 'You're thinking of Mick the Lampshade. It was Mick who got shot in Glossop. No one knows what happened to the Beast. They never found his body. He disappeared along with Heidi, Doc and Malcolm Priest. All dead in a fucking trunk somewhere.'

'Yeah? I heard Priest isn't dead,' said Snowy. 'I heard he'd retired because he was getting too fat. They did liposuction on him, sucked off all the blubber. Now he lives in a French chateau with a gorgeous nineteen-year-old blonde. That's what I heard, anyway. He's a bit like Elvis. People keep getting sightings of him, but no fucker can pin him down.'

'I heard Elvis was dead,' said the stranger in the ski goggles.

'Fuck off,' said Pest. 'Who asked you?'

The stranger shrugged and inched further down the bar. 'What can I get you?' said Snowy. He eyed the man in ski goggles sternly, as if to warn him that if he was no match for Pest, he was certainly no match for the yellow-toothed landlord of the Old Cow.

'Rémy Martin. A double.'

Pest and Jammer, overhearing the order, sniggered at its ponciness.

Privately, Snowy was impressed by the stranger's request. Normally he catered for the worst inhabitants of Glossop, punters that were one step up from the meths bottle. Few of them had heard of champagne cognac, let alone drunk it. Despite his bizarre appearance, the stranger was clearly a man of discernment. Snowy pumped out two shots from a bottle encrusted with dust and grease. But for the sake of appearances, he slammed the glass down insultingly and snatched the proffered note from the stranger's hand.

Pest wasn't about to let Snowy get off so lightly. 'I don't know who you've been talking to ... probably the cockroaches in your filthy fucking toilets. But anyone who's anyone in Manchester knows that Priest's dead.'

'Yeah?' said Snowy. 'Well, it's facts that impress me. Not rumours.'

'What's more, everyone knows who fucking killed him,' continued Pest. 'Rawhead. That's fucking who. The Priesthood was the greatest gang in Manchester. The greatest gang anywhere in the globe – Leeds, Newcastle, you fucking name it. Rawhead was this fucking legend, the law couldn't get near him.

'Then Mal Priest does something to piss him off and Rawhead goes on the rampage. Next thing you know, the Beast, Heidi, Priesty all vanish off the face of the earth.'

'Who the fuck was Rawhead?' said Snowy rhetorically. 'No cunt knows.'

'He always wore a hood. That's what's so bloody clever about it,' marvelled Jammer, wishing *he'd* thought of wearing a hood. 'For all we know, Snowy could be Rawhead. I could be Rawhead.'

'No, you fucking couldn't,' said Pest. '*I* could. You couldn't.'

Jammer went quiet.

Pest wouldn't let it rest. 'Who's number one? I am. Who's number two? You are. Repeat after me, "I'm number one, you're number two."'

'I don't want to,' said Jammer.

'Say it!' warned Pest, spraying spittle across the bar.

Jammer shrugged. 'I'm number one, you're number two.'

Pest pulled a Beretta. 'You fucking what? Are you fucking saying you're better than me?'

'No,' admitted Jammer. 'I was just repeating what you told me to say.'

Pest held the gun to Jammer's head. 'Say "I'm a hairdresser."'

'Pest.' Jammer sighed. 'What're you pointing that at me for? You know as well as I do that gun ain't real.'

'Of course it's real. It's a real copy.' Pest placed the replica Beretta on the counter and shoved his empty glass over to Jammer. 'It's your round, dear.'

'It was my round last time.'

'And it'll be your round every time 'til kingdom fucking come, unless you stop behaving like my aunty fucking Mabel.'

'These are on the house, lads,' said Snowy, not wanting another death on the premises just yet. 'You were telling me about the Priesthood, Pest.'

'Now Chef's in charge of the gang,' said Pest, 'no one sees him.'

'He's shared the power out with Little Malc, Priest's son,' said Jammer. 'Chef lives out in Knutsford. Little Malc runs the club at Salford Quays.'

'It all comes down to money,' lamented Pest. 'Without capital, you can't even set yourself up as a criminal no more. Little Malc inherits his dad's club – what do I inherit? Me mother's false teeth and the piss-pot from under her fucking bed. Guys like me, with brains and balls but no fucking money – we're caught in the poverty trap.'

Pest thought he heard laughter to his right. He turned to ask the prat in the ski goggles what was so funny, but there was no one there.

*

It was after three on a dark January afternoon when Pest walked home to his lonely terraced hovel in old Glossop to sleep off the seven pints he'd drunk at lunchtime. A knackered-looking Ford Sierra was parked outside his front door. Pest didn't own a car but resented people parking outside his house. He kicked in the nearside headlamp as he passed it.

Pest entered his house, bent down to pick up the notice of eviction that was lying on the doormat and felt something cold brush his left temple.

'Don't turn your head,' advised a calm, low voice.

The warning was uttered with such quiet conviction that Pest froze, remaining bent over the doormat. In the corner of his eye he could see something dark and knew that a handgun was touching his skull. 'If this is about the money I owe Phil Haye, he'll get it back on Wednesday when I get me giro.'

'Get up and walk over to the sofa. Don't look at me. Just sit down.'

Slowly, Pest did what he was told. Rawhead, standing behind him, noticed that he was shaking. 'There's an envelope on the sofa. Open it.'

Pest peered into the envelope. It was full of ten-pound notes. 'What's this?'

'One hundred. You get the same again when the job's done.'

'What job?'

Rawhead dropped a Browning automatic over the back of the sofa. The gun had belonged to one of his victims. 'Have you heard of Malcolm Priest Junior?'

'Fucking hell!' said Pest.

'Do you know what he looks like?'

'Yeah, but . . . he's in the fucking Priesthood.'

'Used to be. Let's just say Little Malc has passed his expiry date.'

There was silence as Pest struggled to absorb and interpret this information. If this was a commission from the Priesthood, perhaps glory beckoned. 'Why don't you do it yourself?'

'I'm not here to satisfy your idle curiosity.'

''Cause you don't want to get fucking shot,' sputtered Pest.

'Shut up and listen,' said Rawhead. 'Little Malc is regular in his habits. He leaves his club every morning just after four. No one'll be with him. He has a driver who picks him up in a Rolls.'

'Does Little Malc carry a piece?'

'No.'

'What about the driver?'

'No. A hairpiece, maybe.'

Pest shook his head and lit a cig. 'Maybe I've got a bad head for figures,' he said, 'but two hundred don't seem enough for a job like this.'

Miraculously, a set of car keys fell into Pest's lap.

'Plus you get to keep the car that's parked outside.'

'That Sierra? Fucking hell! Why didn't you tell me before? I just smashed one of the fucking lights.'

'Should teach you to look after your things. As for the fee, it's the same for all hitmen. Shit money at first, then the money gets better on the next job, when we know we can trust you.'

'You're making me a hitman?'

'Yeah.'

'For the Priesthood?'

Rawhead didn't answer.

'Even so,' mused Pest. 'Two fucking hundred?'

'I don't see you getting any better offers.'

'And what if I say no?'

'Then you'd better lie down. Face down on the floor.'

'No need, mate. I'll take the job. I'm up for it.'

'Lie down anyway.'

Pest forced a laugh. 'I said I'd do the fucking hit, didn't I?' There was panic in his voice as he outstretched on the stained and ragged hearthrug. 'I don't want to fucking lie down.'

'Face down on the floor. Hands by your sides.'

Pest lay there for a long time, waiting and listening, inhaling the stale piss-smell of the rug under his nose. Finally, emboldened by the heavy silence, he raised his head and looked around. The room was empty.

*

There was a full moon that night. Even Pest, who never noticed a fucking thing, saw how bright the moon was and the way it washed the streets of Glossop and the surrounding hills with milky blue light. He was shocked – he thought he hated nature. In fact, Pest thought he hated everyone and everything. Yet tonight life was a magical thing.

Just that lunchtime Pest had been the same old loser. Now he had a gun, not just a reconditioned copy. A genuine illegal firearm, with a full seven shots on the clip. Bang, one dead fuckface. Bang, another dead fuckface. Bang, bang, bang, three dead fuckfaces squealing in a row. Not only that, but he had wheels, licensed and insured until March. He had a hundred notes to spend on a single night out. In his own eyes, he had become a glamorous figure.

He'd arranged to meet a woman in the Old Cow, a divorcee called Margaret. She was in her forties, hard-faced, with a pointed, argumentative nose. According to Jammer, Pest had fucked her once after a party. Pest had no memory of this event. But the bitch kept phoning for no reason, so he supposed it must be true.

He ordered a chicken vindaloo for himself. As he was eating, he noticed Margaret was sulking.

'What's the matter with your fucking face?' he said.

'"And what about you, Margaret?"' she answered. Doing an impression of Pest as a considerate suitor. '"Would you like anything to eat, Margaret?" Yes, fucking thank you. Because I'm out with Pest, and he'd see me fucking starve before he'd offer me a meal!'

At first Pest didn't know what she was talking about. Then the penny dropped. 'What? You expect me to buy your fucking food?' He was so angry he grabbed her by the hair and tried to force her face down in his curry. It wasn't easy. She had strong neck muscles. So it really didn't look as good as Jimmy Cagney. But eventually he managed to thrust her argumentative nose into the vindaloo.

She slapped his shoulder and ran out screaming.

It was a Friday night. The pub was full. For a while, everyone stopped talking. When the chatter resumed, Snowy came over to Pest's table and said, 'Out.'

'You fucking what?' said Pest, not understanding what the fuss was about.

'Out of my fucking pub,' said Snowy. 'And don't come back.'

'OK. But I haven't finished eating. So give us me fucking money back,' said Pest.

Snowy walked off to the bar and returned with four quid.

'What's this?' said Pest.

'The meal cost seven ninety-five. You've eaten half of it, so there's half your money back.'

'What the fuck is the matter with you?' said Pest.

'I'll tell you, shall I? That woman you were with . . . her ex-husband is a fucking copper, you pillock. And you assaulted her?'

'Assault? She got a bit of curry sauce on her fucking conk.'

'You don't seem to understand, dickbrain. If this pub gets any more bad publicity, it gets closed down. That's my livelihood down the fucking Swanee. Now fuck off.'

'All right,' said Pest, getting to his feet. 'Just one more thing . . .'

And then he drew the Browning.

But before he could remove the safety catch, Snowy hit him. It was a wonderful, direct punch in the mouth that sent Pest careering over chairs and tables. Pest tried to get up, but Snowy hit him again, this time splattering his nose. Pest was vaguely aware of being dragged through the narrow, crowded bar before being ejected into the cold night.

He lay on the pavement for a while, gathering his thoughts. The night was turning out quite badly. Ten minutes ago he'd had a pint, a curry and a guaranteed shag. Now his front teeth were loose, his aquiline nose looked more like a viaduct and his reputation as Glossop's hardest man had taken a serious dent.

Pest rolled over onto his side, hawking and spitting to clear the blood from his throat. He felt intensely humiliated. It is always uniquely embarrassing when a man you feel sure you can beat has the audacity to turn round and hammer you. Who'd have thought a fairy like Snowy could pack a punch like that? It wasn't as if the fat yellow-toothed bastard went to the gym or anything.

No, Snowy wasn't hard. He'd just been lucky. Pest knew he was still the hardest man in Glossop, and possibly the north-west of England. He got to his knees, coughing. Cars went by but no one stopped to help him. Good. Because if they had, Pest would have given them the same treatment he'd given his own car. Kicked their fucking headlamps in, that'd teach them to take pity on him, the patronizing four-wheeled bastards.

Then he remembered the gun. It was still inside the pub. He'd dropped it somewhere between the first and second punch. He got to his feet, realized it hurt to breathe. His ribs ached, although he wasn't sure why. Swearing, he walked back into the crowded pub and up to the bar. 'Gimme my fucking gun.'

Snowy looked at him and sighed. Pest could see regret in his eyes as the landlord studied his shattered face. He whistled to someone out of view. Pest felt a supportive arm slip under his left armpit. He looked to see who it was and saw Jammer.

'You're not to start any more trouble,' said Jammer sternly.

'Take him to a hospital, would you?' pleaded Snowy. 'I'd appreciate it.'

Jammer nodded. Pest hung his head for a moment to drip blood onto the floorboards. Then Jammer marched him out.

Pest didn't want to go to a hospital. He insisted that he'd be better off at home. They were halfway to Pest's house when he remembered the Browning again and tried to turn back. 'I need it.'

'I've got your fucking gun,' said Jammer. 'Here. Take the bloody thing. I don't know where you got it and I don't fucking want to know.'

'Fuck off.'

'Listen. Don't come back to the pub tonight. Get me? I'll smooth things over with Snowy, leave that to me. Give it a couple of days to blow over, he'll come round. But tonight you're staying home. OK?'

'Just fuck off, will ya?'

Pest hugged the weapon to his heart until they were at his front door. Jammer asked if he needed any more help. Pest took a swing at him, missed and fell over. Jammer walked away in disgust. Pest struggled to his feet, found his door key and let himself in. He turned on the light and lay down on the sofa. Still clutching the gun, he passed out.

*

The fat man with curly hair that Rawhead had butted in the face was called Fats Medcroft. On Rawhead's second night Medcroft was on duty, eyes swollen, a plaster on his nose. 'You wouldn't

DAVID BOWKER

believe the cunt who did it. Some cunt in a pair of goggles – the stupidest twat you ever saw – nuts me and shoots another lad's foot off. First rule of running a door: just because a fella looks like a daft prick, don't mean he ain't dangerous.'

Fats Medcroft was about forty-five. He refused to call the new boy Abraham, feeling it was a puff's name. So he called him Stoker. Everyone else did the same.

In his youth, Fats had been a promising boxer, but had found it difficult to keep within his weight category. Forty thousand meat pies later, Fats was the most disgracefully unhealthy bouncer Rawhead had ever seen. He smoked constantly and kept a flask of brandy in his hip pocket.

While they controlled the door, a third bouncer called Sirus patrolled inside to check for trouble and drug dealers. Sirus had a peroxide crew cut. He looked like a low-grade villain from a Bond film, one of those poor fucks who get thrown to the piranhas and never makes another movie as long as they live.

Tonight was a dance night. Fats hated dance nights, not because of the lasers and the noise but because of all the illicit dealers trying to unload their talcum powder on unsuspecting posh kids from Bramhall and Cheadle Hulme. Pockets and handbags had to be searched, it took time, and there were only two of them. 'Why doesn't Mr Priest employ more staff?'

'Because he hasn't got the money,' said Fats.

'How come? This place must make a fortune.'

'Yeah. But Malcolm only gets to keep a share. Most of it goes to the big man.'

After they'd searched a coachload of kids from Rochdale, Fats went for a cup of tea and a sit-down. Little Malc appeared and asked Rawhead how he was doing.

'Fine, Mr Priest.'

'Good,' said Little Malc, walking about in a great cloud of

70

citrus-scented cologne. 'Now, don't take this the wrong way, but I've got to search you.'

Rawhead frowned. 'I thought you'd already done that?'

Little Malc, hands working all the time, shot Rawhead a sly glance. 'Just because you came in clean don't mean you still are.'

'Fine. I just wouldn't want you to search the wrong guy . . .'

Little Malc glared at him. 'Listen, fuckface,' he said, suddenly sounding and looking like his father's son. 'You're just a fucking doorknob with a stupid name. After tonight, you might not even be a doorknob.'

Fats returned from his tea break as Little Malc was storming off. 'He gets like that,' Fats said. 'Pay no attention. He hasn't seen his wife for a few nights. The lad gets grumpy when he hasn't had his whistle blown.'

It was Rawhead's turn for a break. He went to the gents for a piss, but the door was jammed. He kicked it open and saw a man in a dinner jacket slam into the opposite wall. It was Sirus. Two hundred and fifty pounds of rippling muscle and the guy couldn't even hold a door shut.

Angry and humiliated, Sirus turned on Rawhead. 'Use the fucking bog upstairs.'

His eyes were wide and shining, like he'd just seen a vision of the Virgin Mary. But Rawhead thought it was more likely that he'd been nosing coke. Rawhead didn't move, so Sirus tried to shove him. Rawhead didn't like being touched, especially by low-grade Bond villains. He punched Sirus in his six-pack and Sirus doubled up, yelling: 'Oof!'

Rawhead was surprised. He thought people only said 'Oof!' in comics.

Rawhead looked past the injured doorman at the two other guys who were standing by the sink. Between them lay a black attaché case. The case was open. Rawhead couldn't make out the contents. But he recognized the two men. It was the Medina brothers. They stared at him, not moving, too startled to be angry.

'Tell you what,' said Rawhead, turning to leave. 'Why don't I use the bog upstairs?'

*

Just before midnight, a silvery sports car screeched to a halt outside the club. A man with a sequinned beret got out, followed by a blonde woman with very long legs and a very short skirt. Leaving the car running, they walked to the door. Fats nodded respectfully. The man in the beret tossed his car keys to Rawhead.

'Park the car, would you, my good man?'

You could tell he thought he was a witty guy. His girlfriend certainly thought so. Rawhead tossed the keys back. 'Park it yourself.'

'My friend doesn't understand,' said Fats, shooting Rawhead a warning glance. He nodded at the beret-wearing prick, then at the poster on the door. 'This is Zippa Jay, Manchester's coolest DJ. Park his car.'

Zippa Jay and his girlfriend smirked as Rawhead grimly accepted the keys and walked out to the car. He was beginning to wonder if he was temperamentally suited to being a doorman. The car was a Porsche Boxter with a number plate that read:

ZIPPA 1

If there was one thing that Rawhead hated more than personalized number plates, it was DJs. They reminded him of the fourteen-year-olds who open their bedroom windows wide on summer afternoons so the entire neighbourhood can hear their record collection. Such behaviour is forgiveable in a naive kid. But not in a thirty-five-year-old twat in a beret.

Rawhead motored round to the private car park behind Diva and slotted the Porsche into a reserved parking space. He took a penknife out of his pocket and scraped a diagonal line across the car's bonnet.

Suddenly, Zippa's car didn't look nearly so expensive.

*

When Pest came round, he didn't know where he was.

His first impression was that he was still on the pavement outside the Old Cow. He could feel freezing cold air on his face, ankles and the base of his spine. He opened his eyes slowly and recognized that he was at home, lying on the torn, shiny sofa stained with ketchup, brown ale and stray jism. It was winter and his house had no heating apart from a two-bar electric fire that he'd forgotten to put on. Cold air poured in through the gap under the front door.

His face hurt, but not unbearably. What hurt more was the memory of the severe pounding Snowy Rains had given him. Something hard was burrowing into Pest's chest. He reached for the cause of his discomfort, felt the muzzle of the gun. With a rush of anxiety he remembered the job he'd been given. Stiffly, he turned his head to look at the clock and, for a horrible moment, thought it was quarter past six. *Fuck! Fuck!* He sat up and, focusing, saw that it was in fact thirty-two minutes past three. This was still very bad. He had half an hour to get down-town.

He went upstairs to relieve his bladder, farting curry fumes as he waited for the piss to flow. When he looked in the mirror, he was dismayed. He looked like one of the losers after a bout at 'Fight club'.

He could still smell bile, but couldn't see where the stench was coming from. Above the neckline of his leather jacket, he could see he was wearing a speckled brown scarf. He couldn't recall owning such a scarf and opened the jacket for a closer look. A solid lump of cold vomit sagged forward and slapped to the bathroom floor like a jelly.

Pest had no time to wash or change his clothes, no time to study for a fucking PhD either. Stinking and unsightly, he went downstairs and had a brief panic while he searched for his gun. It was on the floor by the sofa. A horrifying thought occurred to him. What if Snowy had unloaded it? His heart hammered like an injured bird's until he released the clip and saw that he still had his seven shots.

It was now three thirty-six. *Move it, you twat, you loser.*

He rushed into his kitchen, walls and ceiling black with the grease from a thousand filthy fry-ups. In a cupboard above the sink, he kept some sulphate in the bottom of a cracked china cup. The grey powder was hard and old. He chipped a lump free with the end of a teaspoon and swallowed it. Almost instantly, he felt the speed lighting him up, window by window, like a tall building at night.

Then he went out to the crappy Sierra and started it up.

His journey to the club was fast and berserk. He jumped every available light. The speed he'd taken made all the red lights leave weird, wiggly trails. If there had been any pedestrians on the roads, he would have mown down the fuckers and laughed about it. He was a killer.

At the mouth of Water Street he rolled down his window and slowed to a crawl. Pest didn't know the time. He didn't have a watch and he'd forgotten to charge up his mobile phone. He had no idea whether he was late or early. Probably late. The street outside the club was surprisingly busy, taxis coming and going, girls standing about in groups, laughing and talking. At four in the fucking morning.

Outside Diva he had to wait for a black cab to load up and move away. This gave him a chance to see who was on the door. There was just one guy there, some lanky bonehead in a suit. Absolutely no fucking problem.

Pest had planned on waiting in his car with the engine running until Little Malc came out, but there were too many cars. He was scared that if he parked, some inconsiderate fucker might box him in. Then he'd be in trouble after the hit. *Excuse me. Would you mind moving your motor? I need to make a speedy fucking getaway . . .*

Instead he found a dark side street, parked the car and walked back to the club. After the sulphate, he was well revved. He was fucking buzzing. Tonight he was going to kill Little Malc. *The son of Malcolm Priest.* This would make his reputation. In a few months, with a few kills under his belt, he'd give Snowy Rains an ultimatum: free beer for life or I'll kill all your customers, one by one.

He found a dark doorway across the street from the club and lay there. Nothing unusual about a guy lying in a Manchester doorway. The wall beside him reeked of rotting fish, but Pest didn't smell much better. A couple of young women clicked by, all lip gloss and powdered pubes.

Pest took out his gun, slipped off the safety catch and waited.

An hour passed. As he watched, the lights outside the club went off. The bonehead on the door emerged once, to glance up and down the street. Then he disappeared again. A couple of loud rich guys came out of the club, then went back in, then came out again, like indecisive homos. For what seemed like ages, the two ponces stood outside the club, laughing and talking in rich plummy voices. It seemed obvious that they were waiting for a cab, but then they broke away abruptly and walked off in opposite directions.

In the space of about fifteen minutes, the street had emptied. Above the doorway, high above the ugly roofs and chimneys, the full moon looked down at Pest, its pale mouth open as if it was about to gob in his face. A block away, some guy was singing unaccompanied in a sweet tenor voice. 'I wonder what is keeping my true love tonight, I wonder what is keeping her from my sight . . .'

The voice echoed, lonely and sad, a stab of poetry in the piss-stained night.

Instinctively, Pest moved further back into the doorway. A moment later, a silver Rolls-Royce oozed past and parked outside the club.

Engine purring comfortably, the Rolls waited, completely blocking Pest's view of the main entrance. He got to his feet for a better look and saw the uniformed driver getting out of the car. Pest heard voices and started to walk, adrenalin wiping out the reassuring glow of the sulphate. The gun's handle and trigger were now slippery with his sweat. His legs felt unsteady as he raced round the side of the Rolls to perform his first-ever hit.

A short, wide-shouldered man in a grey suit was approaching the car. The chauffeur, stout and grey-haired, held the passenger door open for him. Pest brushed past the chauffeur and said, 'Malcolm Priest Junior?' He had to be sure.

'Yes,' said Little Malc automatically, his eyes widening as he realized he'd made a mistake.

Little Malc saw the gun and outstretched the palms of his hands. As if he was Clark Kent, and his hands could deflect a speeding bullet. The chauffeur, who could have intervened, hadn't yet worked out what was happening. Pest could feel his own heart bouncing around in his chest, like a bird trapped inside a room, crashing from wall to wall in its panic.

Time seemed to slow down. Pest thought, this is it, I cannot fail. He's standing right in front of me. Now I shoot him. He's just fucking standing there. All I have to do is point the gun and squeeze the trigger. Don't snatch at the trigger, that'll fuck up your shot. Aim at the target and squeeze slowly. But oh, the gun feels heavy. So very heavy.

The thing was, Pest had never killed anyone. He'd slashed guys, burned and stabbed them, kicked them in the head. But he'd never deliberately pulled the 'off' switch on another human being. It was a little harder than he'd expected.

Shouting and swearing, hands over his eyes, Little Malc threw himself on the ground and curled up in a ball, as if this would somehow protect him from a bullet fired at close range. The chauffeur was crouching behind the bonnet of the car. He was shouting, too. Pest was about to shoot Little Malc when he was distracted by someone walking towards him. It was the tall bonehead who'd been standing on the door.

Pest should have shot Little Malc there and then. But as the doorman drew closer, Pest saw he was holding an oversized revolver, the kind of weapon Clint Eastwood used in the *Dirty Harry* films. He appeared to be in no hurry. He moved like a man going out to buy a newspaper. His gun, held loosely in his right hand, was pointed at the ground. Obviously an amateur. Pest decided to shoot him first.

Pest fired. The tremendous ringing blam of the shot made him jump. There was more smoke than he'd expected. The smoke smelled sweet, like the cap guns he'd played with as a kid. Although Pest had aimed at the doorman's midriff, or thought he had, the bullet hit the Rolls, blasting a hole through the rear passenger door. The car rocked on its beautiful springs.

The doorman kept on coming.

Pest fired again. This time, the gun went *Myoww* like a startled cat. The second bullet hit the wall beside the doorman's head, showering him with brick dust and sparks. The doorman did not flinch, merely raised his own weapon and fired.

The big gun made a noise like the earth cracking open. The bullet hit Pest in the chest, severing his aorta. He rocketed backwards, flying five feet through the air. He landed on his back, already confused and blinking. Two seconds later he was dead.

6

He gives me wealth; I give him all my Vowes:
I give him songs; He gives me length of dayes

'Canticle', Francis Quarles (1592–1644)

When he heard the shots, Fats Medcroft ran upstairs to the gents' lavatory and hid. His departure was prompted by ambition, not cowardice. He was fat and old, his tits were getting bigger by the year, but Fats still dreamed of making something of his life. He was not about to get mourned for a man who paid him five pounds an hour.

After what seemed a long time, but was in fact seven minutes, he heard footsteps on the landing outside. He flushed the toilet and caught a glimpse of himself in the mirror. Under the naked bulb, his sagging face looked white and scared. His hair curled upwards, vertically, like a dollop of whipped cream. The light was on in Little Malc's office. He could hear soft voices. Cautiously, Fats walked across the landing and stood on the threshold. Then he rapped softly on the door and peered into the room.

Little Malc, his chauffeur and Abraham Stoker were inside the room. Stoker and Little Malc were sitting at the table. The chauffeur, Frank, was slumped on the sofa. He was in shock, twitching and shaking. He flinched at the sound of Medcroft's knock.

Stoker was curiously relaxed and watchful. Little Malc was agitated. 'Where the fuck were you?' he asked Fats.

'I needed a dump, Malcolm.'

'So did I when I saw that fucking gun pointing at me.' Little Malc jabbed his own chest. 'I've just been shot at, I have. Some fucking nutter just tried to box me.'

'What? In the club?'

Quietly, Rawhead told the story of the shooting.

Fats wasn't surprised. Anyone who puts a price on a hitman's head is crying out to be deeply mourned and sadly missed. Fats had told Little Malc as much to his face. 'Don't do it, boss. You're endangering yourself and the lives of your family.' Then Little Malc had got angry and called Fats a white wog. Fats wasn't quite sure what Little Malc meant by this, only knew it was intended as an insult.

'So where's the body?' said Fats.

'In the boot of my fucking Roller!' said Little Malc. 'That car was my dad's. Now it's covered in blood and shit.'

'And puke,' added Rawhead.

'That's right.' Little Malc pointed at Fats. 'And you? Where were you? You big fat ladyboy.' Then he pointed at Rawhead. 'I might be dead, if it weren't for this lad. Do you hear me? This brave bastard, who isn't even on the payroll, fucking shielded me! He did the job I pay you to fucking do!'

'Really?' said Fats. 'That's funny. 'Cause when I saw this job advertised at the jobcentre, I don't remember "human shield" being part of the fucking job description.'

'Don't be smart, it doesn't fucking suit you,' snapped Little Malc.

'I better ring my wife,' said Frank, the chauffeur. 'She'll be wondering if I'm all right.'

'What're you on about?' demanded Little Malc.

'She'll want to know if I'm all right,' said Frank, 'if she's heard about the shooting.'

Little Malc was incensed. He got up and shook his finger in

Frank's face. 'How could she have heard about the shooting, tug-boy? No one knows about this but us.'

'Bad news travels fast,' said Frank lamely.

'You'll travel fast in a minute,' Little Malc told Frank. 'You'll travel right through that fucking window, head first.'

Frank looked stunned, so Little Malc punched him on the shoulder to underline the point. 'You breathe one word about this, Frank, and I'm warning you. I don't know what I'll do . . .'

Everyone went quiet apart from Frank, who started to blub. Little Malc poured brandy into a dirty glass and passed it to him.

'I don't drink and drive,' said Frank.

'Fucking drink it!' snarled Little Malc. Then he poured a glass for himself.

'So what do we do now?' asked Fats.

'Answers on a postcard to Strangeways Prison, No-hope-of-parole, Losershire,' said Little Malc, with some bitterness. 'What a fucking night! Someone trashes the fucking DJ's car and it's *me* he threatens to sue. Then I end up with a body to hide.'

'You could ask Chef for help,' said Fats.

'No fucking way,' said Little Malc. 'It was probably him that paid for the fucking hit!'

There was another long silence.

Rawhead cleared his throat. 'If you'll forgive me, I've got a suggestion,' he said quietly.

*

Rawhead drove into rural Staffordshire and found a quiet leafy road. He opened the boot and attended to the stinking mutilated corpse. When he was satisfied that the dead man carried no ID, he dumped the body in a drainage ditch and drove away.

Normally Rawhead took pains about concealing bodies, sometimes driving about with them in the boot of his car for days. But he guessed, rightly, that no one would be able to identify Pest's remains. The Staffordshire police would make a half-hearted appeal on *Crimewatch* and give up. Pest had no dental records. He had no dentist. Apart from his many creditors, no one would care that he was missing. People had wanted Pest to go missing for years.

*

Rawhead spent the rest of the day cleaning up the car and himself. He took out the carpet from the boot and dumped it at the local tip. Then he washed the Rolls by hand, scouring every inch of it for blood and tissue. He found quite a lot. When he'd finished, he phoned Little Malc on his mobile.

Little Malc asked Rawhead round to his house in West Didsbury, a nice three-storey house in a desirable road. His neighbours were actors and TV personalities.

Rawhead rang the bell and Little Malc's wife opened the door. She looked stupid and pretty. She had kind eyes and a layer of brown mud on her face that Rawhead supposed was make-up. Two little girls ran into the hall to see who it was. They looked like their mother, only less used.

Little Malc was in the vast fitted kitchen. He'd just got up. He was wearing his dressing gown and nothing else. He had his father's tits and his mother's hips. A huge pan of bacon, eggs and mushrooms was cooking on the stove. Little Malc asked his wife for a little privacy and shut the kitchen door.

When they were alone, he asked Rawhead what he'd done with the body. Rawhead told him he didn't need to know.

Little Malc nodded and narrowed his eyes. 'Yeah? Something tells me you've done this kind of thing before.' Rawhead smiled politely. Little Malc dished the food out onto two plates. 'You eating with me? You might as well. There's enough for two.'

Rawhead was hungry. He sat down at the table with Little

Malc and ate. Little Malc finished first and got up to brew a pot of tea. As he waited for the kettle to boil, he stood by the window, serious and watchful, the veins showing in his pale ankles. 'Maybe you could tell me what your real name is.'

'The name isn't important,' said Rawhead.

'So why are you here? You're not from Manchester, you've got a London accent. And you're certainly not a fucking doorknob. Are you?'

Rawhead continued to eat. When he'd finished, he looked at Little Malc and smiled. 'It doesn't matter who I am. I think I could help you. You admit you need help?'

Little Malc blew air out of his mouth like a child playing puffer trains. 'You shouldn't have been packing a gun. That was naughty. I told you not to. All I can say is, thank God you didn't listen. Otherwise I'd be dead and me kids would be orphans. Well, I suppose they'd still have a mother. So maybe orphans isn't the right fucking word . . . anyway, you get me drift.'

'You want me to work for you?'

'Yeah. If you want it, you're guaranteed a job on the door of my club for life.'

Rawhead laughed. It was not a pleasant laugh.

Hurt appeared in Little Malc's eyes. 'OK, then. Tell me what you want. Don't just fucking snigger. I've got half shares in a restaurant, too, you know. The Moroccan in Deansgate. I'll give you a job there, if you'd rather. How does head waiter grab you?'

'Listen. In a year or so, you won't have a restaurant. You won't have a club either, if the drug dealing carries on.'

'What drug dealing?'

'Are you kidding me? Those scumbags the Medinas are playing you like a flob.'

'A what?'

'A flob. A flobadob. A flowerpot man.' Rawhead sighed to

convey his immense weariness. 'You're supposed to be in the Priesthood and you don't even know Priesthood slang?'

'Ah. But who said I was in the Priesthood? I'm not. I'm a "business associate" of the Priesthood.'

'You're nobody's associate, Malcolm.'

'All right. Fuck off, then. Don't work for me. See if I care.'

'No. I'll work for you.'

Little Malc looked distinctly sceptical. 'What as?'

'I'm going to be your mentor.'

'What kind of mental? You mean like a spackhead?'

Rawhead wondered whether Little Malc was putting on an act or whether he really was this stupid.

*

When Rawhead explained it, Little Malc grew to like the idea. Rawhead – or Stoker as Malc knew him – would act as his bodyguard, his financial advisor and his personal trainer. It sounded like value for money. 'But it's the bodyguard bit that's important. How do I know you're any good?' he asked. 'OK, you shot that crazy bastard. No offence, but it don't prove a thing. At that range you couldn't have fucking missed.'

'OK,' said Rawhead. 'Come with me.'

They drove into town, to an Irish pub called the Peggy Gordon. It was smoky and crowded. A sign on the door read: 'No Bikers, Leather Jackets, Etc.' When Rawhead and Little Malc walked in, the bar was full of men in overalls.

A TV above the bar was showing rugby. Rawhead ordered two pints of Guinness extra-cold from a barman who looked as if he was auditioning for Darby O'Gill & the Little People. He had red hair and a scar above his nose. When he saw Rawhead, his eyes darkened. He had worked rough pubs all his life and knew trouble when he saw it.

'What're we doing in this fucking shithole?' said Little Malc.

'Why? Don't you like the Irish?'

'I don't care one way or another,' mumbled Little Malc. 'Protestants, Catholics, they can all blow the living fuck out of each other for all I care.'

'You think the Irish are a violent people?'

'No more than most.'

'How do you feel about Catholics in particular?'

'I'm not bothered one way or the other. But I think it's time they stopped propping the Pope up. I wish they'd just let the poor old cunt lie down and die.'

To Little Malc's amazement, Rawhead suddenly shouted, 'Hey! My friend here says the Pope is a poor old cunt!'

Little Malc sputtered beer down his chest. 'Jesus!'

'What's that?' said Rawhead, pretending to listen to Little Malc. 'He says Gerry Adams wears a dress and bakes fairy cakes.'

It was the barman who attacked first. Roaring like a warrior, he pulled a wooden club from under the counter and swung it at Little Malc, missing his head by a fraction. Rawhead caught the barman's hand, held it against the counter with his left and hit the barman in the centre of the face with his beer glass.

Apart from the shard of glass protruding from his left cheek, the barman was relatively unhurt. But he was surprised, which was why his mouth was open when Rawhead punched him. Rawhead heard a crack and knew he'd broken the man's jaw.

The barman held his left hand to his face and Rawhead twisted the club out of his grip and swung it round, almost hitting an old man in a cardigan who had got up to object to Rawhead's comment about His Holiness, the Pope. Realizing he might get hurt, the old man changed his mind and hurried back to his stool.

One of the mechanics ran up next. A little guy with jutting ears and a long, James Joyce chin. He seemed to have been influenced by James Joyce, too, because he was shouting something that sounded like, 'I what dogs turd wanker!' Little Malc held out his fist and the guy ran straight onto it. Then his friend, huge and long haired, weighing about twenty-four stone, lunged at Rawhead, who fell to the sawdust with the fat mechanic on top of him.

For a moment, Rawhead couldn't move or breathe. The mechanic was gritting his teeth and bouncing up and down on him. It was like he was trying to fuck him. Rawhead could smell motor oil and dirty cock, and the beer on the guy's breath. He could see the hairs up the bastard's nostrils, thick and tufted like tobacco.

Someone was shouting, 'Kill him, John. Fucking smack him!' in a high-pitched Mancunian voice. Rawhead tried to find his gun, couldn't reach it. But he groped in his pocket and found his lighter. He held it up to the mechanic's nose–hair and set fire to it.

The mechanic screamed and jumped off Rawhead. The James Joyce lookalike sloshed a pint of beer in the mechanic's face. A moment later, while he was rubbing his eyes, Rawhead hit the mechanic so hard that he slid over the floorboards, smashed the back of his head on the jukebox and blacked out.

Little Malc had seen enough and was edging towards the door. Rawhead followed. A stout red-faced woman with an outraged expression tried to bar their way. Little Malc stopped to reason with her, but Rawhead could see the barman was back on his feet and hungry for vengeance.

Rawhead was afraid that if they stayed around any longer, things might get violent. So he hit the woman, right in her outraged expression. The woman went down.

*

They got in the Rolls, Rawhead at the wheel.

'You punched a lady,' said Little Malc. 'I can't believe you sunk that low.'

'She was about to deck you.'

'Are you seriously implying a woman could beat Malcolm Priest Junior?'

'Yep,' said Rawhead.

'Right!' said Little Malc. 'That's it. Stop the fucking car and get out. I'll drive meself home. I'm stronger than any fucking woman and you're fucking sacked.'

Rawhead ignored him. He drove south out of the city, all the way to Macclesfield Forest. When they parked, Little Malc refused to get out. Rawhead sat there in silence, just staring at him. The power in his eyes was so intense that Little Malc had to look away. He was getting scared now, having finally deduced that the man at his side was not remotely like anyone else he'd ever met.

Suddenly, a little fresh air seemed like a good idea. They walked for about half a mile, meandering through the trees, Little Malc complaining that the ground was frosty and he could feel the cold through the soles of his Italian shoes. Rawhead was dressed more sensibly in heavy walking boots.

Squirrels chased and chattered in the trees above them, claws scrabbling as they raced upside down, apparently defying gravity. The light was fading, the sky streaked with pink and mauve, as pretty and sad as a bunch of hospital flowers.

Finally, Little Malc got pissed off. 'Right. I'm not walking any fucking further.'

'This'll do fine,' said Rawhead. He pulled the Ruger out of his belt and fired up at the trees. In his alarm, Little Malc gave an impromptu little dance. Overhead, a squirrel exploded. Blood and fur rained down from the branches. Rawhead fired again and a second squirrel fell, this one merely wounded. As it fell, Rawhead shot it again and it burst apart like the first one.

'Jesus Christ,' said Little Malc. 'I like animals, I do. We're animal lovers in our house. My little girls'd be heartbroken if they saw what you just did.'

Rawhead turned and pointed the gun at him. Little Malc's mouth dropped open. There was a long silence before Rawhead lowered the gun and said, 'There. That's how easy it'd be.'

'How easy what'd be?'

'To kill you,' said Rawhead, walking away.

'Know what? You're a fucking psycho!' yelled Little Malc. 'You start a fight in a pub and nearly get us both killed, you shoot some cute little furry fuckers that have never done me any harm, then you point a gun at me? Some fucking bodyguard!'

*

Rawhead drove to Knutsford, Little Malc prattling all the way about what a maniac Rawhead was. 'Mentor? More like a fucking mental case.' They cruised down the wide avenue where Chef lived and ran his business. The house, once the home of Little Malc's father, was now protected like a fortress.

'Did you live here once?' said Rawhead.

'No,' said Little Malc. 'I never did. Dad moved here after him and Mum divorced.'

There were security lights, high fences and surveillance cameras. A tall man was standing behind the gate, face in shadow, looking out as they cruised by.

A little further down the road, Rawhead parked the car and switched off the engine.

'Why've we stopped?' said Little Malc.

'I want to ask you something.'

'What?'

'Do you want to stay alive?'

Little Malc glared at him. 'What kind of stupid fucking question is that? Do you?'

'Well, explain this to me. You work in Manchester – the city of guns. You put out a contract for a guy that took out eighty per cent of the Priesthood, then sit around with no protection. You don't seem stupid, no more stupid than most people I come across.'

'Well, *thank you.*'

'But you're not armed. The people around you aren't armed. If he's alive, is this Rawhead guy going to sit back and let you insult him? I don't think so.'

'Anyone who thinks they can kill my dad and get away with it has got another think coming.'

'Then at least defend yourself. You don't even carry a weapon.'

'It's something me and Chef have agreed on together. None of the guys in the Priesthood carry weapons.'

'You really believe that?'

'My uncle Chef wouldn't lie to me.'

'Your uncle Chef?' Rawhead had to laugh.

'I've known him all me life. He was my father's best bud. They built up the Priesthood together. This guy used to sit me on his knee when I was little. No way would this man fucking lie to me.'

Rawhead turned in his seat to look at Little Malc. 'He *is* lying to you,' he explained. Very calm, very patient. 'In fact, I think he'd be very happy to see your coffin going by.'

'No way,' said Little Malc.

'Those friends of Chef's, the Medina brothers. I suppose you know they've been dealing in your club?'

'No way. In the past, maybe. My dad, God rest his soul, used to have us dealing drugs from behind the fucking bar in them days. When he died I told Chef. I told him, I said, "Top entertainers are staying away from the venue because they don't want to be associated with a low-life drug den." Chef gave me his word there'd be no more of it. I've got his word.'

'They're dealing. I've seen it with my own eyes. That's what Chef's word is worth. You know nothing illegal goes on in Manchester without the Priesthood taking a share. So what does that tell us? The Medinas are dealing in your club with Chef's permission. Otherwise they'd be dead. Don't you see that?'

'No.' Little Malc's eyes seemed to tremble in their sockets. You could see him battling the sheer logic of what he was hearing. 'He wouldn't do that to me.'

'Does he still use you for recruitment?'

'Eh?'

'Chef. Does he still pay you to send him new boys?'

'Now and then.'

'Didn't Bryan Edwards used to take the coats in the club?'

Little Malc sniffed. 'Take the piss, more like.'

'I'm right, though, aren't I? Bryan was one of your dad's sops. Now he's an altar boy. In a couple of years he'll be ordained.'

'What's your point?'

'That you're treading water. If you find good people, Chef takes them off you. Leaving you to look for new people.'

'People move up when they see the chance. That's the way it's always been.'

'Yeah? When are you going to move up?'

'Eh?'

'What are your promotion prospects? I'd say they were non-existent.'

'Hey, pal. Don't you worry about me. I'm happy enough. I'm not a gangster, I'm a showman. Give me a song and a glass in my hand, I'm happy as Larry.'

'Malc, listen,' said Rawhead. His eyes gleamed oddly, reflecting light from nowhere. 'Is it all right to call you Malc?'

Little Malc either nodded or suffered an involuntary neck spasm. Rawhead wasn't sure which. 'I saved your life. Do you admit that?'

'Yeah. I admit it. Thanks.'

'So you can trust me. Yes?'

'Maybe.'

'Well, look. Your "uncle Chef" is fucking you over. Completely and comprehensively. What did he say when you put out the contract for Rawhead?'

'He said he understood,' said Little Malc. 'He said the love between a father and son was special. He didn't agree with me, but he understood. He said if that was my decision, he wasn't going to interfere.'

'I bet.'

'Look. Everyone knows Chef and me are partners. If I was in trouble, he'd come to help me. Course he would.'

'Yeah? Where was he the other night when that punk tried to waste you? You're alone. You're so wide open, I can see the sky. And there's Chef, safe in his electrified kingdom, with a whole army around him. *Vive la différence.*'

Little Malc sulked like a small child.

Rawhead sighed and looked straight ahead. A rather shame-faced man was walking a little dog in a red velvet waistcoat. When the dog crapped on the pavement, the man instantly bent down and scooped it up. It was that kind of neighbourhood. Rawhead wouldn't have been surprised if the owner had wiped the dog's arse.

'It's like this, Malcolm. I can protect you. I can protect you from *anyone*. If that's what you want.' He appraised Little Malc coolly, offering his hand. 'Well?'

Little Malc felt excited, confused and scared, all at once. Mostly he felt excited. He took Rawhead's hand and clasped it. 'It's what I want,' he said.

*

Rawhead got Little Malc to drop him off at a bar in Sale. As soon as the Rolls was out of sight, he stepped out of the bar and walked back to his lodgings. Mrs Munley was sitting in the living room, watching a game show on TV. Rawhead could hear her laughing indulgently as the young morons went through their carefully rehearsed routine. 'I'm easily bored,' said the girl who was choosing a date. 'I enjoy fine wines, particularly champagne. Contestant number one: how would you wine and dine me?'

As Rawhead went upstairs, he imagined an honest answer to the mindless question. 'Well, Sarah ... I'd take you to a nice little wine bar. We won't need champagne: your beauty will be more than enough to make this boy fizz. When I'm chilled, you can help to pop my cork. Then you can taste my fine vintage.'

Rawhead took a bath, dressed and cooked himself an omelette. Then he made tea for himself and Mrs Munley. He'd bought her a box of Lindt chocolates and she ate them while she watched some laughable shit about a casualty ward, in which all the accident victims gave lengthy speeches to let the audience know how they were feeling. 'Oh, Victor, it's a long time since I've had company on a Saturday night,' said the old woman.

*

After his landlady went to bed, Rawhead sat in his room reading *The Oxford Book of English Ghost Stories*. When the house was still, he loaded his gun and went out in the BMW. He drove to Prestbury. According to the guidebooks, Prestbury was a picturesque Cheshire town at the foot of the Pennines. It had a thirteenth-century church, many of its shops occupied listed buildings and practically none of its citizens pissed in the streets. And now Billy Dye, Rawhead's blood brother, had exchanged his three-storey slum in one of the poorest parts of Manchester for a house in this pleasant bourgeois village.

Prestbury was a retirement village for *Daily Telegraph* readers, not a gifted writer who had once spat on society's corrupt values. To Rawhead, living in such a place was proof that Billy had fallen a long way.

Billy's new house was on a country road at the edge of the village. Rawhead parked in a lay-by round the corner. The house was only a century old, a mere stripling of a dwelling by local standards. Its black and white timbers conveyed money without taste rather than the Tudor opulence that was intended. There was a stone fountain on the front lawn. The house had land on all sides, at least five acres. As Rawhead strolled by in the dark, it seemed to him that cosy yellow light shone from every window.

With ease, he climbed the low wall and strolled over the front lawn to the house. There were two cars: a nice little Rover 45 and a battered Nissan Bluebird. Billy obviously wasn't as rich as he'd like to be – not yet, anyway.

Rawhead rounded the house. None of the curtains were drawn. As he drew closer, he could hear raised voices. Billy was standing with his back to a massive widescreen TV. He looked tired and dishevelled. He was arguing with somone out of sight, not angrily but forcefully. Then, waving his arms, he walked out of the room.

Rawhead moved round to the kitchen. From the bushes nearby came the sound of a hedgehog snuffling and grumbling. Rawhead stepped to one side of the window and peered in. Nikki was in the kitchen. She had her arms folded and was staring into space, waiting for the kettle to boil. The kitchen window was wide open. Rawhead heard the click of the kettle as it turned itself off.

Like Billy, Nikki looked far from happy. Unlike Billy, she was wearing nothing but a T-shirt and knickers. Rawhead looked at her legs and the long dark hair tumbling down her back and felt an unexpected pang of desire.

Billy walked into the kitchen and for a moment Rawhead thought he'd be seen. Billy's eyes seemed to be staring directly at him. Then he turned to his wife. 'It isn't just my fault,' he said. 'You should have reminded me.'

'Reminded you?' Nikki couldn't believe what she was hearing.

'Why not?' he said. 'Next time you're in bed with me, give me a nudge.'

'Billy, every night since the wedding, I've been practically dancing naked in front of you.

'Oh, is *that* what you were doing?' said Billy. 'I thought you were trying to lose weight.' He laughed uproariously at his own joke. His wife's face darkened. 'I was *joking*. Don't be ridiculous. You're not overweight.'

'No, but you are.'

'No, I'm not.'

'If your arse gets any bigger, it'll start appearing on ordnance survey maps.'

'Well, at least it isn't sagging like yours.'

'A moment ago, I wasn't overweight.'

'You're not. Doesn't stop you from sagging.'

'Your soul's sagging.'

'Fine.' said Billy. 'If I'm that unappealing, why do you want to shag me?'

'I don't. But as long as I'm stuck with you, I think our relationship should include sex.'

'Or we could just hit each other with baseball bats. It'd achieve the same effect. In fact, it'd be more fucking fun.'

Nikki folded her arms and glared at him.

There was a long pause. With a hearty sigh, Billy started to undress.

'What are you doing?' said Nikki.

'We're arguing about not having sex. So I think we should just do it.'

'Don't be stupid.'

'It isn't stupid. Why not? A quickie. Right here on the floor. It'll be just like the old days.'

She sighed despairingly. 'Jesus Christ Almighty . . .'

Billy wobbled, balancing on one foot with the other leg trapped in his trouser leg. 'What?'

'You,' she said.

'What about me?' said Billy.

'You just don't understand, do you?'

'Understand what?'

'Everything. Sex isn't about sticking things up people.'

Billy looked baffled. 'Isn't it?'

'Is it hell.'

'Well, what's sticking things up people called?'

'Why does it have to be so basic? Why can't we try non-penetrative sex?'

'I haven't got the faintest idea what you're talking about.'

*

Rawhead had heard enough.

Thanking God that he'd never been in a steady relationship, he tapped one ear as if to knock the bickering voices out of his head. Then he explored the rest of the garden. A glass-fronted summerhouse purchased from a garden centre stood at the far end of the lawn. The summerhouse was brand new. Rawhead tried the door. It slid open. He stepped inside, to the sweet smell of new pine. There was a picnic table and two chairs. A folded sun lounger rested in a corner.

At the back of the house lay a deep ditch, and beyond the ditch a vast field. Rawhead inhaled the darkness, the air cold in his lungs. Overhead, stars shivered in a Spielberg sky. The waning moon blazed. He spat into the dark and turned back to the house.

Nikki was still in the kitchen, pretending to be preoccupied with wiping and tidying the work surfaces. As Rawhead watched, Billy re-entered the kitchen and quickly folded Nikki in his arms. There was tenderness in the action, but there was also need.

Rawhead, who thrived on his separateness from the rest of humanity, found that need baffling. He had never wanted to own a woman, or be owned by one. To him, the women he'd slept with had never been quite real. He could live with this. It was when they became real that the problems started.

With a woman, you had to pretend, you had to sacrifice your true self. You couldn't even walk into the darkness without them asking where you were going or what time you'd be back. Rawhead found the whole charade obscene. No woman would ever prevent him from walking into the darkness.

Having seen what he came to see, he walked round the house and exited via the drive. At the front gates he felt a slight tingling at the back of his neck, a nagging suspicion that he should move faster. Rawhead quickened his step. There was absolutely no one in the lane.

He passed a lamp-post, its tired light flickering. He wondered why rich people always lived on ill-lit roads.

The BMW was waiting in the lay-by, black bonnet gleaming coldly. He unlocked the door and slipped behind the wheel. The engine fired instantly, a low murmur. The Ruger Blackhawk was sticking into his thigh, so he withdrew the gun from his belt and lay it on the passenger seat.

As he looked into the rear-view mirror he saw car lights rounding the curve in the road. The vehicle was some distance away, but he decided to let it pass before driving on. Then the car slowed down beside him and he saw it was a police patrol car. The officer in the passenger seat rolled down his window and leaned out. Rawhead did the same.

'Hello,' said the officer. He had blond highlights in his hair. Apart from the pretty hair, he was rather plain. 'Do you mind if I ask what you're doing?'

Rawhead smiled. 'I was just out for a drive. Can't believe what a beautiful night it is.'

Blondie wasn't listening. 'Only we've had reports,' he said, 'of a prowler in the district.'

'Ah. That was me,' said Rawhead.

The policeman laughed amiably enough. 'Oh. That was you, was it?'

'I got out to stretch my legs and look at the stars.'

'Why was that?''

'I told you. I was admiring the glittering firmament, officer. No law against that, is there?'

Apparently there was, because Blondie got out of the car. The driver, a sullen, bearded bastard, followed as quickly as his regulation police paunch would allow. Rawhead picked up the revolver and held it between his legs. Freud would have been proud. Blondie poked his head through the window while Beardie circled the car. The radio in the patrol car bleeped and prattled.

'What's your name?' said Blondie.

'Montague Rhodes James.'

'That's a funny sort of name, isn't it?'

'It's a funny sort of world, officer.'

'Is this your car?'

'Don't do this, officer.'

'Let's see your licence.'

'Drive away, why don't you?' urged Rawhead. Never blinking, never raising his voice. 'While you've got the chance.'

Blondie exchanged a glance with Beardie, who was peering in through the front passenger-door window. 'You. Get out,' said Blondie.

'Just think of your family,' said Rawhead.

'Out!' barked Blondie. He tugged at the door, found it was locked.

Beardie, less patient than his buddy, hammered on the opposite window. 'Unlock these doors this fucking minute.'

Almost indolently, never once removing his eyes from Blondie's, Rawhead unwound the opposite window and fired a shot through it. He didn't see the policeman totter back into the darkness. But he heard the heavy slump as he fell.

Blondie gaped. The driver door opened, sweeping him off balance.

Then Blondie did something Rawhead hadn't counted on. He started to run. Rawhead was fast, but the speed of the policeman startled him. The guy moved like a professional sprinter, cheeks puffing, head erect, arms and thighs pumping him forward.

Blondie was fit and he wanted to live. It was as simple as that. When he'd been running for eight seconds, he stole a quick glance over his right shoulder. Rawhead was close behind him. Blondie put on a fresh spurt and vaulted over the wall of the house next door to Billy's.

Rawhead followed, but caught his foot on the wall and tumbled over onto the lawn. Blondie raced down the side of the 7house. Rawhead hauled himself to his feet and charged after him. It was as he was passing the side porch that he heard a loud bang.

At first, Rawhead thought that the officer had drawn a gun and was firing at him.

He threw himself onto his belly and aimed the Ruger at the back lawn. Full-length statues, fake Grecian, lined its oval perimeter. When Rawhead reached Blondie, he was lying on his back, his breath coming in quick gasps. There was a smoking black hole through the centre of his chest.

Someone had gunned him down.

It was impossible, it made no sense. But somene else had got to Blondie before him. Rawhead searched the garden for the killer. He found no one.

He returned to the dying man, whose face was now so white that it glowed in the dark. 'Who shot you?' he asked softly.

'Too dark,' said Blondie. Then he died.

Rawhead didn't know whether he was talking about his killer, the night or the world he was leaving.

*

Rawhead, silent and damned, walked past the bungalow and across the front lawn. Behind him, the click of a lock. He glanced back and, to his utter disbelief, saw a nice, bespectacled old man in pyjamas and a silk dressing gown running after him. 'No through way! No through way!' he was shouting.

As famous last words go, they were pretty piss-poor.

Aiming carefully, so as not to cause unnecessary suffering, Rawhead shot the nice old man through the heart. The nice old man lurched backwards and fell, skidding and hurtling over the lawn, getting mud over his nice dressing gown. Rawhead heard a woman scream, turned and fired at the sound. Then there was no sound at all.

Rawhead kept walking.

Past the flickering lamp-post with bats swerving round it.

Past Billy's house where the newly-weds, oblivious to the chaos around them, were still arguing.

Over to the hedge beside the lay-by, where the policeman lay sprawled. After checking the bearded officer was dead, Rawhead stole the retractable baton from his belt. He'd always wanted a police baton.

He drove away with his lights off, guided only by the moon. The road was narrow, with many turns. Sometimes it was so dark he couldn't see where he was going. Rawhead didn't care.

This was the story of his life.

It was always dark.

He could never see where he was going.

He never cared.

7

Leave this gaudy gilded stage,
From custom more than use frequented,
Where fools of either sex and age
Crowd to see themselves presented.

'Song', John Wilmot, Earl of Rochester (1647–1680)

Early on Sunday morning Billy woke to the sound of church bells. Billy liked the sound. From a distance, churches filled him with longing and affection. It was only when he got close, close enough to smell the Christians, that he drew the line.

And what else was wrong with churches? As he lay drowsing in bed, Billy tried to think. Then he remembered. Rawhead. Rawhead, who loved tombs and spires and swirling mist.

Billy heard the doorbell ring. Then Maddy squealing and Nikki talking to her softly. The bedroom door juddered as air rushed in through the front door. Billy heard distant voices, then footsteps on the stairs. The door opened. It was Nikki, carrying Maddy. As soon as he glanced at Nikki's face, Billy knew something had happened. 'What's the matter?' he asked her.

'The police are here. They want to talk to us.'

'What about?' said Billy.

Nikki didn't know. 'You haven't done anything wrong, have you?'

Billy wasn't sure how to answer this, but shook his head anyway. He kept thinking, 'It's Rawhead, it's something to do with Rawhead.'

He got out of bed and slipped into a sweater and jeans. Then he walked to the window and drew back the curtains. Nikki came and stood beside him, holding up their daughter so she could see the scene below. A row of men in white boiler suits were crawling over the front lawn on their hands and knees. The road outside was cordoned off and lined with vans and police cars. A stretcher was being carried into an ambulance.

'It's Mrs Reisler,' said Nikki.

'What the fuck's going on?' said Billy.

The driver closed the doors and the ambulance moved off.

'Car,' said Maddy happily. It was the only word she knew.

*

Detective Superintendent Janet Harrop was a fine, rather fierce-looking redhead. Although Prestbury was under the jurisdiction of the Cheshire Constabulary, Harrop was on loan from Greater Manchester because of her vast experience in the investigation of gun-related crime. It made sense, especially for such a high-profile inquiry. The Greater Manchester Force had infinitely more money and equipment than their neighbours across the border, who struggled to get by with outdated computers, radios that didn't work and patrol cars that routinely failed their MOTs.

Harrop's bag carrier, Detective Sergeant Hughes, was also from Greater Manchester. Hughes was neat and unassuming with a baby-face and prematurely white hair. Billy made the mistake of assuming that Hughes was in charge, forcing the sergeant to correct him.

'Sorry,' said Billy.

'It takes more than that to offend me,' said Harrop, her lips forming a thin smile. But her eyes told Billy to go and fuck himself.

Amidst constant interruptions from their daughter, Billy and Nikki tried to answer Harrop's questions while Hughes took notes. 'So you heard or saw nothing strange last night? Nothing at all?'

'Like what?' said Billy.

Harrop just looked at him. She had very clear sea-green eyes and had chosen to sit on a straight-backed wooden chair while Nikki and Billy slumped on the sofa. This enabled the Detective Superintendent to look down on them, something she found easy to do. 'Neither of you are hard of hearing?'

'No,' said Billy. 'Although I sometimes get a build-up of wax in my left ear. Always the left ear, for some reason. Never the right.'

To Billy's amazement, Hughes jotted this down.

'What did you both do yesterday?'

'Nothing,' said Nikki. 'We stayed in.'

'All day?'

'All day and night,' said Billy.

'Neither of you left the house for any reason?'

'No,' said Billy. He thought about this for a few seconds. 'Actually, that isn't true. I think I went out to the car. I'd left the *Radio Times* on the front seat. I went to get it.'

'What time would this have been?'

'After putting Maddy to bed,' said Nikki. 'It must have been about seven.'

Harrop stared at Billy for a few moments. 'Did you see anything unusual? Think carefully before answering. What may have seemed unimportant to you might turn out to be absolutely vital to us.'

Billy thought for a moment. 'When I went to the car,' he said, 'I remember noticing that a bird had crapped all over the windscreen. It really annoyed me, because the car had just been through the car wash.'

'Anything else?' asked Harrop.

'Yeah,' said Billy. 'The bastard thing had crapped on the bonnet as well.'

Nikki sighed despairingly. Billy turned to her and shrugged. 'Well? Who's to say that bird shit isn't evidence?'

'Mr Dye,' said Harrop carefully. 'I *very much* hope you don't find this amusing.'

Billy shook his head and mumbled an apology.

'Because two of our colleagues died last night. Along with your neighbour. A man whose wife is now so badly traumatized she may never lead a normal life again. Now, you may find that amusing, but I can assure you we don't.'

'Which neighbour?' said Billy, instantly chastened. 'Which neighbour died?'

'Dr Reisler.'

Rawhead, Billy was thinking. *It's got to be.*

Nikki, now tense and pale, had to ask Harrop to repeat what she'd said.

'How well do you know the Reislers?' asked Hughes.

'Not very well,' admitted Nikki. 'It sounds awful now, but we didn't actually hit it off.'

'Why was that?' said Harrop, sitting bolt upright in her chair.

'Oh, just silly little things. When we first moved in, we sometimes parked our car out in the road. We had builders in, sometimes three big vans at a time, so we parked our car outside the gate. Dr Reisler came round to lecture us about why we shouldn't park in the road when we had a drive.'

'What happened?'

'We started parking in the drive,' said Nikki.

'OK,' said Harrop. 'I have a slight problem with what you're telling me and I'll explain why. Three people dead. All of them killed by what looks like a high-calibre firearm. That's at least three shots. Out here, where it's so peaceful, that's got to be pretty noticeable. Yet you both maintain you heard nothing.'

'We were having an argument' said Billy.

Harrop wasn't impressed. 'Then you must have very loud voices.'

'We really didn't hear anything,' said Nikki. Harrop was beginning to grate on her.

'What were you arguing about?'

Nikki began to say something but Billy got in first. 'Whether the police are all bastards or whether it's just ninety-nine out of a hundred.'

Harrop sighed. 'All right,' she said. 'That's enough for now. We may need to question you further. If you could stay close to home for the next week or so, we'd appreciate it.'

The officers took down a series of contact numbers and got up to leave. At the door, Billy felt he had to say something, but didn't know what. So he said the first arsehole thing that came into his head. 'Is it OK to wash my car? Or are you planning to take any bird-shit samples?'

*

On the Monday, Billy had an early script meeting at Granada studios. In televisionland, early meant eleven o'clock. Billy sat in the lobby, where two large TVs broadcast simultaneous daytime dross, and portraits of successful soap stars smiled ingratiatingly down at the poor bastards being kept waiting. Many of the actors had appeared in Granada's most famous soap, *Coronation Street*. A soap about ordinary northern people. Its actors, unsurprisingly, were chosen because they looked and sounded ordinary.

Nonetheless, this didn't prevent many of them, particularly the younger ones, from leaving after a year or so to try their luck as movie stars. None of them ever became movie stars. Like Billy, most of them spent their lives waiting in lobbies. Some didn't even make it that far.

Billy didn't look down on the actors, even though their portraits looked down on him. He knew success was a fragile thing.

At Manchester Grammar School, where he and Rawhead had been uneducated two decades before, Billy's teachers had assured him that he had a great deal of talent. That if he worked hard – which in those days he seldom did – he would thrive in our society, a society that rewards effort. In other words, Billy only had to pass his exams and he would become a well-paid middle-class arsehole, with a big house, two children, an erotic car and a neurotic wife.

It hadn't worked out that way. Billy had passed his exams but had gone to art school to study painting. In two years he studied only one painting, and that was by someone else. Billy spent the rest of the time getting blasted. After the second year he got thrown off the course for being so chronically lazy that even his deadbeat, failed-artist tutors produced more work.

Desperate for money, he wrote a review of a Nirvana concert he hadn't seen and sent it to a music paper as a sample of his work. The editor thought he showed promise, sent him off to review bands. People noticed he was funny, so magazines asked him to write satirical pieces about topics like dying young or having a cock. Soon Billy noticed that all the best jobs went to a small group of writers who all drank together and went to each other's weddings. These people were never going to invite him to join their club. Billy wouldn't have joined if they had. He thought they were a bunch of ugly, boring fuckers and made no secret of his disdain.

Hoping to carve an escape route for himself, Billy decided to fulfil a childhood ambition and write a book. He translated his love of classic ghost stories into a novel called *Unholier Than Thou*, telling the story of one night in the lives of a group of ordinary, everyday necromancers. Billy concentrated all his passion and acquired skill into the book, convinced that it would make his name. The book found a publisher. Surely a new golden age was dawning?

What Billy forgot was that a book needs publicity and reviews. And many of the journalists he had snubbed over the years, those ugly, boring fuckers, had gone on to edit the very magazines and papers he hoped to be reviewed by.

So Billy had floundered, for five bitter years. His books were published but unreviewed and largely unread. Until a film director called George Leica had picked up a copy of *Unholier Than Thou* in a London bookshop, read it on the plane home and had arranged for his assistant to phone Billy the next day.

The subsequent deal had led to representation by Fatty Potts, one of the best-fed agents in London, the commission to write about Manchester gangland and the meeting Billy was about to attend.

Billy looked up and saw Artemesia, the script editor. The first time Billy had heard her name, he'd almost pissed himself. She was a little like Uma Thurman, only not as tall or dirty-looking. Artemesia asked Billy how he'd got in to Manchester, as if she fucking cared. But he told her he'd got the train, just so they had something to talk about in the lift upstairs.

Artemesia led the way to Larry Crème's office. Larry, head of drama, was sitting behind his desk. To his left sat Tim, the director. Larry was in his fifties, well-groomed and likeably insincere. Always watching his back or knifing someone else's back or making promises he couldn't keep, because Larry knew fuck-all about drama and never knew which horse to back. So he backed every horse, told everyone they were wonderful until the ratings proved otherwise.

Tim was thin, nervous and bespectacled, skin bluish grey, looking more like a consumptive eighteenth-century country parson than a TV director.

There were croissants and Danish pastries on the table and a pot of fresh coffee. For the first ten minutes everyone quizzed Billy about the shootings in Prestbury. Larry Crème, not to be outdone, told a story about getting hit in the leg by an air-rifle pellet when he was a kid. Smiling, Larry rolled up his right trouser leg. There was a peanut-sized scar under the knee. The leg was tanned. Larry owned a sunbed.

Larry's leg effectively killed the conversation. Billy took advantage of the lull to ask what the meeting was about.

Larry turned to Tim. 'Tim? Would you like to get the ball rolling?'

Tim looked as if he'd sooner lie face down on the floor while a rat gobbled a Mars Bar out of his arse. 'Well, we all love your writing, we think you're absurdly talented and we're all thrilled to be working with you.'

'And?'

'That's why we've called this emergency meeting.'

'What's the emergency?'

'Your second script, basically.'

'What about it?' said Billy.

Tim sighed and bit into a croissant.

'None of us think it's quite there yet,' said Artemesia.

Larry nodded in sombre accord.

'Quite where?' Billy demanded.

'Not filmable,' said Tim, brushing crumbs off his tweedy trousers.

'But Larry said he loved it,' said Billy, going red in the face. 'He told me it was one of the best first drafts he'd ever seen and I shouldn't change a word of it.'

'Yes. I did say that,' conceded Larry. 'But, in my own defence, that was before I'd actually read it. Then we showed the first episode to Sheila.' (Sheila Burman was the head of drama at ITV.)

Tim took up the sorry tale. 'She said that if it goes out this year, as planned, we couldn't have anyone getting shot. Especially after those policemen getting shot in Prestbury. So basically, the last episode needs a complete rewrite.'

'But you were all happy with it,' protested Billy. 'What happened to the outline? I thought Sheila had approved it.'

'She may not have read it,' said Larry with a shrug. 'She's a busy woman.'

'It was only one page long,' said Billy.

'It's really a question of journeys,' suggested Artemesia. 'If the hitman, Bonehead, is cold and frightening all the way through, where can we take him? What's his character arc?'

'What the fuck are you talking about?' said Billy. 'You worked on the script with me. You told me you loved it.'

'I think what Artemesia is saying,' offered Tim, 'is that if Bonehead starts off nasty, then just gets nastier, it makes his character too unsympathetic.'

'He's meant to be unsympathetic,' said Billy through gritted teeth. 'He's a fucking murderer.'

'But if it's all played on the same level, it becomes monotonous to film and boring to watch,' said Tim. 'Why not make Bonehead all jolly and friendly at the end of the story? So we know he's moved on.'

Larry Crème sat upright in his chair when he heard this. 'That's it. We could make him a kind of conjuror. He could tell jokes and juggle with oranges. If it's done right, it could be really fantastic.'

'We just think,' explained Tim, 'that the first episode is very funny. All that stuff with the gangsters and Melvin Feast made me laugh out loud. But as soon as Bonehead comes into the story, everything gets a bit depressing. I'd like to see more laughs.'

'There are laughs,' countered Billy. 'What about when we find that Bonehead has killed hundreds of people and buried them in his cellar?'

'To be honest, that's one of the things we're concerned about,' admitted Larry. 'Because dead people really do end up in cellars in real life. And it's no laughing matter for them or their families, I can tell you.'

Billy couldn't believe what he was hearing. 'So you think Rawhead should tell jokes?'

Artemesia frowned and began to leaf through her copy of the script. 'Rawhead? Is there a character called Rawhead?'

'Uh, I meant Bonehead,' said Billy.

'No,' said Larry. 'But how about this? At the end of the story, we find out that it isn't just Johnny's life he's spared. That's it! Maybe he's been fooling everyone. He hasn't killed a single person, just moved them to a safe place!'

'Like where?' said Billy. He hadn't felt as bewildered since Malcolm Priest had ordered his execution.

'The cellar?' said Artemesia.

'Might work,' mused Larry.

Tim nodded. 'Think of it from the audience's point of view, Billy. They'll have decided Bonehead is a cold-blooded monster. Then they'll learn that he's Oskar Schindler. It's not that he doesn't shoot people often – he's never shot anyone in his life. He's a complete fraud!'

'Also,' said Tim. 'We don't think there should be as much violence.'

'It's a gangster story,' said Billy wearily. 'Violence is part of that world.'

'It's the guns, really,' pointed out Larry. 'You need to get rid of the guns.'

'I can't do that,' said Billy. 'It'd ruin everything.'

'Well, you definitely need to do *something*,' said Tim, 'because I start filming this in ten days' time, and I can't film the script as written. It won't hold, I fear.'

'Hold what?' said Billy.

'Hold the attention of a television audience,' said Artemesia primly.

'Would it help if we put you up at the Malmaison for a week?' suggested Larry pleasantly. 'Nice suite, no interruptions, order whatever you like on room service. You can send the new scenes to us as and when they're written.'

Billy sulked.

'Oh, go on,' urged Larry, who wanted the meeting to end so he could go to lunch. 'Who needs guns? We can still show the gangsters pushing people around.'

'Bonehead in particular needs to be more sympathetic,' added Artemesia. 'If he just shoots people and buries them in a charnel house, how can you expect the viewers, especially female viewers, to care about him? Why would Johnny care about him?'

'Whereas if he juggles oranges,' said Larry, 'people will know that he's basically nice. Because who ever heard of a nasty juggler?'

'You know, I rather like that idea,' said Tim. 'Bonehead could have a day job as a conjuror – and what does a conjuror do? Like a hitman, he *makes people disappear*.'

'Clever!' enthused Artemesia.

'Of course, we'd have to change his name,' admitted Larry. 'Bonehead doesn't sound right for a stage magician.'

Silence fell as they all mused on this problem. 'How about Marvo?' said Larry. 'Marvo the Magnificent.'

They all turned to look at Billy as if the incandescent brilliance of their ramblings was beyond question.

'I've given everything you've said very serious consideration,' said Billy. 'And you can all go and fuck yourselves.'

*

In his youth Dad Cheeseman was a locksmith. It was said of him that he could open any door or safe in the city. Now he runs a gym and a snooker hall on the outskirts of the city. Walk down Market Street in a straight line from Piccadilly, past St Anne's Square and Deansgate. Just as you're wondering how an atomic bomb could have gone off in Manchester without you ever hearing about it, you come to an old red-brick Methodist church on a corner. The church stands alone in a desert of shit and rubble. This is Cheeseman's place. The windows haven't seen glass for some years. There are metal grills over the window frames and boards under the grills. The only hint that the building isn't condemned comes from a peeling orange Day-Glo sign above the door. The sign reads POOL ALL DAY, FULLY LISENCED.

The snooker hall is upstairs. The lower floor is a shabby gym where amateur boxers train at weekends. The gym reeks of feet and armpits.

Dad was once a boxer himself, but started losing his hair at an early age. He took to wearing a wig. No matter how much adhesive he used, the wig kept falling off during bouts. Not wanting his fans to see him bald, Dad retired early. People liked and respected Dad, so had learned not to comment on the toupee, or to ask why the toupee was bright orange when the hair at the back and sides of his head was iron grey.

On the day Rawhead came to call, Dad was sat on a stool, smoking and chatting to the bored mother of five who served behind the bar. A couple of kids skiving off school were the only customers in the otherwise deserted hall. When Rawhead sat down on a stool next to Dad, the old man gave him a brief glance and flinched slightly. Then he remembered to smile, but it was too late. Rawhead had already seen fear in his eyes. 'Steve,' said Dad. 'How are you?'

The old man had known Rawhead since he was a boy. But in his time, Dad had met many crazed and vicious men. Some of them turned the stomach, some of them – the truly dangerous ones – chilled the blood. Steve fell into the latter category. Dad knew in his heart that Steve was a killer. Steve knew that he knew. It was not a matter either man cared to discuss.

'It's been too long,' said Rawhead gently.

'What've you been doing with yourself?'

'I took a sabbatical,' said Rawhead.

'That's a big word,' said Dad, spinning round on the stool. 'What the fucking hell does it mean?' Rawhead didn't answer. He was looking at the purple and brown bruise around Dad's left eye.

'Fancy a drink?'

'Thanks. Mineral water'd be fine.'

Dad mumbled to the woman behind the bar, who went to the cooler and came back with a bottle of fizzy water and a glass. 'Your health, ' said Rawhead.

'What can I do for you, Steven?'

'Malcolm Priest Junior needs doormen for his club. Five quid an hour and all the drunks they can beat up. I need strong, honest guys with no extra additives. I'm definitely looking for the additive-free variety.'

'A few names spring to mind.'

Rawhead threw a notepad and pen onto the counter. 'Write down their names and numbers on there.' Dad picked up the pen, holding it like it was a giant banana. He stuck his tongue out as he wrote.

'What happened to your face, Dad?'

'Oh, that.' Dad finished writing and took a pull of his cigarette. 'You know what this place is like. We get some right fucking Tonys in here.'

'I thought the Priesthood were supposed to protect you. Thought that was why you paid them.'

'Yeah. So did I. But if you're with Little Malc now, I better watch what I say.'

'I'm not *with* anyone,' said Rawhead. 'Say what you like to me. It'll go no further.'

Dad thought about it as he squashed his cigarette stub into an ashtray.

'OK,' he said. 'Here's the story. When Chef took over, a lot of people said, "Great, now the city's a safer place." Bullshit. Say what you like about Malcolm Priest Senior, but when he was around, no one pissed on your carpet. You paid for protection, that's what you fucking got. Plus it didn't cost the earth.'

'Yeah?'

'Then Chef's in charge. He puts the fucking subs up, didn't he? Two hundred a month. Doesn't sound much, but it's practically two and a half thou a year. That's a nice holiday, presents for the grandkids, the car's annual service and MOT. Worse thing is, when I got fucking bopped, Chef does fuck all about it.'

'Who was it?'

'Those two bastards who rule Salford. The Medinas.'

Rawhead grimaced.

'I see you've heard of them? They came in here before Christmas. Said that Chef said I was to give 'em hospitality, free drinks all fucking night. It's the first I've fucking heard of it, but I give 'em a couple of pints to shut 'em up and phone Chef. One of his monkeys picks up the phone, listens to what I have to say, then goes off to ask the boss. Then he comes back and says Chef says I've not to worry, just run a tab and he'll settle up with me later. Two days pass. No fucking cheque.

'The next Wednesday, they're back again with a couple of ugly girlfriends. Do they pay for a single drink? Do they fuck. All this gracious hospitality comes out of my fucking pocket.

'In the end I get tired of this, I phone up Chef. This time I get him. I say I've got a drinks bill for six hundred quid here, and when's he going to settle it? He says not to worry, he'll see to it right away. Next Wednesday, in they come again. The older one, Keith, says, "I hear you've been telling tales, but we're prepared to overlook it if you keep on being nice to us." I said: "Sorry lads, I'll serve you, but only if you pay for your drinks."'

'So Chris points a gun at me while Keith smacks me in the face. In the old days I'd have fought back, but I'm fucked if I'm going to get shot for six hundred notes.

'So what do they do? They get me down, sadden me big time.

'I end up having to go to hospital: bruised ribs, stitches in me mouth where they knocked me fucking dentures into me gums. To top it all, I lose half the hearing in my left fucking ear. When I'm back in the club, in comes one of Chef's boys. Big hefty lad, thinks he's a cut above. They call him the Philosopher. In for the monthly sub, would you believe? I said, "You expect money for protection. Where the fuck were you when I was getting smacked around?"

'This guy thinks it's a real fucking joke. Know what he says to me? "Just because you're covered for fire damage, it don't mean the insurance man has to stand in your house while it fucking burns down."'

'I take it you haven't seen your money yet?' said Rawhead.

Dad scowled. 'There's no fucking chance of that. I suppose I could take it out of Chef's monthly subs. But, somehow, I don't think he'd like that.'

Rawhead sipped his drink and thought for a moment. He

turned his face to Dad and his eyes glittered coldly. Dad knew he'd seen those eyes before. Deep in a dream, many years ago. A bad dream that had soaked his chest with sweat.

Dad shivered.

Rawhead gazed at him and through him. 'What would you say if I told you I could get your money for you?'

Dad didn't say a word.

8

Follow a shaddow, it still flies you;
Seeme to flye it, it will pursue:
So court a mistris, shee denyes you;
Let her alone, shee will court you.

'That Women Are But Mens Shaddowes', Ben Jonson (1572–1637)

In the hall of the school at Dale Brow, Prestbury, Detective Superintendent Harrop made an announcement to the press. Because she knew the TV cameras would be there, her hair had been recently cut and coloured. Talking to journalists was part of her job, despite her innate loathing for them. Her face remained impassive while the cameras rolled.

'PC Mather and PC Broadhurst were two fine officers, cut down in their prime. They will be sorely missed, both by their families and by their fellow officers.

'A post-mortem examination has revealed the vital information that two separate attackers were involved. We are still trying to establish a motive for what happened, and it is vital for anyone who may have seen anything unusual in Prestbury on Friday evening to come forward.

'We are following a number of lines of enquiry, and one of those is that the officers may have intercepted a robbery, but it is too soon to say.

'Did you see or have you heard of anyone who was bloodstained on that Friday night, especially in the Macclesfield area? Did you see anybody acting in any way suspiciously in the Old Prestbury Road area on that evening?

'Anyone who may be able to help is urged to contact the incident desk directly. Do not – I repeat – DO NOT attempt to confront any suspicious persons directly. It is believed that the men responsible for these crimes are highly dangerous and would have no compunction about killing again.'

*

After the broadcast, Harrop and Hughes drove to a pub for lunch. Harrop ordered a chicken sandwich. Hughes had cod and chips. While they were eating, Hughes opened his briefcase and took out a novel with a gaudy cover. The title was *Complicated Monsters*.

'What's this?' said Harrop.

'A book by William Dye. I thought it might interest you.'

'Oh.' She seemed disappointed. 'So that little cunt actually gets stuff published, then?'

'Yeah. I've flicked through it. There's a scene that might interest you.'

'I doubt that very much.'

'It's about zombies. And there's this scene near the end where the zombies eat someone alive.'

'Charming.'

'Yeah. But the point is, the guy they eat is a *police officer*. They roast him over a slow fire and cut off the choice bits of meat while he's screaming and begging for mercy.'

'Do you mind? I'm trying to eat.'

'All I'm saying is, you've already pointed out that Dye didn't seem too upset when we told him about the murders. The murders of two innocent bobbies. On top of that, we now find he's written a novel in which a police officer is sadistically murdered. So maybe he's got a grudge against the service?'

'Pardon?'

'A grudge against the police service.'

118

'Sorry, Hughes. For a mad fucking moment I thought you called the police force a "service".'

'Sorry.'

'I'm not interested in being a service. I joined the police so I could push people around. Why did you join?'

'Er, so I could help my fellow citizens and be a useful member of the community.'

'Bollocks.'

'I haven't finished telling you about this book. The most sickening thing is the way it's written. As if it's all a bloody big joke. Every time they cut a slice off him, the bobby says, "I must caution you . . .". Anyone who finds that funny has got to be warped.'

'Is it selling?'

'I shouldn't think so. I mean, there's only one review, and that's from the *Poynton Post*. "A lot better than I expected."'

Harrop laughed, spraying white wine over the table.

'Exactly,' sneered Hughes. 'The *Poynton Post* is a bloody *free* paper.'

'This is all very interesting, but it's got fuck all to do with the inquiry.'

'How do you know?'

'Because I know,' said Harrop. 'He doesn't look like a murderer. He just looks like a prat. He's got no form. No MO. I bet he doesn't do anything with his life apart from write his wanky books.'

Detective Sergeant Hughes was not convinced.

*

Little Malc called a lunchtime meeting, just for the door staff. They met on the dance floor, suspicious and resentful. Dressed, as instructed, in sports gear. The cleaners had finished early. There was no one about.

Everyone turned up. Fats and Brando, Sirus and Rawhead. Little Malc was wearing a Manchester City strip, his short pink legs dangling from a pair of oversized shorts. 'OK. Everyone listen up. As of now, I'm doubling your wages.'

Blank stares and sardonic snorts. No one believed him. Little Malc was forced to repeat his pledge. 'Whatever you're earning now, times it by two. That's the good news. The bad news is that you're going to have to earn your fucking money. Firstly, by being able to stand up. It's come to my attention that some of you aren't as fit as you ought to be. For men in your line of work, that's a fucking problem. So Stoker here has very kindly offered to act as our personal fucking trainer.'

'What the fuck does he know?' demanded Sirus, speaking for the majority. He was wearing a black karate suit tied with a black belt.

Rawhead, who was dressed in his normal clothes, walked to the centre of the dance floor. 'If you'll give me a chance, I'll show you. I need a volunteer.'

No one offered.

He pointed to Sirus. 'You'll do.'

'You can't teach me anything about fucking martial arts,' complained Sirus. 'I was a karate black belt by the age of fucking ten.'

'Give him a chance, Si,' said Little Malc quietly.

When Sirus was standing in front of him, Rawhead pointed to his bleached hair.

'Nice highlights.'

Sirus sighed.

'Did you go to John Frieda or Vidal Sassoon?'

Sirus was about to answer when Rawhead punched him in the adam's apple. Sirus staggered, choking. Rawhead turned to the others.

'Rule number one,' said Rawhead. 'Don't talk. Real life isn't a spaghetti western.'

Sirus was still gagging and clutching his throat. Before he had time to recover, Rawhead bounded forward and swung his right elbow up into Sirus's face.

Sirus opened his mouth to complain and a torrent of blood and teeth poured out. Afraid of looking helpless, he launched a respectable roundhouse kick. Rawhead caught the offending leg and swept it upwards, throwing Sirus heavily onto his back.

Fats, who didn't like to watch an unfair fight, looked at his own feet. Brando chewed gum thoughtfully, surprised to see a fit man like Sirus despatched with so little effort.

'You fucking bastard!' screamed Sirus from the floor.

Rawhead bent over and slapped him. 'Shut up.'

It should have been enough. But Sirus wouldn't do what he was told. 'Right! You cunt,' he yelled, blood lining the cracks between his remaining teeth. 'My mates are going to hear about this.'

Rawhead smashed his heel into Sirus's ribs. Sirus doubled up with pain.

'Tell them about that as well,' said Rawhead.

It was violence as God intended. Fast, businesslike and thoroughly unpleasant.

Little Malc and Brando stared in amazement.

'See that?' said Rawhead. 'He knew I didn't like blond hair. But he still bleached it. Rule number two: Don't be a ponce.'

Sirus was crawling away across the dance floor, mouthing threats.

'You're a fucking maniac,' marvelled Little Malc, giving voice to the feelings of the majority.

Rawhead smiled. 'As long as that's understood.'

*

Nikki got out of the bath to hear the doorbell ringing. She didn't want to answer in case it was the police or another journalist.

Mrs Dye, one of your neighbours has been murdered. How do you feel about that? 'Relieved.'

Whoever it was wouldn't go away. Nikki suspected the caller was her mother. It was meant to be Nikki's time off, the day her mum looked after Maddy. It would have been just like the old cow to get bored and bring the child back early.

The caller tired of the bell and resorted to the knocker. A volley of deafening raps rang through the house like pistol shots. Finally, overcome by curiosity, Nikki slipped into a dressing gown and went down. She stumbled on the stairs and had to clutch the banister for support. She was drunk. Although it was not yet noon, she was already on her fourth rum and coke.

It was only when she was unbolting the front door that she thought of the shootings. What if the killer had returned? So fucking what, she thought. Her life was complete shit anyway.

It took her a few seconds to recognize the tall man in the porch as Billy's friend. Steve was dressed like a rock star. A long fur coat, a simple black top that showed off his hard chest and belly, jeans supported by a studded belt. He was holding a bottle of Taittinger. 'Hi. Is Billy coming out to play?'

He was standing side on, like he already knew the answer and was ready to walk away.

'No,' she said. Suddenly feeling vulnerable.

He smiled again. Like many people who habitually scowled at the world, Steve had a great smile.

'He's in town,' she said. 'He's gone to a meeting.'

'Yeah? When will he back?'

'Good question.'

'Oh. OK.' He seemed disappointed, gazing wistfully down at the champagne bottle. 'Well, tell him I called, will you?'

'Was it about anything in particular?'

'No.'

'You sure? What's the champagne in aid of?'

He laughed to himself and shook his head. 'OK, I'll tell you the truth.' *I'm the greatest murderer who ever walked the earth.*

'Yes?' she said.

'It's my birthday,' he told her, 'and I just thought it might be nice to share it with an old friend.'

'Oh, no!' she said, holding her hands to her face. 'And he isn't even here.'

'Oh, woe is me,' he said, clowning for her. 'Woe, woe. When will he back?'

'This is Billy we're talking about,' she said, as if no further explanation was required.

'He must have given you some idea?'

'Maybe teatime. Maybe midnight.'

First he'd looked hopeful. Now he looked crushed.

'But you must have something else planned,' she said. 'On your birthday.'

'Nope.'

'No, you *must*.' Nikki was almost pleading with him. 'You've got other friends, surely?'

He gave her a shy smile. 'Not like Billy.'

'Aw! That's so sweet.'

When women talked this way, Rawhead wanted to slap them. He felt like tying them up with bows and ribbons and burying them alive. See how sweet they found the maggots and the worms.

Yet Rawhead was all gentle manly grace as Nikki leaned forward to hug him. As she bent forward, he inhaled the booze on her breath and glimpsed one of her tiny girlish breasts.

The black funeral pyre that was Rawhead's heart began to smoulder.

'I'll phone him, shall I? Let me phone him. Come in for a minute.'

He stepped into the bright bourgeois hall, catching sight of himself in a long oval mirror. His eyes gleamed madly, as if he'd taken acid or seen the kingdom of heaven. He turned away, watching her make the phone call. Predictably, Billy's mobile was switched off. Rawhead thanked Nikki and moved towards the door.

'You could always wait,' she said.

'No. Like you say, Billy could be all day. I'd just be in your way.'

'I'm not doing anything,' she said. *Ever.*

He stood there, pretending to consider it.

When what she was proposing was exactly what he had in mind.

*

Rawhead insisted on opening the champagne. It was colder than a Salvation Army bed. Nikki got dressed and they sipped Taittinger together in the vast living room. While they were chatting, a delivery man called at the house to drop off a parcel. Nikki opened it in front of Rawhead. It was full of paperback books.

'Oh,' said Nikki. 'It's Billy's latest. I'd forgotten all about it.'

She passed a copy to Rawhead. The title was *Not Dead, But Creeping*. Like all Billy's books, it had a bad cover – a corpse crawling on all fours through a graveyard. 'I didn't know he had a book coming out,' said Rawhead.

'Yeah. He wrote that soon after Maddy was born. I think he got an advance of about two thousand for it.'

Nikki watched Rawhead leafing through the book.

'You actually read those things?'

'Yeah,' said Rawhead. 'I think Billy's a great writer.'

She looked at him sideways, as if there must be something wrong with him. His face suddenly registered mild shock. 'Have you seen this?'

'What?'

He took the book over to her. On page three there was a dedication. TO STEVE ELLIS, FRIEND AND BROTHER.

Nikki was delighted. 'Hey! How about that? You got a birthday present. Take that copy away with you. Happy bloody birthday'

Rawhead nodded and sat down. For a long time, he browsed through the paperback, his face dark and intense.

'How old are you?' said Nikki eventually. 'Same age as Billy?'

'I think so,' he said.

She thought he was joking. 'How do you mean?'

'My mother abandoned me when I was small.' He said this cheerfully, without a trace of self-pity.

Nikki didn't know what to say.

'I was adopted when I was thirteen, and my mum and dad chose today as my birthday. I don't know when my real birthday is. My real mum was a chronic alcoholic, you see. One day was very much like the next to her.'

'I know the feeling,' said Nikki.

Rawhead nodded, his eyes taking in the suburban decor, two goldfish swimming forlornly in a huge bowl, a framed wedding photo above the fireplace.

'Did you ever know your father?' she asked him.

'He was probably some wino who traded a sip from his meths bottle for a fuck. And, believe me, if you'd seen my mother, you'd realize the wino was getting the raw end of the deal.'

Nikki looked at him for a long time. 'That's sad, Steve.'

'Is it?' He smiled. 'I wouldn't change anything about my life.'

'I think I'd change practically everything about mine,' she said. 'Apart from Maddy.'

'You and Billy are having problems,' he said. It wasn't a question.

She nodded. 'It's hard, living with a person all the time. After a while, you stop noticing the good things and just home in on the faults. When I met Billy, we were both art students. He was Modigliani, I was Frida Kahlo. Except better. We were going to be the greatest painters ever born. But somehow, I got side-tracked. Billy ended up with a writing career. I ended up with nothing.'

Rawhead looked around him. 'Not bad for nothing.'

Her eyes shone with anger. He realized she was probably drunker than she looked. 'You think I wanted to live in a house like this? Surrounded by right-wing pricks who toast the Queen before every meal?'

'Billy isn't like that.'

'Billy's hardly ever here.' She pointed to a National Trust magazine on the coffee table. 'Look at that. We could have supported a charity for the homeless, a charity that feeds children in Africa. And what do we do? We become members of a charity that helps aristocratic scroungers to keep their country mansions. And get this: joining was Billy's idea.'

Rawhead shook his head in sincere disapproval. He had occasionally fantasized about killing every member of the National Trust.

'So OK, I live in a big house. But I feel I'm living the wrong life,' said Nikki. 'With the wrong person.' She looked at him. Her eyes dark and huge, full of fear and desire.

Fear and desire will destroy the world.

'Er, maybe I should go,' said Rawhead. Knowing that if he left now, she would keep thinking about him.

He saw her flinch as if he'd slapped her. 'We haven't finished the champagne.'

He waited a while, holding the paperback against his chest. 'Billy's my best friend. And I don't much care for the thoughts that are running through my mind.'

She leaned towards him. 'You can't help having thoughts. Thoughts only become a problem if you act on them.'

'No, I'll go,' he said. 'I think I should.'

She followed him out into the hall. Disappointed, vaguely thwarted. At the door, she threw her arms around him. 'Will you come back?'

He shrugged. 'When's a good time?'

'Any time that Billy isn't here.'

Before he left, she wrote her mobile-phone number on his hand.

*

That night a concert in aid of the Sunny Bunny Trust was held at Diva. The concert was followed by an auction. The worst of Manchester's comedians and recording artistes had turned up to perform for nothing. In addition to his role as master of ceremonies, Little Malc sang a song he'd written especially for the occasion.

> *Have a care for the children of tomorrow,*
> *Give them a future that they will not be denied.*
> *They may be crippled, but keep them free from sorrow,*
> *They may be coloured, but they still have their pride . . .*

Little Malc was so moved by his own lyrics that he wept during the song. So did many members of the audience, albeit for different reasons.

Mercifully, Rawhead wasn't there to witness this disgraceful performance. He was on the door with Brando.

'But I don't understand,' said Brando. 'I thought I was just promoted.'

'This is your last night on the door,' promised Rawhead.

Halfway through the charity gala, a battered Daimler stopped outside the club. The Medina brothers got out. Tonight they were alone.

'OK,' said Rawhead. 'You know what to do?'

Brando nodded.

Chris Medina got out of the car first, raising his left leg and farting like a horse. Then his brother appeared, laughing and complaining about the smell. Rawhead stepped out into their path. 'Sorry, sir. Tonight it's invitation only.'

Chris thought it was a joke. 'Yeah. And I'm Cinderella.'

'That's right,' said Keith. He nodded at Brando. 'And if we don't leave on the stroke of midnight, that nigger's suit turns back into a grass skirt.'

They pressed forward. Rawhead pushed them back. Now Keith was standing at his little brother's side.

'Hey. Who're you fucking touching?' demanded Chris. 'Hands off, you fucking pleb.'

Rawhead stood firm.

'Acting the big man, are you?' said Keith. 'You couldn't take my three-year-old kid.'

'Just show me your invitations,' said Rawhead calmly.

'Oh, grow up, you cunt,' said Chris.

'We don't need no spacko invite,' added his brother. 'We rule fucking Salford.'

'But this isn't Salford,' said Rawhead patiently.

'Bring me Sirus. Now,' demanded Keith. 'I want to talk to him.'

'He's in hospital,' said Brando.

'Who asked you?' said Chris.

'Yeah? Who asked you?' echoed Keith. 'You fucking chimp.'

'Goodnight, gentlemen,' said Rawhead with an air of finality.

Chris was about to take a swing when he glanced to his left, saw a police car slowly approaching. Instead, he got out his mobile to call back his driver.

rawhead in love

'I don't blame nigger boy,' said Keith Medina, looking directly at Rawhead, 'because no way would he have thought of this all by himself. So that just leaves you.' He leaned forward and with laudable accuracy spat on Rawhead's left shoe. 'You are fucking dead, my friend.'

9

That evening, all in fond discourse was spent,
When the sad lover to his chamber went,
To think on what had past, to grieve and repent

'The Dejected Lover', George Crabbe (1754–1832)

Billy fully intended to abandon his TV series. He really did. He longed to be an artist again and write just for himself and his only fans: Rawhead and the ghosts of other dead artists.

All television had going for it was large audiences. Nobody reads novels, but at least a novelist has only one editor to contend with. It seemed to Billy that in television the writer was accorded no respect. He was like the poor peasant who grows the food but is not invited to the feast.

In a television script meeting, everyone except the writer had a better idea. Before a script exists, no TV executive alive has the faintest idea how to write it. But when the writer has delivered the first draft, virtually any dimwit who happens to be walking past the producer's office is invited in to comment on the writer's script and scribble all over it with red ink.

Yet the evening after the disastrous meeting, Billy logged onto his computer and found five emails waiting for him. Two of the messages invited him to enlarge his penis, one invited him to lick a fat girl today, the fourth was from a credit-card company and the fifth was from his agent, Fatty Potts.

rawhead in love

Thought you should know that George Leica phoned. Brad Pitt
didn't like the book, Nicole says she's too busy. George says we
shouldn't be downhearted, it's early days yet. Best wishes, Fatty.

The message contained an underlying hopelessness that made
Billy's cheeks burn. His stomach churned as he felt his Hollywood dreams receding. Two per cent – that was what George
had told him. Only two per cent of published novels get
optioned by movie companies. Of the books optioned, only two
per cent ever turn into films. It was always going to be a long
shot. But Billy had believed, truly *believed*, that his dreams of
fame and riches were about to be fulfilled. Hadn't God given
him talent for a reason? Not just to bring light and meaning into
a wretched world, but to make Billy rich. Having kept his
beloved son, William Edwin Dye, waiting for so long, surely the
creator would get his act together this time?

Now Billy saw the truth. The Lord wasn't rooting for him.
God didn't even know who he was. To God, Billy was just
another of those nasty little talking monkeys that he'd invented
for a joke, one rainy afternoon in heaven.

*

This was how Billy ended up occupying a suite high in the
Malmaison Hotel, gazing down on a dirty brown river and
miles of derelict buildings when he should have been writing.
He had a house in Prestbury with a big, fat mortgage that he'd
stupidly believed would be paid off this year when Brad Pitt
said yes to the part of hell's emissary in the movie of *Unholier
Than Thou*.

A day before, in Billy's imagination, Brad Pitt had invited
him to his beach home in Malibu. In reality, Brad may not have
owned a home in Malibu. But in Billy's fantasy he did. Billy had
played with Brad's children and shared his ice-cream cone while

they discussed their next project. In the fantasy, Brad had laughed wildly at one of Billy's jokes. Then he had placed his hand on Billy's shoulder and said, 'Man, you are like the brother I never had.'

Today, Billy was no brother to Brad. He was not even an insignificant boring cousin who Brad had never particularly liked. In Brad's personal universe, Billy was nothing. Brad Pitt, the handsome, talented fucker, thought Billy's work was shit. Furthermore, if Billy had been able to get hold of Brad at that moment, he would have given him a damned good kicking.

Suddenly, the TV series about gangsters looked like Billy's sole source of income. His fifth novel, *Not Dead But Creeping*, was about to be published, hardly a cause for celebration. People weren't exactly going to be queueing round the block for a signed copy.

Once again, Billy's dreams had turned to shit. It was like climbing the tree of life only to find a waiting noose.

His suite was like a gilded prison cell. With its modernistic, arty decor, the hotel seemed to be pretending it wasn't in Manchester. Billy wasn't fooled.

As a child, he'd sometimes visited the printing works in Ardwick that his dad managed. The building stank of ink and rats, and commanded a panoramic view of poverty and desolation. The Malmaison, for all its charm, overlooked a similar landscape. It was like staying overnight in his dad's printing works, this time with room service.

Billy phoned reception to ask what the nearby river was called, but no one knew. The worst thing was, no one offered to find out.

'Is it the Cuntington Canal?' Billy asked the assistant manager.

'I honestly couldn't say, sir.'

In the distance lay the railway station. Late at night he heard the trains rattling in on the wind. Drunks shouted and sang in the street below.

It was lonely in Billy's tower. Rain spattered the windows in sad little spurts.

Because someone else was paying, Billy ordered the most expensive items on room service. Prime Scottish sirloin with *pommes frites,* accompanied by icy cold Perrier-Jouët. Vanilla rice pudding and a glass of aged Calvados. Then a box of chocolate truffles.

One by one, he squashed the chocolates against the bathroom mirror. This was Billy's idea of trashing a hotel room.

He sat down to write. This is what he typed:

Int. Bonehead's House. Night.

JOHNNY, clutching a knife, descends the steps leading to the dark cellar. The cellar door is shut. JOHNNY stands beside the door and listens. From within, the sound of manic laughter. JOHNNY reaches for the door handle and turns it with agonizing slowness. The laughter continues. JOHNNY pushes the door open, afraid of what he might be about to see.

Golden light shines on JOHNNY's face. His fear turns to amazement. Inside the cellar a pleasant little party is in progress. A dozen people, including BEASTLY and THE SURGEON, and TERRY THE POLICEMAN are sitting on comfortable sofas, sipping wine. The laughter comes from Billy's missing publisher, DAN PERRY, who is eating a giant cream cake. In the centre of the room stands BONEHEAD, juggling with oranges. At the sight of JOHNNY, everyone falls silent. Only BONEHEAD, who continues to juggle, seems unconcerned.

BONEHEAD

Hi, John. Get yourself a drink, will you? I've got my hands full here.

JOHNNY

But . . .

BONEHEAD

Yeah?

JOHNNY

All these people . . .

BONEHEAD

What about 'em?

JOHNNY

Well . . . they're alive!

The onlookers laugh and nod.

BONEHEAD
(Mildly exasperated)
Of course they're alive. What do you take me for?

JOHNNY

A murderer?

More laughter. TERRY THE POLICEMAN comes up to pat
BONEHEAD's arm.

TERRY
There's something you should know about this man . . .
this man . . .
(Emotional)
. . . this man is a saint.

The others applaud. BONEHEAD looks bashful.

BONEHEAD

Hey, folks . . . just because I like saving lives, doesn't make me special.

*

Little Malc kept phoning Chef, asking for a meeting.

'What about?' demanded Chef.

'I'll tell you when I see you.'

'Tell me now,' said Chef. 'Then I'll know whether it's worth going out of the door for.'

'It's worth it.'

'What is it, then?'

'Meet me and I'll fucking tell you.'

Chef didn't care for the way Little Malc sounded. A bit pushy. More confident than usual. 'What? What is it? No, let me guess. Your balls have finally dropped. You're pregnant with Tony Bennett's love child.'

'I just want to talk to you. Face to face. That's what business associates are supposed to do, isn't it?'

'Stop fucking around. If you want something, tell me what it is and I'll think about it.'

'It's business.'

'What kind of business?'

'The kind of business you don't fucking discuss over the fucking phone.'

*

Chef kept putting him off, but Little Malc was persistent, phoning every day until the big man caved in.

They met in the Moroccan at lunchtime, sitting down together in the back room where the private parties were held. Chef was flanked by the Philosopher and Average. Average was a thick-limbed ex-biker with long hair, rings and amulets. His real name

135

was Andrew Aspin, but they called him Average because he looked like a bear. Not Yogi Bear, who was smarter than the average bear. This guy was strictly average, hence his name.

Little Malc turned up with a big, solemn tool who he introduced as Stoker.

Chef had already heard about this Stoker guy from the Medinas, who wanted an example to be made of him. They said he'd insulted them. Either Chef made him pay, or they'd do it themselves. All Stoker had done, as far as Chef could tell, was bar the Medinas entry to the club. It wasn't enough to maim a guy for.

Right away, the Philosopher and Average started needling him.

'Hey, Average,' said the Philosopher, 'I think the new boy here's been seeing Sidney.'

'Eh?' said Little Malc.

'Sidney Scud. The Sadhouse Stud. Lick his lollipop and win parole.'

The Philosopher and Average chortled comfortably. Little Malc didn't know what the fuck they were talking about.

'They're saying your friend here looks like a convict.' explained Chef.

'They should fucking know,' retorted Little Malc.

Stoker behaved as if Chef's boys hadn't spoken. It was as if a couple of house flies were trying to intimidate a lion. Although Chef didn't like to admit it, the guy was impressive. He looked fit, but carried himself like he had nothing to prove. Not a bully or a braggart – Chef despised men that acted tough. This guy seemed different.

Little Malc was looking different, too. He was wearing a dark, funereal suit and seemed to have stopped dying his hair, allowing the grey flecks to show at the neck and sides. Apart from a few perfunctory wisecracks with Average and the Philosopher, Little

Malc maintained a steady emotional distance. The man at his side, Stoker, said nothing at all. When it was time to order the food, he just shook his head and poured himself a glass of water.

Chef noticed that the back of Stoker's left hand was disfigured. Chef, who had set fire to a few men in his time, could see the hand had been burned. On his right hand, Stoker wore a gold ring in the shape of a skull. Something about that ring troubled Chef. For the life of him, he couldn't think what.

'I've been doing a lot of thinking,' announced Little Malc, his face very serious. 'My dad set up the Priesthood with you. And he always said that one day, when it was time to retire, that I'd take over his share of the business.'

Immediately, Chef saw what was coming. 'He may have said that to you,' he said calmly. 'He never mentioned it to me.'

Little Malc carried on as if Chef hadn't spoken. 'So there's my dad. OK, we never found his body, but we all know where he is. Floating on a cloud in the Big Blue Swoon. Meanwhile, down on earth, you're in control of the skew, the card games, the porn, the drugs, the whores, the free gifts, the anonymous donations. You're worth fucking millions. And all I'm thinking is this: when do I get mine?'

The room went deadly quiet. The Philosopher and Average were staring at Little Malc with thin smiles on their faces. Stoker was staring down at his glass of water.

'You already got yours,' said Chef. 'You got half shares in this place and the club. You never had to work for these things, they just fell out of the sky into your lap. Just be fucking grateful. The economy is in trouble. Average has got a brother who hasn't had a job since 1989. That right, Average?'

Average gave a sombre nod.

Little Malc smiled. 'Don't give me that. The economy hasn't harmed your fucking business.'

'Just leave it,' warned Chef.

Little Malc didn't want to shut up. He was just getting started. 'My father shared the profits with you. That's right, isn't it?'

'Don't raise your voice to me. I don't talk to people who raise their voices.'

Little Malc looked to Stoker for support. Without appearing to move his head, Stoker nodded. Little Malc took a few deep breaths and waited.

'We didn't quite share the profits,' volunteered Chef. 'I got forty per cent. He got sixty. Which was fair, I admit that. Your father got the whole thing going.'

'OK. I'll accept forty per cent.'

Chef held up his hands. 'Whoa. You go pretty fast for a little fat guy.'

Chef's men laughed.

'I'll go even faster unless you answer me this one fucking question,' said Little Malc. 'Do you think my dad would be happy with the way you've shared out the pie?'

'What pie? I don't see any pie.'

'Why won't you answer the question?'

'Because it's the wrong question,' insisted Chef. 'What you should be asking is, would your old man be happy with the way I'm carrying on his business?'

'Well, I'm not fucking asking that. I'm asking if you think he's happy with the way you've treated me. Come on. You're a Catholic. You believe he can see us, don't you? Is my dad laughing or crying?'

'This is hypothetical bullshit,' said Chef. 'You might as well ask me what your dad thinks of Legoland or the latest TV commercial for Lloyds fucking bank. I don't know what he thinks, he isn't here to ask. All I can say is that I've been fair with you; I've always been fair with you. And, frankly, it hurts me and incenses me that you should think any different.'

'OK,' said Little Malc. 'Either you give me a share, or you hand over all rights in the club to me. Plus, I start collecting insurance from all the local businesses that aren't happy with the service you're providing.'

Chef laughed. 'Yeah? Who isn't happy?'

'Lots of people.'

'Name one.'

'I'm not about to betray the confidence of my investors,' said Little Malc.

Average whistled in mock admiration.

'I'll tell you what,' said Chef. 'All these businesses you say aren't happy – take them over, with my blessing. Why don't you? Build your own crime empire.'

The Philosopher and Average laughed heartily at this suggestion.

'That's right. Give the people a choice.' Chef was enjoying himself. 'And who do you think they'll root for? A fat little compère from a back-street club or the gang that rules Manchester? Duh, that's a hard one.'

Little Malc had gone red in the face. By way of contrast, the man called Stoker looked bored and unruffled, somehow contriving to watch everyone without ever making eye contact.

When Little Malc didn't answer, Chef felt he'd scored a victory. 'And another thing,' he went on. 'What gives you the right to turn my friends away from *our* club.'

'You mean Dumb and Dumber? The hairy menks from Salford?'

'I mean anyone who *I* do business with.'

'They were dealing.'

'Who says?'

'What do you mean, "Who says?"? The kids who were buying fucking shit off them, that's who.'

Chef sighed. 'You better apologize to them.'

'Yeah. I'll go round to all their houses and say, "I'm sorry you didn't get high, the Medina brothers burned you off."'

'You call up Keith and Chris. Tell them there's been a misunderstanding, that your man here got a bit overzealous, that he's still learning the job. Say they're welcome at the club any time. You can do that, can't you?'

Little Malc and his bodyguard got up to leave.

'Hey,' said Chef. 'Sit down. Please. Come on. This is stupid. How long have we known each other?'

'I'm needed at the club,' said Little Malc.

'Malcolm, you've ordered food. You might as well eat it.'

Little Malc started pointing the finger. 'All these years, I trusted you. And all along, you've just been taking me for a flob.'

'A *what*?'

'A flobadob. A flowerpot man. You're in the Priesthood and you don't even know Priesthood slang?'

'That's not Priesthood slang,' scoffed Chef. '*Flob?*' He turned to the Philosopher and Average, who were rolling about, laughing hysterically.

'Malcolm,' said Chef, 'go home, take an asprin and have a nice lie down.'

'Yeah,' said Average. 'And take your girlfriend with you.'

Rawhead stared at him, very cold and calm.

'Whooh,' said Average. 'I'm scared.'

The Philosopher got up to escort them out, serious now, trying to show Little Malc they were still friends. 'We had a juice night out at your place the other night,' he said, holding the door open for them. 'You've really turned that club around.'

'Oh,' said Little Malc humbly. 'Thanks.'

'Take care, mate,' said the Philosopher to Rawhead, playing

the magnanimous victor. 'We were only joshing around, hope you know that.'

'Fuck you,' said Rawhead as he walked out.

'*What?*' The Philosopher thought he must have misheard. He stood there, still holding the door open, watching the two men walk to their car. 'What did you just say to me?'

*

Rawhead drove Little Malc back to Diva, crawling through the rush-hour traffic.

'Flob!' said Little Malc. 'Why did you tell me there was such a word when there fucking isn't? You made me look like a right 'nana.'

'Don't you mean a flob?' said Rawhead. And he laughed quietly.

'Hey, pal. They were laughing at you, too,' said Little Malc. 'You needn't look so fucking pleased with yourself.'

'Let 'em laugh,' said Rawhead.

'What kills me is, today was your fucking idea. Then you just sit there and say fuck all while those twats rip it out of me.'

'They did exactly what I wanted them to do.'

'Right. That's it. You're fucking sacked.'

Rawhead was getting used to this. Little Malc sacked him at least once a day. He was like a child. Ten minutes later, all was forgotten and he'd shuffle back to Rawhead, asking him to help tie his shoelaces.

'This may surprise you,' said Rawhead, 'but you did a great job in there.'

'Bollocks. You saw it! They don't take me seriously.'

'They took you very seriously when you mentioned drugs. In fact, I think I've finally worked out what's been going on. The Medinas have been dealing Chef's gear for him in your club. It's all part of Chef's plan to become respectable.

'First of all, he stopped selling guns. Now he's got subcontractors to take care of the dope distribution. Little by little, he's distancing himself from all his criminal activities. If the club gets busted, you blame the Medinas, they blame their social worker. No one blames Chef.'

Little Malc sighed, bitter and resigned. 'Way I see it, there's fuck all we can do to stop the bastards.'

'Believe me,' said Rawhead, 'they have no idea what's coming.'

'What's coming?'

'You. You're going to beat them. You're going to be number one.'

'Fuck off,' said Little Malc. Grinning because he was flattered. 'Now *you're* taking me for a flob.'

When they got to the club, a sorry scene awaited them. Someone had sprayed 'CUNNT' on the entrance doors in letters eighteen inches high. Fats Medcroft was out there, ineffectually dabbing at the offending red paint with a damp tissue.

'Oh, Jesus fucking Christ!' said Little Malc. 'Who the fuck did this?'

'We didn't see, boss,' said Fats. 'I was down the cellars when it happened.'

'I wouldn't mind,' complained Little Malc, 'but it isn't even spelt right. Who do we know who's got a grudge against me and can't spell?'

10

Come away, come away, Death
And in sad cypres let me be laid;
Fly away, fly away, breath;
I am slain by a fair cruel maid.

'Dirge of Love', William Shakespeare (1564–1616)

The meeting with Little Malc put Chef in a foul mood. He ate his lunch alone. For lunch he always ate the same meal. Fillet steak with a hint of blood, served with fries and vegetables of the day. Usually he drank only water. Today he consumed two and a half bottles of chianti.

Chef's eyes were turning as red as the wine when Bryan walked in holding Billy's first draft of episode one of *Gangchester*. After a quiet chat with Average, who was spinning on a stool at the bar, Bryan walked over to Chef's table. Chef slammed down his fork in disgust. 'What now?'

'Sorry to interrupt.'

'So you fucking should be.'

'I think you should hear this. You'll thank me for it.'

'Sit down,' said Chef grudgingly. He picked up his fork and stabbed a lump of steak.

'It's this fucking script, boss,' said Bryan. He was half smiling, eyes wide, as if what he'd discovered was simultaneously thrilling and appalling. 'It's about us.'

'Does it use real names?'

'No, but it might as fucking well. The gang boss is called Melvin Feast. His number two is called . . . get this . . . *Chief.*'

'Chief?' Chef's fork hovered between his plate and his mouth. 'What's this character like?'

'That's just it,' said Bryan.

'Just what?'

'He's gay.'

'He's *what*?'

Bryan opened the script. In a halting, unconfident voice he read: 'Chief sits in his office. He's pushing fifty, a closet queen with mafia pretensions. He studies images of male bodybuilders in a glossy magazine.'

Chef plucked his napkin from his lap and slammed it down on the table. A vein on his forehead was throbbing. Bryan had never seen him so angry. He looked like he was about to explode. 'And you say this shit's going to be made?'

'Shonagh says it's been green lit.'

'What does that mean?'

'That's what you call it in tellyland. Green lit. When something's going to be made.'

'Well, listen. You don't work in fucking tellyland. Neither do I. So stop talking like an arsehole. What's the guy in charge called?'

'Larry Crème.'

'Do you know where we might get hold of him?'

'I could find out.'

*

Larry's affair with Artemesia had lasted seven months. For Larry, this was a record. Initially he'd hired her as a PA, hoping she'd be willing to accommodate a stale middle-aged man with dyed hair in exchange for career advancement. Happily, she was. Two dozen blow jobs later, Artemesia was a script editor on *Second Thoughts*, Larry's most popular programme. In the afternoons, when they could, they went to Artemesia's flat in West Didsbury for a sandwich, a glass of wine and a one-minute fuck. Larry knew a minute wasn't long enough, but at least it proved Artemesia excited him. When Larry had sex with his wife, it sometimes took him all night to come.

When the doorbell rang, Larry was lying on Artemesia's bed, surrounded by teddy bears.

Artemesia was in the shower, rinsing Larry's scud out of her hair. Larry wanted to ignore the doorbell, but it kept ringing. He got up, swearing and walked to the intercom. 'Hello?'

'Parcel for a Mr Larry Crème.'

'I'll be right down.'

Larry was intrigued. The only person who knew where he spent his lunch breaks was Artemesia. Had the little darling bought him a present? He dressed, left the flat and descended to the main entrance. A thin young man with no eyebrows and tousled blond hair was standing on the step.

'Mr Crème?' he said hopefully.

Larry nodded. The young man smacked him in the jaw. Larry Crème fell over.

*

Rawhead phoned Nikki, to check she was in. She said yes, come by for tea. He drove round that afternoon. The little girl was playing on the rug. Every time Rawhead looked at her, she screamed for her mother.

Nikki looked great, eyes and hair shining. 'Where's Billy?' said Rawhead.

Nikki told him about Billy, locked in the Malmaison Hotel like Rapunzel.

'Do you think he's doing any work?'

'I don't know. When he phones, all he does is swear. Last night he was crying.'

'*Crying?*'

'Yes. He thinks he's betraying his soul. I told him he'd better get writing. His soul is going to feel a lot more betrayed if we lose this house.'

The sun was shining so they put Maddy in her pushchair and went for a walk. Nikki wanted to know about Billy, so Steve told her all about when they were thirteen. The times that Billy stayed over at Steve's, the two boys reading ghost stories aloud by candlelight when they were meant to be sleeping. He missed out the stuff about going to prison for stabbing a kid at the school dance. In Rawhead's experience, stabbing was not an aphrodisiac.

'You like Billy a lot, don't you?' she said.

'Why? Don't you?'

'Course. I love him. But creative people tend to be very selfish. They're not easy to live with.'

'But you're a creative person, too.'

'Nice of you to say, but no. I used to be creative. At the moment I'm just a housewife and a mother.'

'So you resent Billy for that?'

'Yeah.'

'It's not his fault.'

'I know. I can't help it.'

Rawhead nodded sympathetically. 'Why did you come back?'

'Sorry?'

'You left him once, didn't you? If he's such a pain, why did you come back?'

'I was pregnant. I had no money, nowhere to live. It's not that I don't love Billy. He thinks I don't, but I do. He complains that I don't admire him any more, but he's wrong about that, too.

He's focused, he's determined. Why wouldn't I admire him? But the truth is, I'm thirty-three and I can't work out what I've been doing or where my life went.'

Rawhead was thinking, *You talk too much, bitch.*

'Pills, therapy, I've tried everything,' she went on. 'I didn't know what was wrong, but I went to the doctor and she told me I was showing all the classic symptoms of depression. Not sleeping, inertia, thinking the world is a horrible place.'

Just to shut her up, Rawhead pulled her towards him and kissed her.

Nikki didn't respond. It was like kissing an inflatable doll. He stepped back to look at her. Her face was now sad and stricken, as if he'd imparted some catastrophic news. 'Sorry,' he said. 'Maybe I shouldn't have done that.'

She shook her head, grabbed the back of his neck and returned the kiss. A tender girl's kiss, that probed and coaxed and took its time.

*

Chef appeared to be upset when he saw Larry's swollen face. Not as upset as Larry. No one had ever hit Larry that hard before, although many had been tempted. Nothing was broken, but his jawbone ached. Not the muscles around it, but the bone itself. Larry was amazed, not having realized that bones could hurt.

Larry had never heard of Chef, but he found the height and bearing of this swarthy, broken-nosed killer hypnotic. Chef had more presence than practically any actor that Larry had met. And, crucially, Chef was for real.

This didn't stop Larry from having a tantrum when Chef apologized. 'Do you realize who I am? Anything happens to me, and half the country's TV drama grinds to a halt.'

Like this was a threat.

Chef took Larry into his games room (tastefully refurbished

since Malcom Priest had burned to death on the carpet) and gave him a large glass of brandy. The Philosopher positioned himself by the door in case Larry had hysterics and needed to be hauled off the boss.

When he saw the brandy and the thug standing guard, Larry finally started to grasp the gravity of the situation. 'What do you want with me?'

'Only that we should talk. Man to man.' Chef turned his liquid brown eyes to the TV producer.

'About what?'

'This show you're making: *Gangchester*. I don't want it.'

'You don't *want* it? Don't want it to do what?'

Chef just leaned back in his seat and scratched his chin. It occurred to Larry that it might be a good idea to be polite.

'To be honest, sir, I'm a little surprised you've heard of the programme.'

'It's about my organization, the Priesthood. The writer, Dye, has been here. In this house. He spent a few weeks with us, researching a book that was never written. You knew this?'

'No,' said Crème. 'I did not know this.'

'It's true. We paid him, welcomed him into our lives. And he shows his gratitude by ridiculing us. According to his script, I'm a homosexual! To take real people and rubbish them for the sake of a piece of entertainment – how can that be justified, Mr Crème?'

Crème needed to gulp, so gulped down brandy. 'It can't.'

'That's good. So the programme doesn't get made.'

'It isn't as simple as that,' said Larry.

'Why? Has it been filmed?'

'No. But it's been scheduled. We'll have a great hole in our drama schedule if we don't go ahead.'

'You'll have a great hole in your head if you do.'

'Are you serious?' said Larry.

'No.' Chef forced a smile. 'That was just a joke. But I will say this. You'll anger a lot of people in my line of business if you depict them as fools.'

'But it's comedy drama. The characters have to be foolish.' He looked at Chef searchingly. 'So this Johnny character. The writer. You're saying he's based on Billy Dye?'

Chef nodded.

'But he's stupid, too,' said Larry. 'It's not as if Billy is ridiculing gangsters and making himself out to be special. Everyone gets the piss taken out of them.'

'You don't really know who I am, do you?'

'Not really.'

'That's good,' said Chef, secretly annoyed. 'I don't want to be well known. That's the last thing I want. A programme like this will bring me and my organization unwelcome publicity.'

Larry Crème shrugged helplessly. 'I see that. But I don't know what you expect me to do about it.'

'I've already told you. I don't want this programme to be made.'

'Would it help if you were heterosexual?'

The Philosopher was so shocked to hear this insult that he drew a .38. Seeing this, Chef gave a subtle shake of his head. By the time Larry had glanced round to see what was going on, the gun was back in its holster.

'I am heterosexual,' said Chef coldly.

'Sorry, sorry,' said Larry. He moved to touch Chef's forearm, felt the chill and withdraw his hand at the last moment. 'I meant your character in the show. I mean, the character that you *think* might be based on you.'

'I wouldn't trust the writer to do anything I approved of. I've met him, remember. He's a very disrespectful person.'

'You're not wrong there. He told me and my colleagues to go fuck ourselves.'

Chef sniffed. 'You're just proving my point. I don't want you to make any programme written by Billy Dye.'

'What? Ever?'

'Ever.'

Larry Crème sighed.

'Are you a man of honour?' said Chef. 'Do you give me your word?'

Larry allowed himself a small cackle. 'You sound like one of them Mafiosi fellas.'

Very coldly and deliberately, Chef looked Larry up and down.

'Sorry, sorry. I give you my word. I promise.'

Chef realized that Crème would tell him anything that he thought would get him out of the house alive. Without changing his expression or the tone of his voice, the gang boss reached a decision.

'Anyway, have another drink. Come on. No more business talk. Let's relax. Do you like women?'

Larry wasn't sure he'd heard correctly. Chef nodded to the Philosopher, who got up and opened the door. Two women walked in, both dressed in white frilly underwear. One of them was fair haired, young and slim, with a flat stomach. The other was big and beefy, with huge breasts and a sullen face.

'My friend here is an important man in TV. There are four bottles of champagne on ice next door. Give him a good time and he'll get you a part in *Coronation Street*.'

The women looked startled. But not as startled as Larry. 'I . . . this isn't . . .'

'Please. Don't thank me,' said Chef firmly. 'It's all part of the service.'

*

The two women wore Larry out. When Average came to collect him, Larry was lying on his back on the floor of the guest bedroom. Average picked him up, sat him on the bed and passed him his clothes.

'OK, Mr Crème. I think it's time to take you home.'

Larry looked around the room. He was finding it difficult to focus. 'Where's the big girl?' he slurred. 'I want the big-titty lady.'

Average smiled tolerantly. 'We can take her with us, if you want. You wanna take her with us?'

'Yes, please,' said Larry.

'Now, put on your trousers like a good boy.'

Larry started giggling. 'Know what you look like? You look like one of them heavy-metal fellas.' And he started playing an air guitar to illustrate the point.

'That's funny,' said Average. 'Now get fucking dressed.'

*

It was a cold night. Larry's breath turned to mist as he followed Average out to the waiting Jag. The Philosopher was already at the wheel, gunning the engine. The big girl, Fiona, was waiting in the back seat, wearing an enormous mink coat. She snuggled up to Larry and wrapped the coat around them both. 'You're a naughty boy, aren't you? Does your wife know how naughty you are?'

'I shouldn't think so,' said Larry.

The Philosopher and Average laughed. The car moved off and the security gates opened. Soon they were on the motorway. Larry groped Fiona, felt something hard and metallic. It was a pair of handcuffs.

Larry laughed. 'Have you seen what she's got here?'

'Only way she can get laid,' said Average.

'Look who's talking,' sneered Fiona. 'When was the last time you had a fuck you didn't pay for?

Larry and the Philosopher tittered. Average sulked.

Unhurriedly, the car swept off the main road and stopped before a set of iron gates. Average got out and unlocked a heavy padlock. He opened the gates and got back into the car. Larry watched this in a kind of happy, drunken daze. Fiona stroking his hand as if to reassure him.

The car moved forward down a tree-lined avenue. The trees writhed and bowed in the wind. Then the car turned into a circular avenue. Out of the window Larry could see hundreds of graves. 'Why have we stopped here?' he said.

'Because I'm dying for a fucking piss,' said Fiona.

The gangsters laughed. 'Sheer class,' said Average.

'Working class,' said the Philosopher.

Fiona opened the car door, then looked at Average in the mirror.

'Will one of you come with me? It's horrible out there.'

'Fuck off,' said Average. 'Just squat down by the car. We won't look.'

'I'm not doing that,' said Fiona. 'What do you take me for?'

'A big fat whore,' said Average.

The gangsters guffawed.

'Hey,' said Larry, feeling gallant. 'There's no need for that.' He patted Fiona's hand. 'I'll come out with you.'

Fiona led Larry away from the car, down an aisle of tombs. She linked his arm, guiding him past the crosses and the graves. Swearing, Larry paused for breath. He was wearing a thin lilac shirt without a jacket and shoes without socks and was feeling the cold. He was still very drunk. Fiona turned and pushed him against a set of ornamental railings. 'Give me your hand,' she said.

Without thinking, Larry offered her his right hand. She

snapped one of the handcuffs onto his wrist and joined the other to the railings. Larry laughed. 'You kinky bitch . . .' With his free hand he tried to grope one of her breasts. But his hand seized nothing but the cold air. Fiona was already walking away.

Larry rattled the handcuffs, saw that he was trapped.

'Oi!' he shouted. 'Come back this fucking minute!'

He was shivering with cold and fear.

Directly in front of him was an elaborate tomb with a grinning skull carved on its side. The skull had little angel wings sprouting from each temple. Larry glanced to his left and thought he saw something moving. He narrowed his eyes to peer into the dark. He could see nothing and thought he'd been mistaken. But, no. There was another flicker of movement.

Someone was coming.

They were walking slowly down the path towards him.

It was a figure in black. The stranger approached with excruciating slowness, stopping a few yards away from Larry. Larry couldn't see the face, only the outline of a boyish head.

'Listen,' said Larry. 'I don't know who you are or what you want. But I've got money. We can work something out.'

Larry's voice, like his body, was shaking violently.

'There's nothing to fear,' said the stranger, in a calm, low voice.

Larry's hopes soared. It was a woman's voice. He was talking to a woman.

'Jesus Christ, you had me worried for a minute . . .' said Larry.

Larry had always had luck with the ladies. Surely a woman wouldn't hurt him?

'I'm not going to hurt you,' she said. As if she'd read his mind.

Larry's eyes filled with tears of gratitude. 'Could I have a drink of water?'

She seemed to consider this.

'Please?' said Larry.

In the gloom he saw her nod. Then she turned sharply to Larry's right.

'Bring him some water!' she shouted.

There was no one there. But Larry didn't know this. As he turned to see who she was talking to, the woman shot him in the head.

She had kept her promise.

There was no pain.

There was nothing to fear.

11

You are crueller, you that we love,
Than hatred, hunger, or death;
You have eyes and breasts like a dove,
And you kill men's hearts with a breath.

'Satia Te Sanguine', Algernon Charles Swinburne (1837–1909)

When Chris and Keith Medina began to make money, they refused to let success change them. They remained the same vicious, nasty, self-centred vermin they'd always been. Instead of moving out of their old house in Salford, they bought the entire street.

Because no one wanted to live in an area where blood flowed in the gutters, the houses were going cheap. Twenty soot-black terraced slums at four grand apiece. The brothers knocked three of the houses into one and lived there. The other seventeen homes remained empty and boarded up.

The advantage of living this way was that the Medinas had no neighbours. Any cars found parked in the street were fire-bombed. Any person found walking down their street, with the possible exception of the postman, was liable to receive a serious kicking. When the brothers created a disturbance – as they often did – no one in the surrounding estate felt inclined to call the police. Even if they had, the police would have been too scared to call.

The Medinas loved to make noise. They were the kind of people that let off fireworks at five minutes to midnight on New

Year's Eve and then again at 1 a.m. and 2 a.m., and then all over again the following night. They kept two huge Rottweilers that snarled and barked into the early hours while their owners lay on the floor with cocaine snot foaming from their nostrils. When the dogs were quiet, the brothers would be shouting at their girlfriends or each other. When they were bored, they sometimes walked round the estate shooting out the street lights.

When the brothers were stoned beyond redemption, they vandalized the buildings on their own street. They held mock trials, in which they found their property guilty of being working class and shot it. So far, they'd spared the lives of the houses they lived in, but it was only a matter of time before these dwellings also faced death by firing squad.

Whenever they went anywhere, Chris would drive and his big brother would wind down the window to shout obscene abuse at innocent bystanders.

Joggers. ('You running bastard!')

Fat people. ('You fat bastard!')

Girls they wanted to fuck. ('You sexy bastard!')

Girls they didn't want to fuck. ('You ugly bastard!')

Women in saris. ('You wog bastard!')

People in wheelchairs. ('You crippled bastard!')

Middle-aged women. ('You menopausal bastard!')

Middle-class women. ('You posh bastard!')

People who looked terminally ill. ('You dying bastard!')

Old people. ('You dribbler bastard!')

The Medinas believed they could do or say what they liked to anyone, without fear of comeback. In most cases, this was true.

But spitting on Rawhead's shoe?

That was a bad mistake.

*

The street the Medinas owned was called Stainer Street. A fitting name for a thoroughfare spattered with every conceivable form of human and animal filth. Even without a map, Rawhead would have found the Medinas easily.

Rawhead was wearing his long black coat. He had a pair of matching Ruger magnums in his trouser belt and a short, wide-bladed knife in the side pocket of his overcoat. On foot, he skirted Stainer Street to familiarize himself with the geography of the battle ground. Stainer Street marked the end of a block. To the south lay several identical roads. In the opposite direction stretched a vast area of dogshit-encrusted waste ground, where Rawhead had paid two kids twenty each to guard his car, with the promise of the same again if he returned to find it still had wheels.

Rawhead crossed the end of Stainer Street. A big, fat intellectual was standing guard in the middle of the road. Behind him, party-goers were dancing in the street, whooping and shrieking in a desperate attempt to convince themselves they were having a great time. The intellectual spat on the ground as Rawhead walked by. Without reacting, Rawhead turned right into the neighbouring street. The windows of the houses were vibrating with the noise.

An old man in a vest was standing on his doorstep. He addressed Rawhead as he passed. 'Twice a week we get this fucking lot! My wife's fucking bed-ridden. I've written to environmental health. Have they done anything? Have they fuckers like!'

Rawhead nodded politely, walked back the way he'd come and watched the big fat prick waving a taxi full of party guests into the street. When the car had driven off, Rawhead whistled to the fat intellectual. The intellectual glared at him. 'What?'

'What's the capital of Denmark?' said Rawhead.

'What?'

'It's a general-knowledge question,' explained Rawhead calmly. 'Name the capital of Denmark.'

The intellectual took a step towards him. 'Fuck off! You stupid fucking pillock . . .'

'If you don't know the answer, just say so.'

As the guy walked forward, Rawhead stepped back.

'What about Holland? Surely you can name the capital of Holland?'

The intellectual swung a kick at him. The kick almost connected. Rawhead felt the breeze against his knees.

Before the aggressor could recover his balance, Rawhead stepped forward, drove the knife behind his windpipe and twisted. The intellectual staggered, his lips moving as if he was trying to say something. Blood spurted freely.

'Say it, don't spray it,' said Rawhead.

Wearily, the victim sank to his knees and lay down. A seismic shudder passed through him and then he lay still.

He died as he lived. Pointlessly.

*

Keith Medina was upstairs in his room with two teenage stinks. The music was so loud that the floor was humming. The girls were meant to be putting on a show for Keith. Chris had asked them to wear corsets, frilly knickers, stockings and suspenders and loaned them an enormous vibrator. But the teenagers looked more like two dumb supermarket check-out girls pricing a cucumber. It was obvious that they weren't really lesbians and it was debatable whether they even made the grade as whores. So far, their efforts had been so lame that Keith couldn't even get a hard-on.

It was conceivable that his lack of enthusiasm owed something to the mound of cocaine on the dressing table. Every few minutes he returned for another snort. That was the maddening thing about coke. Once it had got you as high as you could go, high enough to make any further dosage pointless, you still went back for more.

Keith dipped his forefinger in the white powder and then reached down the back of his boxer shorts. He'd read somewhere that taking cocaine up the arse helped avoid nosebleeds. Hadn't Stevie Nicks from Fleetwood Mac done it? But what about arsebleeds? There was only one fucking way to find out. He shoved his finger as far up his rectum as it'd go and waited. Nothing.

One of the girls on the bed belched. They both rolled about laughing, as if flatulence was the very pinnacle of wit. For them, it probably was.

There was an Uzi sub-machine pistol on the dressing table. Keith picked it up, eyes watering as he turned back to the bed. Over the pounding music he thought he could hear a woman screaming.

'You idle fucking stinks, I've seen more convincing dykes in fucking pantomimes. Now make a fucking effort or I'll shoot your tits off.'

Uncowed, the girls continued to snigger. It was amazing, the ignorance of modern youth. Keith was glowering down at them, wondering which one to maim first, when he registered that the woman was still screaming. The sound was coming from outside.

He looked out of the window and saw a man capering round in circles, blood fountaining from his cranium. It seemed impossible that he could be losing so much blood yet still keep upright. It looked like Barney, who used to play rugby for Salford. Barney was one of their best men.

Barney flopped forward onto his hands and knees and Keith saw his open mouth and realized it was him who was screaming. There were shouts, more screams. There was a loud bang.

Then a crowd of people surged away from the house into the middle of the street. People panicking, fighting, pushing each other out of the way.

A woman with blood on her face and dress took off her stilettos and ran away down the road. Keith didn't know what the fuck was going on. He hurriedly pulled on a pair of jeans – the thought of being attacked in his boxer shorts appalled him.

*

Zippa Jay was in the long living room. He was using the smaller rig that he reserved for private houses, yet his speakers still reached the ceiling. These days, it was literally an act of charity for Zippa to play a house party. He made more money as a producer/mixer than he'd ever made as a club DJ. One of his own masterpieces was on the turntable, a fucked-up Psycho remix of the theme from *The Magic Roundabout*, yet no one in the house seemed to realize how clever he'd been.

From his place at the mixing desk Zippa could see all three entrances. He kept watching the doors, hoping that no one in the dance community would walk in to catch him playing a wanker's private party. Gangsters were meant to be cool. But the Medinas weren't cool. They looked like second-hand-car salesmen.

A bruiser disguised as a waiter offered Zippa a glass of champagne from a tray. Zippa accepted, but he was bored and ill-at-ease. He didn't feel safe. He was only playing the gig because Chris Medina had asked him, and Zippa had heard distressing stories about what happened to people who disappointed the brothers.

Chris Medina pushed his way over to Zippa with a request. As Chris bellowed in Zippa's ear, hand dangling over Zippa's right shoulder in an over-familiar way, Zippa smelled rum on the gangster's breath. 'We got a problem, pal.'

'What?' mimed Zippa.

'None of us recognize one fucking tune you've played so far.'

'Ah. That's because "tunes" aren't exactly my thing.'

'Have you got any proper dance music? Like the Bee Gees or something?'

'Er, no.'

'What about northern soul?'

'Mainly, I've got techno or trance.'

'No northern soul?'

'No.'

'Well, what kind of fucking DJ are you?'

Zippa glanced at the door, saw a man with a hood on his head pushing through the guests. Normally, Zippa would have found the sight alarming. But he was more concerned about how the conversation with Chris Medina was going.

'If I gave you a pile of my own records, would you fucking play 'em?'

'It's kind of difficult . . .' said Zippa, squirming.

'Yeah. And it's also kinda difficult to talk when you've got no fucking teeth.'

'Pardon?'

'I said it's . . . oh, fucking forget it . . .'

The waiter who had served champagne to Zippa asked the man with the hood a question. The hooded man must have given the wrong answer, because the waiter tried to take a swing at him. Zippa didn't see how it happened, but the next second there was a loud bang and the waiter seemed to vomit blood. Some of his blood hit Zippa in the face. People started screaming and running. In slow motion Chris Medina looked towards the sound, reaching into his jacket as he turned.

Rawhead was holding a magnum revolver in each hand. He shot Chris in the right thigh. Chris gasped and fell. The gunman walked over him, using his chest as a stepping stone. Without even glancing down, he shot Chris Medina through the right eye, taking out the back of his head.

Zippa went to the microphone and made a passionate appeal. 'Please. Give peace a chance!'

Rawhead gave peace a chance for precisely one second. It didn't work for him. In order to inflict maximum pain, he shot the DJ's beloved mixing desk. The music died, and Zippa wailed in mourning.

All you could hear now was screaming. There were three staircases. Rawhead took the one to the left, climbing towards a rush of bodies coming downstairs. At the sight of Rawhead they turned round and charged back up. Rawhead ascended steadily, stepping on people, squeezing past bodies pinned against the wall.

On the landing, he avoided the crush by turning into one of the bedrooms. Inside, two men and three women were fucking on a huge bed while three of their friends stood around and watched. One of the spectators was filming the action with a video camera. As Rawhead walked through, the guy with the camera turned to film him instead.

With one swipe, Rawhead knocked the camera out of its owner's hands. It fell to the floor and smashed. The cameraman was about to protest, but fled when he saw who he was dealing with. The people on the bed just carried on fucking.

When Rawhead reached the far door, two holes ripped open in the plaster above the door jamb. An instant later the clatter of automatic fire filled the room. Rawhead turned and saw Keith Medina firing some kind of automatic weapon.

Rawhead fired once, with his left, and saw a bite-sized chunk of fabric fly out of Keith's right shoulder. The Uzi jerked in Keith's hand and he kept firing, cutting down the three spectators standing by the bed but missing Rawhead. There was a pause, then Keith slithered down the wall and his twitching finger hit the trigger again. This time he shot four of the people on the bed.

The survivor, a guy with a shrunken reproductive organ, was cowering on the floor behind the bed with his eyes closed. The thought crossed Rawhead's mind that he'd be hiding too if he had a dick that small. He locked the bedroom door just as someone threw their full weight at it. The door quivered but held.

Rawhead walked over to Keith Medina, who looked up at him helplessly. It was hard to see why a bullet in the shoulder should bring down such a hard man.

But real life isn't like the movies. Getting shot is a terrible ordeal for the body and the spirit.

Rawhead reached into Keith's jacket and withdrew a bulging wallet. Dad Cheeseman's money, plus Rawhead's expenses.

Almost lazily, he tilted the gun in his left hand until it was pointing at Keith's head. Then he squeezed the trigger.

There was shouting outside the door, the bulldog sounds of angry men. Calmly, Rawhead walked across the floor, stepping over the dead and dying.

Soar in eternal bliss, my friends.

At the far door, Rawhead peeled off his hood and threw it down. He thrust his guns back into his belt and buttoned down his coat. He walked out of the room, passed through a small, malodorous bathroom and rejoined the landing. A woman who either was drunk or had fainted was lying in his path, moaning softly. Rawhead scooped her up as if she was a child and made for the stairs.

People were sitting on the stairs, completely stunned by what they'd witnessed. Down below, a man with crazed eyes was waving a handgun about, creating fresh ripples of panic among the fifty or so guests remaining. 'Nobody move. Nobody leaves this fucking house until I fucking say so.'

Doing a perfect impersonation of a shocked, grief-stricken bystander, Rawhead staggered down to the gun-waver, the woman murmuring in his arms. 'Why?' said Rawhead, tears in his eyes. 'Why?'

'Out of the fucking way,' said the heavy irritably, waving Rawhead aside with the barrel of the gun.

It was that easy.

Still carrying the unconscious woman, Rawhead staggered out into the street.

Emboldened by his action, others followed Rawhead out into the night. There was another henchman on the far pavement, pointing a shotgun at the house. He was a kid of seventeen, his eyes dilated by fear. The dead rugby player was lying in the middle of the road.

'Why?' said Rawhead, appealing directly to the kid. '*Why?*' It was a perfectly reasonable question, to which the kid had no reply. Rawhead laid the woman at his feet like an offering. 'Please. Please. Get her to hospital.'

The kid nodded vaguely, not really interested. He was staring beyond Rawhead, back at the windows where the tragedy had occurred. Rawhead joined the flood of terrified party guests and walked calmly away. Behind him, the man with crazed eyes was still shouting. 'Nobody move! Nobody leaves this fucking house . . .'

*

As he drove into town Rawhead kept laughing to himself. He hadn't had so much fun in a long time. He realized how much he'd missed killing, how vital it was to his well-being. It was what he was born for. Like earthquakes, tidal waves and man-eating tigers, Rawhead's sole purpose was to keep down the population.

When he arrived at the car park behind Diva, he rolled a

spliff, still smiling at the memory of the crazy-eyed tool who'd let him walk because he was carrying a woman. After a few minutes, Rawhead got out of the car.

As he closed the door something cold pressed against his face. He heard a man's voice close to his ear.

'Don't you fucking move, you cheap fucking prick.'

Rawhead remained perfectly still.

'Get back in the car. The other door. As slow as you fucking like.'

The man's breath reeked of cigarettes and garlic. When Rawhead had unlocked the passenger door, the gunman instructed him to slide across slowly until he was behind the wheel. Then the gunman got in beside him and slammed the door. Now Rawhead could see who it was.

It was Sirus. His left wrist was in plaster and he had gauze taped over his nose.

'What's this about?' asked Rawhead calmly.

'It's about you acting hard, fighting dirty, putting the boot in on me when I weren't fucking ready. It's about you putting me in fucking hospital. Start the motor.'

Rawhead found his keys and switched on the engine. 'You realize you're about to die a horrible death?'

'Fuck you, cunt!' Sirus jammed the gun barrel hard into Rawhead's cheek.

'You're the one who's gonna fucking die. Now drive.'

12

I saw pale kings and princes too,
Pale warriors, death-pale were they all;
They cried – 'La Belle Dame sans Merci
Thee Hath in thrall!'

'La Belle Dame sans Merci', John Keats (1795–1821)

Like the killings in Prestbury, the massacre in Salford made the national news. The British Government was supposedly cracking down on gun culture, which made the story highly topical. The police remained coy about the precise death toll, but it was clear the Medinas had been the prime targets.

Chef wasn't particularly surprised. Sure, they'd put some good deals his way, which was why he'd given them work. But in his opinion, the Medinas had been arrogant punks with no manners. The brothers had many enemies.

But the gunman had worn a hood. He had walked into a crowded party and killed several people. He had used two identical magnum revolvers with long barrels. Then he had left without being observed.

To Chef, this sounded worryingly familiar.

Then he got a call from the Spirit of Darkness.

*

They met in the churchyard of St Mary's in Nether Alderley. It was a filthy black night, so cold and vile that Chef almost phoned to cancel. He knew that if he did, the Spirit would privately sneer at him, but he didn't want to get wet either. By way of compromise, he took an umbrella.

He drove himself, not wanting anyone to know on whom the ultimate safety of his organization depended. As far as his men knew, the Spirit was a faceless, brooding giant with permanent five o'clock shadow.

He stood in the churchyard under the square tower, watching the rain pounding off the path and dripping from the trees.

Directly in front of him lay a fresh grave, piled high with flowers. The rain pattered on the cellophane covering the wreaths. Chef was slightly surprised to see the grave, didn't even realize that people still got buried. Every corpse he had ever said goodbye to had been cremated.

They had arranged to meet at eight. It was two minutes after the hour. Chef was beginning to wonder why someone so reliable would be late for such an important meeting when he glanced to his right and saw a woman standing next to him. She was about five feet eight, with dark hair, razored short. Chef was startled, but tried not to show it. She'd walked right up to him without catching his eye or making a sound. No wonder they called her the Spirit.

Chef towered above her. He had met her only once and had forgotten how she disorientated him. She looked and moved like a woman, but she was not quite like any woman Chef had ever seen. There was calm, self-contained menace in every movement she made.

Chef coughed to mask his unease but only drew attention to it. 'I'm alone.'

'Not quite,' she said. 'There are ghosts all around us. Every day of our lives.'

'Meanwhile, back on Planet Earth,' said Chef.

'You think we live and die, and there's nothing more?' she asked him.

Chef was struck anew by her soft southern Irish lilt. Few would suspect a woman with such a voice of being a murderer. 'I think we know nothing before we're born,' he said. 'We know nothing after we die.'

'But knowing and existing aren't the same things,' she said.

Chef nodded as if he knew what she was talking about. He had always wanted to ask about her background, but knew such questions were out of bounds. Knowing too much about her would endanger them both.

'Let me buy you a drink,' he said. 'Why not? There are some nice little drinkeries in this neck of the woods.'

He almost blushed to hear himself, knowing he sounded like the office manager trying to get off with the young receptionist.

'No,' she said, in a voice like sudden death.

Absolutely fucking stone-faced.

Chef was slightly in awe of the Spirit of Darkness. Despite his advancing years and general aura of greasiness, most women in Manchester would have crawled the length of the Arndale Centre on their hands and knees just to sniff his crotch.

Not this woman. No flirtation in her eyes or voice. No winsome little smiles. Not only was she unimpressed by his power. She didn't seem aware of his *manhood*.

A lesbian. She had to be. There was no other explanation.

'What if I buy you something to eat?' he asked her.

(Did Spirits of Darkness eat?)

She gazed up at him with genial contempt. 'Why don't we talk in your car?'

*

They sat in the pink Rolls-Royce Chef had inherited from Malcolm Priest Senior, talking quietly while the rain pounded the roof. The warm car smelled of soap and leather. They sat on the vast back seat with a whole body space between them, like would-be lovers that haven't yet taken the plunge.

The Rolls was luxuriously upholstered in cream leather. There was a TV, two phones and a small refrigerator. When Chef opened the fridge door, a light flashed on. He withdrew two bottles of iced Michelob and a bottle opener. He flipped the cap off one bottle and passed it to Spirit, then opened his own.

She held the bottle in both hands, gazing down at it without drinking.

'That shooting in Prestbury. That was you?' he asked her.

'Partly.'

'I paid you to watch Billy Dye. Not to shoot holes through spacks.'

'I only shot one police officer. Nobody else.'

She told him how it had been, watching Billy Dye's house from the neighbour's garden, then turning round to see PC Spack bearing down on her. Chef stared at her. 'What did you do next?'

'What do you think I did? '

'You ran.'

'Right.'

'The way I imagined it,' said Chef, 'the neighbours reported a prowler, you shot the neighbours and the guys in the patrol car.'

'No, I didn't kill those other people.'

Chef nodded to himself. 'So the spack who you thought was running at you, was probably running away from our friend.'

'That's the conclusion I've come to.'

'You were lucky,' said Chef. 'If you'd stayed around any longer, you'd be dead.'

'No,' she said, 'he'd be dead.'

Chef turned away, watched the rain streaming down the

windows. 'Because of Rawhead, I've had to rebuild this organization. From scratch. I don't want to have to do that again.'

'What's your point?'

When Chef's wife talked to him that way, he slapped her in
the mouth. But he needed the Spirit's help.

'The guy beat us. Now he's beating you,' said Chef. 'I pay
you to stake out Billy Dye and what happens? You go all the
way to Scotland, lay a trap for Rawhead and end up stringing
up some fat old poacher.'

'These things happen.'

'Oh, they do, do they? Well, listen. I'm not paying you to box
innocent bystanders. You're meant to be hitting Rawhead.'

She said nothing.

Chef took out a tissue and blew his nose. 'I suppose you
heard about the Medinas?'

'Only what I saw on the news.'

'I'm pretty sure that was him, too.'

'A pair of pimps? Why?' She sounded sceptical. 'Why would
he bother?'

'Boxed sets are this guy's speciality.' Chef shrugged. 'He did
the same thing to us once. He came to the house when everyone
was home. Didn't bother to knock, just walked straight in and
started shooting.'

'What was it like?'

'What do you mean, "What was it like"?'

'I mean, describe it to me.'

His face assumed a defensive look. 'It was like a bad dream.
We saw him coming from a long way off. But none of us quite
believed it. You wouldn't have believed it either. He broke every
rule in the SAS handbook.'

'He was in the SAS?'

'No, no. I'm just making a point . . . if the SAS are the ultimate professionals, this guy behaved like the ultimate amateur. I mean it. He didn't take cover. He had no back-up. He was outnumbered. All he had, far as I know, was a six-shot handgun. It was insane. The guy was wide open.'

'Yeah? How come he got away?'

'Because every shot we fired at him fucking missed. And . . . well . . .'

'What?'

The big man looked down, his bottom lip protruding. '*Daimonas.*'

She turned to face him. 'Sorry?

'A Greek word. Meaning demon, devil. You believe in power? Real, elemental power?'

She drank some beer. He got the distinct impression that she wasn't really listening.

Jesus, she was hard work.

'You know it when you see it,' he said. 'It stops you dead, paralyses you. Coming up against this guy was like trying to fight a volcano, a tidal wave, a fucking lightning bolt. I don't know how else to explain it.'

'And this "elemental force". You still want me to go after him?'

'Yeah. '

'Maybe I should just kidnap Billy Dye. Wait for Rawhead to come to me.'

'No!'

The vehemence of Chef's response surprised her. She turned her head to study him.

'That little writer prick has never been lucky for us,' he explained. 'Stay away from him. Don't watch him, don't go anywhere near him.'

'How do you expect me to find Rawhead?'

'Try going round to his house.'

The Spirit gave a short, mirthless laugh. She thought he was joking.

'I'm serious,' said Chef. 'I know where he lives.'

*

Now he had her attention.

Chef took her to a restaurant called the Wizard, where he already had a table booked. They ate together, the big-boned, gloomy gangster and the dark, watchful woman. They made a striking couple.

His strength was purely animal. It showed in the big hands and the hard face with its jutting jaw.

With her stillness and her huge dark eyes, the Spirit reminded Chef of a beautiful twisted nun. Her fire was internal, intense yet slow-burning. There was a long thin white scar on her left cheek. Maybe that was why she never smiled.

Over dinner he told her about tracking Rawhead down to a vicarage in the Bedfordshire countryside. One by one, Rawhead had picked them off. 'So finally, I decided enough was enough,' said Chef. 'I let him go.'

'You did *what*?'

He lowered his eyes. 'It was a managerial decision. What you've got to remember is, we'd already tried to kill Ellis twice.'

'Ellis?'

'That's his real name.'

She lowered her fork and stared at him.

'Steven Ellis. A Manchester Grammar School boy who let down the old school.'

'This gets better. You know his name, you even know where he lives. And you've done nothing about it?'

'It sounds tapped, I know. But each time we hit him, he came

172

back with more. First and foremost, I'm a businessman. In any business, there comes a point when you just have to cut your losses. I calculated that if I left him alone, he'd leave me alone. So far, that's exactly how it's worked out.'

'So what changed your mind?'

'The fear of what he might do next.'

She marvelled in silence.

A waiter appeared, to refill their glasses. Chef paused until the waiter was elsewhere before explaining. 'My business is allowed to exist because of my special arrangement with the Greater Manchester Police. I'm a big fish, they let me swim where I like. In return, I'm expected to contribute to their retirement fund and keep the peace.

'Now, what happened in Prestbury and Salford broke that peace. It's all over the papers, everyone thinks the Manchester gang wars are starting all over again. Naturally, my friends the spacks are very upset. They don't give a fuck if people are murdered in private. But when questions are being asked in parliament, they get nervous. Understandably. Because every time some arsehole goes on a killing spree, the public and the press blame the spacks for letting it happen. And the spacks blame me.'

She gave a curt nod.

'I can't stress this enough – everything I do in this city depends on the chief constable looking the other way. You could argue that Prestbury isn't Manchester, but try telling him that. So I have to act. You see? Even if Rawhead isn't killing my men, he's threatening my livelihood.'

'You know his name and his address. Do you know what he looks like?'

'As a matter of fact, yes.' He unfolded a computer printout and laid it before her. It was a blurred photo of a bunch of

schoolboys. 'We got it off that Friends Reunited site.' He pointed
to a lean, solemn child on the back row. 'That's him. In the class
of '81.'

'Unless he still wears short trousers, that's no use to me.' She
pushed the crumpled image back across the table to him. 'How
much are you offering?'

She might have been discussing wallpapering his living room.

'The same as before. A thousand a week. Get a result, there'll
be fifty thousand on top.'

'No. Two hundred thousand *at least.*'

'I could go up to seventy-five. That's my best offer.'

'Fine.' She put down her fork and got up to leave.

He waved her down. 'All right, all right.'

'If I succeed,' she said, 'everything you've worked for will be
saved. If I fail, you won't have to pay me. Now, that *has* to be a
good deal.'

Even Chef, who hated spending money, saw the sense of this.
'Either way, I win.' He reached across the table and took her
hand. It was icy cold. 'Now. Do you think you can get this
bastard off my back?'

'Just tell me where to find him.'

*

It was mid-afternoon when she arrived at the Bedfordshire
village of Dudloe. There was a three-quarter moon high in the
sky and the bright sun lingered over the fields. Every so often a
warm wind rose up to shake the trees in the churchyard. Then
the wind died away abruptly, waiting until all was still before
resuming its erratic campaign.

Chef had sketched a map on the back of a napkin, showing
her where to find the house and the church. 'The vicarage is the
next house but one to the church. That's not the place you want.
You want the *old* vicarage, the big house next to the church.

There's no sign outside, but you'll know it when you see it, because it looks like something from a horror film.'

With or without Chef's help, the Spirit would have picked out Rawhead's house. His presence hung over the building like a biblical plague. The walls breathed malice. The house was Victorian, but its true style was American Gothic. All towers, ivy, sweeping gables and an underlying preoccupation with death. It was the kind of house the Spirit of Darkness would have chosen for herself.

She parked her Range Rover on the grass outside the church, adjusting her mirror until she could see the house. She had the window wound down, her elbow resting on the frame. She could hear birds singing, the whisper of the leaves. The stillness came as a shock to her after the noise of Manchester and the roar of the motorway.

She switched on the engine and moved off down the quiet country road. Soon houses began to appear. She turned left and almost ran into a group of teenagers who were playing in the road. She braked so hard that she smelled burning rubber. The kids, two girls and a boy, stared at her blankly, waiting for a rebuke that never came. Unhurriedly, they stepped out of her way and she drove on.

The road brought her to a crossroads, with a school on one corner and a pub on the other. If the village could be said to have any heart at all, she supposed this was it. She waited at the crossing while a tractor chugged by, casting a trail of shit behind it. The pub was called the Ploughboy. She drove into its car park, pulling up near a large notice that proclaimed: BAR MEALS, LARGE GROUPS CATERED FOR.

Besides the Range Rover, there were only two other vehicles in the car park: an ancient Skoda and a Suzuki van. She walked into the pub. She was dressed in a staid black business suit. The scar on her face was camouflaged with a subtle sheen of make-up. She looked exactly like what she was pretending to be: an estate agent in between appointments.

Two old men were standing at the bar. Their conversation dried while she stood beside them, waiting to be served. A sour-faced old cow walked out from the kitchen and addressed the old men without looking at the Spirit. 'No Cornish pasties, Bob. But I could heat up the lasagne if you like.'

Bob, a long-faced man with thick grey hair on his exposed forearms, shook his head. 'No, I don't like any of that I-talian stuff. It repeats on me.'

'Don't you mean retreats?' said his companion. 'Wops always retreat. In fact, they're known for it.'

This pleasantry invoked comfortable laughter.

After ignoring the Spirit for just long enough to be offensive, the landlady eventually turned to her. 'Yes?'

The Spirit gave her a white smile. 'What a lovely welcoming little pub this.'

'We try our best,' said the landlady slowly, obscurely aware that she was being insulted but unable to determine precisely how.

'A vodka and tonic. With ice, please.'

'You're foreign,' said Bob with a wink. 'I can always tell.'

'I was born near Dublin,' said the Spirit.

'That's what he's getting at,' said the other old man. 'You hail from foreign parts.'

'Don't mind Dennis, here,' said Bob. 'He was shot in the war. He's never quite recovered.'

'You mean, I was killed in the war,' said Dennis.

'That's right,' agreed Bob. 'He was pronounced clinically dead.'

'Then I started breathing again,' said Dennis. 'But for a minute or so, I was dead. So when people ask, I always say I died in the war. Technically, it's not a lie.'

Bob laughed. 'Clinically dead. But did they ever pronounce him clinically alive? That's what I want to know.'

The Spirit sipped her drink and smiled along with them. 'Does anyone know who owns the big house next to the church?'

The question spawned a cautious silence.

'The reason I ask,' she continued, 'is that I represent an estate agency. We tend to keep an eye open for unoccupied properties that aren't yet on the market.'

'Oh, it isn't unoccupied,' said Dennis.

'No, that's Roger's house,' added Bob. 'I can see why you think it's empty, but no. Old Roger lives there.'

'There's quite a few round here who don't like to walk that way after dark, if you get my drift,' said Dennis.

'Why's that?' said the Spirit.

'Some people say there's a ghost,' said Dennis. 'I don't believe it.'

'Don't just leave it there,' said the Spirit. 'I love ghost stories.'

'All I know,' said Bob, 'is that a little girl is supposed to have fell off a balcony and broke her neck. Now whether that's true or not, I couldn't tell you.'

'But Roger doesn't mind the ghosts, then.'

'He's never said anything about it,' said Dennis, 'and we've never asked. Mind you, he's hardly ever there.'

'That's right.' Bob shook his head. 'Turns up every few months for a day or so, then he's off on his travels. Works all over the place, does old Roger. One of these high-flying executives, as far as I can make out.'

'And he's quite old?' she said. They looked blank. 'You called him "Old Roger".'

Bob seemed surprised. 'Oh, no. Rodge ain't old. No more than . . . what would you say?'

'Thirty-five?' ventured Dennis. 'No more than that.'

'Nice enough bloke. He does odd jobs for them that are really decrepit,' said Bob. 'Like Dennis here.'

'You're only as old as you feel,' said Dennis.

'And how old do you feel?' asked the Spirit.

'Seventy-eight,' Dennis admitted.

'I'll tell you what,' said Bob. 'He could do with doing a few odd jobs for himself, state of that house of his.'

Bob nodded. 'I don't think that place has seen a lick of paint in years.'

'But you don't think he's home?'

'He may be,' said Dennis. 'He was here a couple of nights ago. He always drops in for a drink and a giggle when he's home.'

*

The Spirit drove back to the church. It was dusk. She gazed up at the octaganol spire with its gargoyles and pinnacles, once again feeling the cold presence of the man she had come to kill.

A drink and a giggle?

From the churchyard she could see the windows of the neighbouring vicarage. They were dark and empty. They told her there was no one home. She walked through a gap in the hedge at the end of the churchyard. On the far side of the graves lay tilled fields and a sky the colour of rotting fruit. The wind came over the fields, cutting through her, colder than ever now that the sun had gone. The winter was old and dying, but it still had its teeth.

The grounds of the old vicarage ran down to the hedge at the edge of the field. Peering through the hedge, she could see the ash of an old bonfire. The garden was rugged and unkempt. A grey statue of Flora stood in the centre of the wild lawn, leaning drunkenly to one side. Beyond the statue, the house brooded and scowled.

*

After dark, she returned. She had exchanged her work clothes for a black jacket and jeans. Although there were no street lights in the lane outside the church, the moon was bright enough to cast blue shadows over the house and lawn. The Spirit went round to the back of the house, scanning the windows for any sign of habitation.

There was an old wooden outhouse, door ajar. She stepped inside and saw tools hanging on the walls. A drill, hammers and garden shears. An axe with a shiny black handle.

When she was satisfied that there was no one hiding in the garden, she approached the house and punched a hole through a window with her leather-gloved hand. Then she reached through the gap and unscrewed the lock. She raised the sash and climbed through to find herself in a room full of crowded bookcases.

She shone a small torch over the room. There was thick dust everywhere. She stopped and listened to the silence. A fly buzzed close to her ear. She didn't react. The Spirit knew that the books she was looking at were priceless. Bound first editions of *The Turn of the Screw*, *The Haunting of Hill House* and, most astoundingly of all, *Dracula*.

She took Bram Stoker's masterpiece off the shelf and opened it. It was a genuine first edition. The ancient yellowed pages smelt of piss and vinegar. She held the book to her face and kissed it. Rawhead was evidently a man of exquisite taste. *Dracula* was the Spirit's favourite novel. She did not intend to leave this house without it.

Still clutching the book, she moved across the room and

opened the door. Now she was looking onto a large, bare hall. The flashlight picked out a white shape that turned out to be a statue of the Virgin Mary, gazing down proudly at the grotesque Jesus nestling in the crook of her arm.

The Spirit moved across the floor, her footsteps echoing on the bare floorboards. The house was a wreck. The ceiling overhead was scarred by a deep, twisting rent. She took a step towards the staircase and trod on something soft. When she knelt down to see what it was, she found herself looking at an enormous dead rat with a crushed skull, brains spilling out of its ears.

The Spirit kicked the rat out of her path and climbed the stairs.

The beam of the torch cast the shadow of the banister rail before her. A shadow that shuddered as she climbed. She felt so at home in the darkness that she didn't even bother to draw her gun.

Only two of the rooms on the first floor had furniture. The largest room, facing out to the church, had a double bed. The other room was across the landing. As soon as she entered, she knew that it was his room. There was a wardrobe, a chest of drawers and a mattress on the floor. At the foot of the mattress lay a pile of blankets, neatly folded.

She looked inside the wardrobe. There were no clothes, but at the bottom of the wardrobe lay a Remington shotgun and a box of shells. In the chest of drawers she found socks, shirts, sweaters, jeans and T-shirts. But no bills, bank statements or photographs. Nothing to pin a face to the man she was hunting.

On the top floor, it was the same story. Dusty, abandoned rooms with windows that hadn't been cleaned for fifty years. One of the rooms contained an old wooden cradle and a rocking horse. The Spirit walked to the window and peered through a wide crack in the dusty pane. She could see the moon sailing through clouds. The wind sang like a ghost, carrying fresh country air in from the fields.

She shone her torch at the window ledge. With a chisel or a blade, a name and date had been scored into the wood.

Meg Gear 1856

The Spirit was halfway down the stairs when she heard a cry. It sounded like a wail of outrage. She stopped breathing to listen. Her father had been a manic depressive, given to making similar noises whenever he mislaid a shoe or accidentally dropped a liquorice allsort on the floor. For a moment she thought she was hearing the old man's ghost.

Perhaps she would have to murder him all over again.

From the soft leather holster nestling over her left hip the Spirit drew her gun and took off the safety. It was a Sig 220 with night sights. The magazine held seven forty-five calibre rounds.

Calmly and methodically the Spirit searched the ground floor. She checked the library again, then secured the only other two furnished rooms. When she entered the long kitchen, she walked into a pocket of foul air that might have been caused by another dead rodent or something rotten in the fridge. The Spirit of Darkness suspected otherwise. She placed *Dracula* on the table and listened.

There was another shrill, pitiful screech of anguish. It seemed to come from beneath her feet.

At the end of the kitchen, a flight of stone steps led down to a blue cellar door. The Spirit descended the steps and tried the handle. Locked. But from behind the locked door came a series of gurgling sounds that rose and fell, like someone singing underwater.

She climbed the steps and searched the kitchen. A fat bunch

of keys hung on a nail by the back door. Not believing that Rawhead would be so reckless, she descended to the cellar door.

For a moment the Spirit stood there, wondering what to do next. She had been sent to kill Rawhead. The man making all the noise was almost certainly *not* Rawhead. So why should she go to him?

Because he was a fellow human being in distress?

Fuck that.

Because he might lead her to Rawhead.

The door was secured by a Chubb lock. The Spirit tried six keys, convinced she was wasting her time. The seventh key fitted. She opened the door. Out from the darkness came a cloud of flies and the most unutterably disgusting smell she had ever encountered.

She shone the flashlight through the doorway. The cellar was long and low with stone walls and a plastered ceiling. The wall to her left was newer, made of red bricks. In the centre of the wall was a door of oak, secured with two strong bolts.

The Spirit wiped sweat from her brow with her forearm. She took a black silk scarf from her jacket and tied it around her mouth and nose to lessen the overwhelming stench. There was no light switch in the cellar. She was forced to rest the torch on a stack of old fruit crates, pointing it in the general direction of the door.

She walked over to the door and, with a struggle, drew back the heavy bolts. When she had finished, the door flew open. A freezing-cold wind blew over her, its wings scented with the odour of human putrescence. A smell so powerful it burned her face. Shit, sweat, bile and ammonia. The perfume of Azrael.

At last, the Spirit of Darkness could hear what the stricken man was saying.

'*Oh God, please, Jesus, don't do this, I'll give you money, anything, me dinner's on the table, Oh, Christ, Jesus.*'

Then a dreadful, retching, heaving groan.

The Spirit unholstered the Sig.

With the gun in her left hand and the torch in her right, she took a quick glance through the doorway. She was looking down a long, claustrophobic tunnel with a low ceiling. The earth walls were supported by pit props. She could smell the damp, bittersweet soil. She could smell the huge grey rats scurrying before her feet. Mostly, she could smell death.

Rather than repelling her, the filthy odour lured her on, like the incense that summons an ancient, bloodthirsty goddess.

'Please, I don't know, what? What? Why? I've learnt my lesson. Jesus. Man City won. He's coming, he's coming.'

The hoarse voice echoed all around her.

Straight ahead lay a solid stone wall. In the wall someone had cut a diamond-shaped gap, large enough for a very fat man to crawl through. The stone was dark grey, but the edges of the hole were ragged and white. The Spirit shone the torch beam through the gap to find herself looking down into a deep oblong chamber, approximately three times the size of the average lift shaft.

It was a charnel house, built into the foundations of the church. In the fifteenth century, when the church was erected, the remains of plague victims would have been laid here prior to burning. Now, showing fine respect for tradition, the man she was hunting was using the chamber for its original purpose. The vault was stacked high with dead bodies.

Her heart rate quickened. Her clitoris contracted. The Spirit of Darkness was impressed.

As she shone her torch over the skulls and the skulls-to-be, insects of all shapes and sizes flitted through the beam. The walls above the bodies glistened with slimy fat. And in the middle of the heaving, humming mass of twisted corpses squatted a living man.

He looked like a pop star, his hair bleached platinum blond. He was trembling and sweating, holding a seething wound in his belly. There was a filthy dressing over his nose, and the front of his shirt was caked with blood and vomit.

He was a pitiful sight. For those capable of pity.

'No, no, mum, did you call the doctor?'

He was delerious.

'What's your name?' she called, her voice echoing in the monstrous cave.

Shock registered on his face as he realized he was speaking to a stranger. 'Who's that?'

'I asked first.'

'I saw your mother's shadow on the wall.' He pointed wildly. 'Look! Look! She's from Ashton-under-Lyne.'

'Tell me your name.'

'I came and he did this and I don't know why and he never . . . and I fucking, fucking never . . . I don't know. I don't know.'

'OK. Can you tell me who put you here?'

'Where's the bus? Is it a double-decker?'

She tried again. 'Who did this to you?'

'Stoker!' he yelled. 'Abraham fucking Stoker.'

'Bram Stoker?' she repeated incredulously.

The dying man screamed as his intestinal tract made a fresh attempt to digest the bullet that was lodged in it.

The Spirit leaned over the edge and shot him dead. Gave him a third eye in the centre of his forehead, just like Shiva. It seemed the only decent thing to do.

The sound of the shot spun around the burial chamber. The bodies in the pit seemed to tremble. Behind her, rats darted about in blind panic. Loose soil rained down from the roof of the tunnel. When the gunshot had dwindled to a hum, the Spirit looked down at the dead man and said: '*Lord have mercy on the souls in purgatory, and especially on those that are most forsaken;*

*deliver them from the terrible torments they endure; call them and
admit them to Thy most sweet embrace in Paradise, Amen.'*

*

The Spirit of Darkness slept on Rawhead's bed, her head on his
pillow.

The next day she drove to Bedford and had Rawhead's keys
copied. She also bought a new window pane to replace the one
she had broken. She fitted the pane herself, smearing the putty
and glass with dust and ash, patiently covering her traces. When
Rawhead returned, she wanted to give him a nice surprise. But
what?

What did you give to the man who had killed everything?

13

Love Lives Beyond The Tomb
The Earth, The Flowers And Dew.

'Love Lives Beyond The Tomb', John Clare (1793–1864)

'I don't get it,' said Brando.

'What don't you get?' said Rawhead.

They were standing in a one-bedroom flat above a dentist's surgery in West Didsbury. The flat was clean, furnished and newly decorated. It didn't smell of anything but paint. There was a bathroom, a living room, a bedroom and kitchen. As well as a fridge, washing machine and cooker, the kitchen even boasted a small dishwasher.

Brando looked at the keys in his hand, then raised his eyes to gaze warily at Rawhead. 'You're setting me up like your girl-friend: that it? You drop by when you're passing, bring me flowers and fuck me?'

'If it's all the same to you,' said Rawhead, 'I'll just bring the flowers.'

'I can't take these keys off you 'til I know what this place is gonna cost me.'

'Nothing. It's one of Little Malc's properties. He's a small-time landlord. It's yours rent-free. All you have to do is pay the bills.'

'He told you to say that?'

'I told *him* to say that.'

'Why, though?' Brando walked to the window and looked

out at the cars and the people. Not happy, just stunned. 'There's going to be a fucking catch, man. What is it?'

'No catch.' Rawhead passed him a Browning 9mm and a box of cartridges.

'This is the catch?' said Brando. 'You want me to shoot somebody?'

'Not unless they try to shoot you first.'

Brando turned the gun over in his hands, looking as worried as fuck.

'Look,' said Rawhead, sitting down on the bed, 'Little Malc can't have people in his outfit sleeping in cars. It makes him look cheap. And it's not good for you. You need to look after yourself now. We need you fit and strong. That means plenty of rest and sleep. That's what this place is for.'

Brando held up the gun. 'What about this?'

'You'll need to be armed. If you're going to be my second-in-command.'

'Your second-in-command?' asked Brando, shaking his head and laughing. 'You're the boss, now, are you? What does that make Little Malc?'

'A funny little guy we all protect.'

'But Malc thinks he's in charge.'

'That's right,' said Rawhead. 'And it's our job to pretend that he is.'

'This is getting weird.'

'It'll get weirder.'

Brando gave Rawhead a long, meditative stare. 'Tell me something: if you rate me, why'd you tell me to stay home that night?'

'What night?'

'The night someone tried to kill Malc. You knew something was going down, you told me to stay home. Why?'

'I knew if you were there, you'd try to intervene. I wanted me to be the hero, not you.'

Rawhead's mobile rang. He left Brando to look round the flat while he answered the call. It was Nikki. 'I was wondering if you were doing anything tonight? Or whether you'd like to come round for something to eat? About eight?'

Rawhead made a quick calculation. By nine Nikki would be drunk. By ten, she'd be in his arms and the final phase of Rawhead's plan to repay Billy Dye for his treachery would be under way.

'See you at eight,' he told her.

*

Billy was back in his hotel room, busily revising the third draft of the unspeakable piece of shit that he rather whimsically described as *Gangchester*: 'Episode 3', when the phone rang. It was Artemesia, calling him to a meeting that afternoon.

'What time?' he said.

'Any time. Me and Tim are here until six.' She sounded despondent.

'Did you get a chance to read episode two?'

'Yes,' she said. 'It's improved two hundred per cent. You've thoroughly addressed all our script notes, we're all more than satisfied.'

'Oh. Great.' Relief and glee charged through him like a cocaine rush.

'Come as soon as you can,' she said.

Like most writers, Billy only had to hear words of praise in order to roll over onto his back like a puppy dog. Rather than wonder why it would be necessary to call a meeting to discuss satisfactory work, he focused on Artemesia's claim that the TV bastards were 'more than satisfied' with his efforts. It was only when he met Artemesia waiting at reception that alarm bells rang.

Her face was deathly pale and there were blue shadows

under her eyes. It was not the face of a woman with something to celebrate.

Tim was waiting in Larry's office. When Billy entered, he smiled nervously. Billy noticed right away that there was no script in his lap. Billy turned to look at Artemesia and then at Tim. 'OK. What is it?'

'We've been forcibly impressed by the quality of the rewrites,' said Tim.

'So impressed that the fucking show's been cancelled,' said Billy.

They both looked sick, so he knew he was right. Billy sat down while Tim related the sad story. 'It's Sheila's judgement – and we tend, reluctantly, to see her point – that the climate isn't right for a series about gangsters.'

'So it's not going to be on?'

'All those deaths in Salford,' said Tim, his voice quavering slightly.

'Shit.'

'There have been other problems,' said Tim. 'Larry's disappearance hasn't helped?'

'What?'

'Larry's been missing for quite a few days now. To make matters worse, we've been getting anonymous threats. "Screen this series and we'll cut off Sheila Burman's legs and ram them up her cunthole." That sort of thing.'

The injustice of it all made Billy rage. 'But I've taken out all the fucking violence! It's the first gangster story in history where absolutely nobody gets fucking hurt. Oh ... I tell a lie ... someone gets pushed against a lamp post in episode one.'

Tim and Artemesia stared back at him listlessly.

'No wonder British TV is such a pile of worm-ridden excrement! Everyone who works in it is either cowardly or thick.'

said Billy. 'No wonder the Americans wipe the fucking floor with us on every fucking level. '

Tim took exception to this. 'Now, hang on. We're not the villains here.'

'Yes, you fucking are,' said Billy. 'You're a gutless old maid with droopy balls. She's a silly posh girly who only got promoted by sucking Larry Crème's cock!'

Artemesia burst into tears. Tim held up a long forefinger. 'There's absolutely no need for that. Throughout all this, Artemesia and I have been your staunchest allies.'

'Listen,' said Billy. 'I know *exactly* how loyal you've been. Sheila Burman said the programme was axed and you two said, "Yes, of course, Sheila, we understand and respect your decision." You're a pair of spineless fucking twats and I hope you both get run over.'

*

After leaving Maddy with her mother for the night, Nikki went home to make herself beautiful. She shaved her legs, painted her nails, washed and conditioned her hair, spent ages choosing the right outfit. She was excited and petrified in equal measure, like a teenager preparing for a crucial date. She felt truly alive for the first time in many years.

After bathing in fragrant oils, she put on a dressing gown and cooked dinner, real home-made lasagne. The meal was Billy's favourite. But tonight, Billy wouldn't be eating it. While Nikki was preparing the sauce, she considered the wine. There was a decent bottle of Australian sparkling plonk in the fridge, but Nikki knew that Billy always hid a bottle or two of the real thing at the back of his wardrobe. It was one of the annoying little discrepancies in their relationship that therapy had made her aware of. When Nikki had something to celebrate – and she practically never did – they drank Pinot Noir or Chardonnay. Billy's little triumphs were always toasted with real champagne.

Nikki wasn't supposed to know Billy hid champagne in his wardrobe, just as she wasn't supposed to know that he called her 'Cowface' in his diary. He presumably imagined Nikki was far too honourable to read his diary or search through his belongings. For an author, supposedly blessed with a modicum of insight into human beings, he could be remarkably naive.

In the far corner of the wardrobe she found two bottles of Bollinger, standing to attention like sentries. As she reached out for them, Nikki was irritated to see a small pile of T-shirts and shorts lying in a crumpled heap. Not an unusual sight – Billy was often too lazy to drop his underwear into the dirty-linen basket. As Nikki picked up the bundle, something fell to the bottom of the wardrobe with a dull clunk.

Nikki retrieved the object. It was a beautiful revolver. She knew just by looking at the gun that it was no replica. This was the real thing. The weapon was dark grey with a black grip and the manufacturer's name on the side: SMITH & WESSON, SPRING-FIELD, MASS. For a device capable of murder, the gun was curiously bland, a neat, lightweight treasure that fitted perfectly into Nikki's slim and elegant hand.

She felt her cheeks burning as an appalling thought occurred to her. What if Billy had shot the Reislers and those two police officers? But this was impossible. Billy had been with her all evening. Then what did he need a gun for? Not for the first time, it occurred to her that she might be sharing her life with a madman.

*

By seven thirty she was wearing her make-up and a tight little black dress, listening to Bach as she laid the table for dinner.

She was setting out the candles when Billy walked in, a big grin on his face.

'Something smells good,' he said.

She stared at him, hoping it was all a bad dream.

'I can smell my favourite meal. You knew I was coming, didn't you? You always were a bit spooky.'

At the start of their relationship, their psychic bond had been so strong that Nikki only had to will Billy to ring her for him to pick up the phone, wherever he was, whatever he was doing. Those days of spiritual closeness were long gone. Nowadays, all they shared was the desire to kick each other up the arse.

Billy toured the house looking for his daughter. On failing to find her, he went down to the kitchen. 'Where's Maddy?'

Nikki didn't answer. She was standing at the sink with her back to him. This was never a good sign. Then Billy saw his Smith & Wesson lying on the kitchen table.

'Where's Maddy?' he asked again.

'Where did you get the gun?' she said.

'I bought it off a guy in a pub. Why?'

'I'd like to know,' she said, not looking at him, 'what you think you're doing keeping a gun in the house when we've got a small child.'

He only hesitated for a second. 'Considering that our next-door neighbours have been fucking shot, I think it was a good idea.'

'Firstly, you're breaking the law. Secondly, it wasn't even properly hidden. It was in the wardrobe. What if Maddy had got hold of it?'

'She never goes anywhere near my fucking wardrobe.'

'What if she did?' Nikki was getting angry now.

He glared at the back of her head. 'I've just come home after working my fucking balls off for this family. Is this the welcome I get?'

'You know what I think about guns.'

'Guns are only dangerous if the person using them is dangerous.' He picked up the gun and stood beside her. 'This isn't
even loaded.'

Now she was taking out her anger on a pan, scrubbing it
clean, refusing to look at him. 'Look,' he said. He pointed the
gun at the window and tried to fire. There was a click. 'See?'

She elbowed his arm. 'Keep it away.'

'Nikki, why are you cooking a meal for me if you don't like
me?'

'I'm not cooking it for you!'

'Yes, you fucking are! Who else do you make lasagne for?'

She slammed the soapy pan down on the draining board and
started on a wooden spoon. He pointed the gun at his own
head. 'What are you so mad about?' He squeezed the trigger.
Another click. 'OK. I bought a gun. Maybe I shouldn't have
done that. I was nervous.'

She turned on him, spitting venom in his face. 'Just go! Get
out! I don't want to see you! You wanker!'

'It isn't loaded, you fucking cunt!' yelled Billy. To hammer
home the point, he aimed the gun at her and squeezed the
trigger.

There was a thunderous bang and a ragged hole opened in
the middle of Nikki's face. Bright red blood sluiced across the
sink and the kitchen window. Nikki toppled over. It was an
awkward fall, jerky and unconvincing. If any actor had executed
such a fall, the director would have demanded an instant reshoot.

Nikki wasn't acting. She was dead before she reached the
floor. Billy had killed her.

He looked at his wife, then examined the smoking weapon in
his hand. The gun was warm to the touch.

His head felt like a Halloween pumpkin, huge and swollen
and hollowed by knives.

Billy was blushing in pity, terror and shame.

'Sweetheart, sweetheart,' said Billy. Trembling as he got down on his knees, hoping to revive his wife by pressing a tea towel against the hole in her face. Knowing she was dead. All the time thinking that her last words to him were, *'You wanker.'* And his final words to her were, *'You fucking cunt.'*

*

Rawhead didn't get an answer at the front door, so went round to the back. Billy was in the kitchen, sitting on a stool. He was crying. Without a hint of emotion, Rawhead looked down at Nikki, saw the globs of brain tissue that were spattered on the kitchen window and realized that any attempt at resuscitation would serve no purpose.

'What happened, Bill?'

Billy held up the Smith & Wesson. In a strange, shaky voice he murmured, 'You told me it wasn't loaded.'

Rawhead sighed and took the gun.

'Why did you tell me that?'

'It was the quickest and easiest way to stop you shooting at me. Have you called anyone?'

'Not yet.'

'Don't. Stay where you are. I'll be right back.'

Rawhead left the house and returned a few minutes later with a loaded syringe. Billy hardly registered his return. A moment later, a generous shot of morphine launched Billy into a state of floating bliss. As Billy flopped, giggling, Rawhead picked him up, carried him into the living room and laid him on the sofa.

When Rawhead returned to the kitchen, the timer on the oven was buzzing. Feeling it was a shame to waste good food, Rawhead took the sizzling dish out of the oven and laid it on the blood-spattered window sill to cool. He looked in the fridge, saw the champagne, opened a bottle and poured himself a glass.

Then he sat down at the kitchen table and raised his glass to the dead woman, confident that the world she had entered was infinitely superior to the world she had left behind.

*

After midnight, Billy awoke. He recalled that something truly dreadful had taken place, but could not remember the details. The sight of Rawhead, who was sitting beside him on the sofa, jogged his memory. As the full horror of his wife's death swept over him, Billy screamed. Rawhead put his hand over Billy's mouth.

'All right. Take big breaths.'

Billy sat up too sharply, felt dizzy and almost fell off the sofa. Rawhead laid a steadying hand on Billy's chest.

'Jesus Christ almighty. Tell me it isn't true.'

'It's true.'

'Is she dead?'

'Yeah. But it was an accident. A complete fluke.'

'It's still against the fucking law.' Billy started crying. 'You said it wasn't loaded.'

'I had to say something. You were trying to shoot me.'

Billy wiped his nose on the sleeve of his shirt.

'Do you deny that?' asked Rawhead.

Billy shook his head.

'OK, listen to me.' Rawhead looked at Billy, his expression stern. 'I know you set fire to the caravan with me in it. And, naturally, I wanted to get back at you for that. But I didn't want anything like this to happen. I didn't trick you into shooting Nikki. Do you believe me?'

Billy nodded. 'Will you do me a favour?'

195

'What?'

'Would you phone the police? I don't think I could.'

'I'm not phoning the police. Nor are you.'

'But they'll find out. They'll notice she's gone.'

'Billy. Look at me. The police do not care about Nikki. The police are ignorant bastards. All they care about is getting easy convictions. Your punishment will be living with what you've done. You're just a writer. You pose no real danger to anyone. What good would locking you up do?'

'Maybe I'll get off.'

'Wake up, Billy. Not only will they nail you for Nikki. They'll try to pin the deaths of your neighbours and those cops on you. You had a *gun*. An unlicenced firearm. That's all they'll need to influence a jury. Tell anyone about this, anyone at all, and I guarantee you will never see the light of day again.'

Billy looked into Rawhead's eyes. 'So what can I do?'

'First of all, you call Nikki's mobile. You do that now, leave a message to ask where she is. Because you've just come home and no one's here. In the morning, you go round to Nikki's mum to pick up Maddy. You ask Nikki's mum where Nikki is, she doesn't know, you call the police.

'The good news is, Nikki has gone awol before. This is what she does. She gets depressed and walks out on everyone. The police aren't going to view her as a priority.'

Billy started crying. 'But the body . . .'

'I'll take care of that. I've cleaned the kitchen. Now I'll bury her.'

'Where? Where will you put her?'

Rawhead could see how important this was to Billy. 'Somewhere peaceful,' he answered. 'Somewhere where she can see trees and blue skies and hear the birds singing.'

*

Three hours later, Rawhead carried Nikki into his house by the church. Her body was swaddled in bin liners. He turned on the light and, showing no respect for the deceased, threw his burden to the floor. Then he walked through to the kitchen. He plucked his keys off the wall, went down to the cellar and unlocked the door. Insects flew into his face as the door yawned open, breathing out its customary stench.

He kept a heavy flashlight under the sink, which he now took into the cellar. Rawhead used the light to wedge open the second door, aiming it down the subterrannean tunnel towards the pit. Then he returned for the body.

Flinging the corpse over his shoulder, he noticed a sweet smell. Parma violets. For some reason, the smell reminded him of childhood. He assumed that the fragrance was something to do with Nikki and blanked it out of his mind. Then he carried her down to the cellar. Where there were no trees, blue skies or birds singing.

Only flies breeding in the mephitic darkness.

Not bothering to remove the bin bags, Rawhead thrust the body in through the gap in the wall. A second passed and then he heard the whumphh! as Billy's wife reached her final resting place. He remembered Sirus and wondered if he was dead yet. So he went back for the torch. On his return, he leaned through the gap in the wall and cast his light into the pit.

Sirus was there, twisted onto his side. Not moving or breathing. Over him, partly covering his legs, lay Nikki in her corporation body bag. To their right lay a middle-aged man in a lilac shirt. The man was lying on his back, grinning like a game-show host. The top of his skull was as jagged as a medieval parapet. While Rawhead shone the beam over the man's middle-aged paunch and middle-aged trousers, his pulse quickened. Because he knew, knew beyond all doubt, that he had never before seen the corpse in the lilac shirt.

14

I did but see her passing by,
Yet I will love her till I die.

Anon.

By noon Rawhead was back at Billy's house. Billy, his face lime green, was playing with his daughter on the living-room floor.

'What did the police say?'

'Very little,' said Billy. 'Nikki's dad came to the police station with me. He could see how fucked I was, so he did most of the talking. It was easy. I never knew this, but, according to her dad, she tried to kill herself when she was eighteen.'

'That's good,' said Rawhead.

'Good? What's fucking good about it?'

'I mean, it's consistent. With someone who walks out on her husband and daughter. So you think they believed you?'

'Nikki's mum and dad did. No question. They think I'm a prat, but they'd never have me down as a killer.'

'Mummy,' said Billy's daughter. Billy stared at her in horror. As far as he knew, it was the first time Maddy had ever uttered this word.

'You found somewhere for her?' he asked Rawhead.

'The perfect spot.'

*

They drove to Disley to drop Maddy off at Billy's sister's house. It was no chore for Carole – she adored Maddy and had always wanted a daughter of her own. And even Carole, hardly Billy's greatest fan, could see her brother was suffering. 'She'll be back. I'm sure she will,' she told him, kissing Billy awkwardly on the cheek. 'Try not to worry too much.'

Rawhead waited outside the house, pretending to be a cab driver. Billy was crying again when he got back into the car. That was how he was at the moment; the slightest sign of sympathy from anyone was enough to set him off.

When they arrived at Billy's house, a Mondeo estate was sitting on the drive. Billy's stomach churned. He thought it was the police. But it was some young black guy in a leather jacket. He and Rawhead seemed to know each other.

'Billy, this is Brando. He's a friend of mine. I'm busy tonight, I've got things to do. But Brando here is going to stay with you, make sure you've got everything you need.'

'No, he's fucking not.' said Billy.

'You'll hardly notice I'm here,' said Brando.

'What? You think I won't notice a six-foot black man sitting in my living room?'

Brando thought this was funny.

'You need someone with you,' said Rawhead.

'No, I don't,' said Billy. 'I need to be on my own. When bad things happen, I don't want to see anyone, I don't want to talk. I just want to go to bed and curl up in a ball. That's what I'm going to do now.

'I'm not suicidal, if that's what you think. If I was, I'd have croaked years ago.'

Brando met Rawhead's eyes and shrugged. 'The man seems to know his own mind.'

Rawhead sighed. 'OK, Billy. You win. But I'm not happy.'

'Who the fuck is?' said Billy.

'Stupid people,' said Brando. 'Lots of stupid people are happy.'

*

Detective Superintendent Harrop was in her office, eating a meat and potato pie and staring into space. Since smoking had been banned in the building, her daily pie consumption had tripled. Hughes walked in. He was smiling, and Harrop knew right away he'd found something.

'What the fuck are you looking so happy about?' she said. 'Did your fiancée take it up the shitter last night?'

Immune to Harrop's rudeness, Hughes held a glossy photograph under her nose. At first glance, it looked like a man falling out of a tree. She looked again, realized the man had no head and shoved the picture away. 'Prick! I'm having my lunch.'

'Don't you want to know what it's about?'

'Is it connected with this inquiry?'

'It might be.'

'Might isn't good enough. Is it or isn't it?'

'Yes.'

'Hughes, if you're lying, I'll twat you.'

'It's about Billy Dye . . .'

'Aw, Jesus.'

'This body was found in Scotland in January. Near a place called the Skene Castle Hotel.'

'So what?'

'Billy Dye stayed at the Skene Castle in January. He got married there.'

'Yeah? At the same time?'

'A week before the body was found.'

For a moment Harrop looked interested. Then her eyes glazed over. 'Nah. He gets married, walks into the woods and kills somebody to celebrate? Doesn't make sense. Any ID on the headless horseman?'

'David Brett. An unemployed labourer. Known to the police

for using high-powered binoculars to gaze into women's bedrooms.'

'A fucking peeping tom.'

'Right.'

'So you think Billy Dye caught this guy watching the bride
take off her wedding dress and taught him a lesson by hanging
him upside down from a tree and chopping his head off?'

Hughes shrugged, disappointed by her reaction.

'What do the Scottish bastards think?'

'They're working on the theory that it was one of the Glasgow
gangs. A kind of underworld execution.'

'Ah.' She nodded, sarcasm tickling the corners of her mouth.
'So they don't think the bridegroom did it?'

'No.'

'Then why are you wasting my time with this shit?

Hughes blushed. For some reason, the red glow of shame
only coloured his lower jowls. 'You've always taught me to go
with my instincts. That's what I'm doing. At the very least, the
man's a jinx. When he's in the vicinity, people die. It may just
be coincidence. But my instincts say it's more.'

Harrop cracked open a can of coke, swallowed half of it and
let out a volcanic belch. 'Fair enough.'

Hughes started smiling again. 'You believe me?'

'I do *not* believe you. But because it's you and you're chal-
lenged in various debilitating ways, I'll take pity on you. You've
got two days. Forty-eight hours to prove me wrong.'

*

Chef was lying in his morning bath trying to work out how
much money he had. The income from the porn and the drugs
alone had probably made him close on eight million. Then there
was the skew, at rates of interest only a desperate moron would

pay. Fortunately, there were enough desperate morons in Manchester to bring in another million and a half a year. Selling off stolen goods at knock-down prices brought in at least five hundred thousand, and that was in a bad year.

Chef could have retired there and then had he not been addicted to power. He enjoyed being surrounded by tough gorillas who blushed and stammered when he called them dickless. He liked the show-business glamour of being notorious. When you were a gang boss, especially a polite gang boss who didn't break wind in female company, you got invited to fancy dinners.

Although Chef appreciated the attention of women, he only fucked prostitutes. Unlike wives, stinks were actually grateful when you only took thirty seconds to come.

On the whole, life was good.

The only downside of being in charge was that sooner or later, someone always thought they could send you to the Blue Swoon. That was why whenever Chef took a bath, there was always a gun sitting next to the soap dish. Just in case some opportunistic little cunt was angling for instant promotion.

So when the bathroom door opened and Boner walked in, Chef sat up suddenly, sploshing water everywhere as he groped for his weapon.

Boner, a gaunt young Asian, bore the racial slurs of his fellow gangsters with good-natured fortitude. Usually nothing ruffled him. But when he saw that Chef was pointing an automatic at him, he danced an excitable little jig. 'Fuck! Fuck! What the fuck are you doing?'

'What the fuck are *you* doing?'

'Sorry, boss. I was bringing you this.' Boner held out a cordless phone. 'There's a call for you. From a woman.'

'What woman?'

'She wouldn't say. She just said that if I said, "Death awaits us all," you'd understand.'

Grudgingly, Chef accepted the call. 'In future, knock.'

'Sorry, boss.'

As soon as Chef held the phone to his ear, the Spirit spoke. Her voice sounded husky and tired. 'I'm at his house. No sign of him yet, but he's been here recently.'

'How do you know?'

'I found a dying man in his cellar.'

'Who was he?'

'I didn't find out. He was too far gone.'

There was a silence. She started to say something, then thought better of it.

'What's on your mind?' said Chef.

'It's probably nothing.'

'Tell me anyway.'

'Just that I asked this guy . . . I asked him who shot him.'

'And?'

'I got a very strange answer. He named the author of this book I'd been looking at five minutes before.'

Chef was listening intently. 'What book?'

'*Dracula*. It's by Bram Stoker.'

'I know,' said Chef impatiently. 'I can read too, you know. So he said Bram Stoker put him in the cellar?'

'No. He said he'd been put there by *Abraham* Stoker. That was Bram Stoker's real name.'

Chef felt his heart speeding up. 'Jesus Christ.'

'What is it?'

Now Chef was sweating so much he needed a second bath. 'It's also the name of a tool who works for Little Malc.'

In a flood of recall, Chef saw the skull ring on Stoker's finger. He realized now why the ring had made him uneasy. He had seen that same ring on Billy Dye's finger.

'This Stoker. You wouldn't happen to know where he is right now?' asked the Spirit.

*

Rawhead waited until it was dark. He approached the vicarage from the east, coming over the fields as the night scent rose from the hedgerows and the the first stars appeared in the sky. He knew in his heart that a great enemy was waiting and that he might not survive the encounter. Paradoxically, the idea of his own death gave him a certain peace. He had lived without fear and would die without fear. How many could say the same?

He crossed the churchyard, entering his garden via the gap in the hedge. The house looked as empty and desolate as always. It was uncared for, but not because he did not care for it. He yearned for its shadows, its aura of decay. A house that was clean, bright and smartly furnished would not be a fit place for ghosts.

Rawhead drew his Ruger, knocked off the safety catch and unlocked the kitchen door. He turned the knob and kicked the door open. There was no one in the kitchen. The cellar door was locked. Rawhead was curious about the cellar, but knew he had to secure the house first. So he walked from room to room, searching for signs of an intruder.

In his bedroom, there was that fragrance again. The smell of violets. He scoured the room, sniffing in every corner, until he traced the smell to his pillow. Rawhead was stunned. Who had been sleeping in his bed? The sheets hadn't been changed for years. Who would *want* to sleep in his bed?

In the library, he noticed a gap on the shelf reserved for his most precious first editions. With a start, he realized *Dracula* was missing.

He went down to the cellar. As a precaution he left both

doors open and put the keys in his pocket. Then, head bowed, he walked down the passage to the gap in the wall and surveyed the dead faces below.

It was as he had expected. There was a fresh body down there. A middle-aged female traffic warden in full uniform, her hat at a jaunty angle, face staring upwards in cold disapproval. She had been shot in the heart.

Rawhead was amazed. The corpse was so perfectly positioned that it might have been his own work. He, the stalker, was being stalked. It was now obvious to him that he could not leave the house. He must stay here, keeping vigil, until his enemy returned.

As this thought occurred to him, Rawhead heard a quiet bump behind him. He glanced round and saw that the door at the end was now closed.

Holding the Ruger steady, he crept down the passage towards the door.

*

On the other side of the door, the Spirit waited, crouching low, the Sig resting on her left knee. Not in front of the door, but slightly to one side. There was a full minute of silence, then three shots ripped through the door, spraying splintered oak over the floor, blasting down dust and gossamer from the ceiling.

The Spirit had expected this.

Moving muscle by muscle, inching sideways with excrutiating care, the Spirit crept round until she was in front of the door. And then she waited, eyes fixed on the wooden doorknob. Ten minutes passed. Twenty. Her knees and thighs began to ache. She placed her left hand on the floor to take some of the weight.

Not daring to breathe or move. Because she knew what was coming.

Once or twice she thought she could hear him breathing. A floorboard creaked overhead and she almost fired, but held on, knowing she must not act until she saw the door handle move. In the end, she was not prompted to act by any visual warning. The door to the passage tremoured. That was enough. The Spirit loosed all seven rounds, aiming at where she guessed Rawhead's chest would be.

When the sound of the shots died away, the silence returned.

Then she waited for a great deal longer, listening out for telltale moans or sighs. There was nothing. The Spirit knew it must be over, but still she lingered. In the end, it was sheer boredom that brought her to her feet. She wiped the sweat out of her eyes with her scarf, then bound it tightly over her mouth and nostrils. After reloading the Sig, she reached for the handle and opened the door.

*

All things considered, Chef didn't think this woman appreciated the subtle dynamics of their business relationship. He was her employer, it wasn't the other way around. He could have been doing anything that evening. He could have been setting up a business deal with the heads of all the New York families. OK, so maybe he wasn't.

The point was, Chef called the shots; no one else.

Because of this, Chef contemplated not travelling to Dudloe at all. If he kept an appointment that she'd called, surely that would compound her view that she held the upper hand? Conversely, not turning up might lead that surly bitch to assume he was scared. In the end, he came up with an excellent compromise.

He was accompanied by Boner, the Philosopher, Bryan and Average. All five men were packing. Chef was carrying a derringer, just the kind of dainty little weapon to shoot a woman with. As the Rolls pulled up outside the dark vicarage, Chef's mobile rang. It was her. 'Is that your car outside?' she said.

'Yes, it's my car,' he said. Then he hung up.

'What the fuck is going on, boss?' said the Philosopher.

'You see that house?' said Chef. 'You're going to go inside it.'

'Why me?'

'You know Stoker? The guy that works for Little Malc? The one who told you to go fuck yourself?'

'Yeah.'

'I want to know if he's in there.'

'You setting me up?'

'No,' said Chef. 'The guy can't hurt you. He's swooned. I just want you to identify the body.'

'Why me?'

'Because I trust you. Because you're my number two.'

'Oh, fuck,' said the Philosopher.

'Just go to the front door,' said Chef. 'A woman's going to meet you.'

'What woman?'

'You don't need to know. Just go in, view the body, come out again.'

The other tools sat in stark silence, relieved that none of them was Chef's number two. Boner peered at the house and thought he saw a ghostly light flitting from window to window.

Chef patted the Philosopher's shoulder. 'If you're sure it's Stoker, hundred per cent sure, tell the woman "four working days".'

'Who is she?'

'Nobody. A go-between. OK?'

'OK.'

The Philosopher opened the door and got out of the car. 'And make sure you don't fucking drive away.'

Average laughed.

'Hey, man,' said Boner. 'Be careful. Don't get yourself boxed.'
The Philosopher shrugged. 'If it happens, it happens.'
No wonder they called him the Philosopher.

*

She met him at the door, a small, dark woman in black, holding a powerful flashlight. She seemed supremely confident, which made the Philosopher even more nervous. As they walked through the house, she turned on all the lights. In the kitchen she passed the Philosopher a clean tea towel.
'What's this for?'
'Hold it over your face,' she said. 'The smell down there is pretty extreme.'
He didn't know what she was talking about, not until she unlocked the door to the passage. When he saw the rats and the flies, the Philosopher didn't want to go in there.
'Where the fuck is he?' he said, his voice muffled by the tea towel.
'Just follow me,' she said. 'Mind your head.'
At the end of the passage she shone her lamp down into the pit and told the Philosopher to take a look. The sight of all the bodies made the Philosopher reel. He covered his face with his hands and felt something crawling over his knuckles.
'Did you see him?' said the woman.
'Jesus fucking Christ.' He peered at her through his fingers. 'What's going on?'
'Did you see Stoker?'
He shivered. 'What is this fucking place?'
She repeated her question.
'No,' he admitted.
'Take another look.'
She shone the torch into the vault. With a monumental effort of will, the Philosopher leaned through the gap and looked

down. The cadavers were all colours: black, blue, green and yellow. And in the centre of the corpses, dead but uncorrupted, lay the man who had accompanied Little Malc to the restaurant.

The Philosopher was sure it was the same guy. Stoker. Hands joined over his open belly, intestines erupting through his fingers.

'Is that him?' said the woman.

'Yeah,' said the Philosopher weakly, already turning away. All he wanted to do now was breathe clean air.

When he got back to the car, he couldn't talk. Not at first. He sat in the front seat next to Chef, sweating and breathing heavily. Chef had to give him brandy.

'Did you see him?' said Chef.

The Philosopher nodded.

'You're sure it was him?'

The Philosopher opened his mouth to say, 'Yes'. Instead he threw up, all over Chef, the windscreen and the beautiful cream upholstery.

15

Oft have I sigh'd for him that heares me not;
Who absent hath both love and mee forgot.

'The Third Book of Ayres', Thomas Campion (1567–1620)

As soon as Hughes had shown Harrop his homework assignment, she picked up the phone and put an internal call through to Alan Cheetham, the assistant chief constable. Twenty minutes later, Hughes and Harrop were sitting in Cheetham's office, surrounded by framed certificates. Top of his year at Hendon College, record fundraiser for the Police Benevolent Fund, winner of the Manchester City Council Humanitarian Policing Award. It made Harrop feel sick.

Cheetham and Harrop didn't like each other much, but Cheetham always pretended she was a personal favourite of his.

'Janet, what can I do for you?'

Cheetham had pale blue eyes and thinning hair the colour of wet sand. He parted his hair at the side, combing it unconvincingly over his bare scalp. He liked to smile and engage in direct eye contact, as if hoping, by an effort of will, to divert attention from his comb-over.

'Or what can you do for me?'

'Well, it's Detective Sergeant Hughes, really,' said Harrop. 'He's the one who's been up all night.'

'Not quite all night,' protested Hughes modestly.

Harrop supplied Cheetham with the background. Then Hughes, flustered by the knowledge that the next few minutes might exert a crucial influence over the rest of his career, consulted a single typed page resting in his lap.

'So I did some research into Mr Dye's past, sir. It makes alarming reading. Two years ago his literary agent was murdered. Her head was cut off and left in her office. The rest of her body was never found. At the time, Dye was known to be unhappy with his agent and his career. Which might account for the disappearance of his publisher at about the same time. The publisher has also never been found.'

Cheetham opened his mouth to speak. But Hughes hadn't finished.

'About the same time, Dye's closest friend, a constable in the Cheshire Constabulary, mysteriously vanishes. Also never found. This January, a headless man is found hanging in a wood while Dye is staying in a nearby hotel. Then two police officers and Dye's next-door neighbours are shot dead. And that's not all.

'Last week the producer of Dye's TV show disappears – this happens after Dye tells the producer to "go fuck himself" during a meeting. This morning I contacted our colleagues in Cheshire to find out if they had anything to add. And, lo and behold, I learn that *Mr Dye's wife* has now joined the ranks of the disappeared. He reported her missing yesterday.'

By the time Hughes had concluded his litany of misfortunes, the bland smile on Cheetham's face had been replaced by a look of consternation. 'I must say, I find this rather incredible. Janet, why hasn't this person been arrested?'

Hughes looked at Harrop. Harrop coughed and stared down at her shoes.

*

On Cheetham's authorization, two Armed Response Vehicles were despatched to Billy Dye's Prestbury home. Each vehicle contained four officers armed with Heckler and Koch MP5s,

211

capable of firing eight hundred rounds a minute. In addition to these assault rifles, the officers had access to M1 carbines and Walther P990 handguns.

The road outside Billy's house was cordoned off. A police helicopter, also containing a marksman, hovered overhead in case the suspect attempted a getaway. Harrop and Hughes, watching the proceedings from a safe distance, used radios to liaise with officers on the ground and in the air. But the actual arrest was commandeered by the Armed Response Unit. Four officers circled the house while the remaining four kicked down the door.

The ground floor was clear. They found a locked door upstairs. An officer fired a burst of three to remove the lock, then kicked the door open. Inside the room, they found Billy Dye sitting on the lavatory. Billy exhibited no surprise. He was smiling inanely, stoned out of his brain.

'Get face down on the floor,' the officer commanded.

'Aw! I'm having a shit,' complained Billy mildly.

'On the floor. Now!'

Billy lay down, trousers round his ankles. 'I suppose this is about me not buying a TV licence?'

The first officer cuffed Billy's hands behind his back while another pointed an MP5 at his head.

'Excuse me,' said Billy politely. 'Would one of you be kind enough to wipe my arse?'

*

They locked Billy in a cell while they searched his house. Finding nothing more incriminating on the premises than an ounce of antique dope, they took him to an interview room. Irrationally, Billy kept waiting for Rawhead to rescue him. Surely it was only a matter of time before he heard the gunshots and policemen screaming?

As the hours passed, Billy began to see that Rawhead's intervention was unlikely. His mood passed from disappointment to sorrow, settling on defiance and quiet resolve. Rawhead was right. The police were the enemy, to be resisted at all costs. Lacking the imagination to think for themselves, they merely upheld laws created by the right-wing elite. Like any ordinary bastards, the police didn't yearn for justice. They yearned for more money, longer holidays, less work, shiny new cars and sexual intercourse without responsibility. Telling them the truth made no more sense than confessing to a camel turd.

Billy wasn't sure how long he could protect himself and Rawhead. Billy was a blabbermouth, always had been. Apart from that one time when he was fourteen and the police had asked him to bear witness against Rawhead. To shield his friend, Billy had stayed silent. If he'd done it once, he could do it again.

Hughes offered to provide Billy with a solicitor. Billy declined, knowing he'd end up with Coco the Clown. Harrop and Hughes sat opposite him in the interview room. The two detectives were visibly encouraged by Billy's refusal to accept legal representation, joking with him and offering him tea and biscuits before the tape started rolling.

'Do you know why you're here, William?' asked Harrop.

'No one calls me William,' said Billy.

'Why? It's your name, isn't it?'

'I don't like it. Any more than you like being called Ginger Minge.'

Billy expected Harrop to get angry. Instead she smiled, pleased that he was making a twat of himself on tape.

'What would you like us to call you?' said Hughes.

Billy mimed masturbation. Hughes leaned towards the microphone. 'At this point, the interviewee made an obscene gesture.'

Then Hughes explained why Billy had been arrested. He talked down to Billy as if he was a child. All those poor people, gone forever. Didn't Billy realize how naughty it was to kill people?

'I'm in the dark as much as you are,' said Billy. 'All I can think is, it's something to do with the Priesthood.'

'The Priesthood?' repeated Harrop.

And he told them how he'd accepted a commission to ghost Priest's memoirs, omitting to mention that Priest had ordered his death.

'Can you verify this?' asked Harrop.

'Yep. I've still got the interview tapes,' said Billy.

Harrop gave Hughes a glance of disgust. Hughes blushed, knowing what she was thinking. That, despite all his strenuous enterprise, his research into Billy Dye was woefully incomplete.

'The project fizzled out,' said Billy. 'Priest and me couldn't agree on what form the book should take. I wanted to write about a gangster. He wanted to be shown as a humanitarian. Every morning he sent his chauffeur to pick me up. One morning the car didn't show and Priest stopped returning my calls. It was around this time my agent was murdered and my publisher and my best mate went missing.'

'Who was your best mate?' said Hughes.

'Detective Constable Holt, of the Cheshire Police,' said Billy. 'I miss him a lot.'

'Are you still in contact with Mr Priest's, er, bedfellows?' asked Hughes.

'No. I've had no contact with them since April. Although . . .'

'Yes?'

'It was probably a bad mistake, but I used my research into Priest and his gang as the basis for a TV series. The show's been cancelled now. The production team have been receiving anonymous threats. And, as you know, Mr Crème went missing.'

'What about your wife? Where do you think she is?'

'I don't know. I'm very worried about her. She did exactly

the same thing before our daughter was born. Just walked out on me.'

'Can you prove that?' said Harrop wearily.

'Check it with her mum and dad. Talk to her doctor. Nikki suffers from depression. When it gets bad, this is what she does. She runs away.'

Harrop and Hughes sat there in sullen silence. Dye's story had the depressing ring of truth about it.

'It isn't illegal, is it?' asked Billy innocently. 'To try to write about gangsters? I hope I haven't broken any laws.'

Pushing his luck as always, Billy winked at Harrop, who felt like vaulting over the table and strangling him. If the Priesthood was involved, she knew that her chances of wrapping up this case were non-existent. Not only did Chef control crime in Manchester. He controlled the chief constable of the Greater Manchester Police.

Harrop had clashed with Chef once before. A man had been shot in the legs for failing to repay a loan. The Priesthood was clearly responsible. But no one would talk, the victim included. Harrop's only reward for weeks of work had been razor blades in her mail, derision from her colleagues and a stern reprimand from her superiors.

Colleagues told Harrop how lucky she'd been. Lucky to have escaped with her job and her life. In future, they said, don't pick fights with the big boys. That way, she might live to collect her pension.

But that was the thing about Harrop. She never listened.

16

Come live with mee, and be my love,
And we will all the pleasures prove

'The Passionate Shepherd to His Love',
Christopher Marlowe (1564–1593)

Rawhead had not been as easy to kill as the Spirit had hoped.

After emptying her gun into the door, she had waited a long time. Listening for the slightest indication of her enemy's survival.

An enormous spider crawled over the ceiling above her head. The cellar had grown so silent that she could hear the arachnid's legs brushing against the plaster. Its legs made a soft clicking sound.

Finally, feeling she was being overcautious, the Spirit tied the scarf over her nose and mouth, slotted a fresh magazine into the Sig 220 and turned the key in the lock. There was no answering volley of bullets.

The door opened by itself, its hinges whining. The Spirit leaned in from the side, shining the torch into the tunnel for an instant. The corpse she had expected to see lying on the ground was not there. It was not anywhere. With her trigger finger poised, she shone her light all over the dark passage. There was no sign of Rawhead.

The Spirit fired a round into the corner behind the door, just in case her quarry had learned his survival techniques from the Famous Five. But Rawhead was not hiding behind the door. Nor was he hanging from the roof.

Indolent, bloated flies flew in and out of the torch beam. As the Spirit drew near the gap in the wall ahead, a jewel of sweat dropped from her left armpit and slid over her ribs. Not once did she break concentration. Not even when a rat brushed against her left foot.

The torch beam danced over a plaque on the wall of the vault. The plaque had a Latin inscription, but the Spirit was too preoccupied to read it. She leaned over to shine her beam into the pit and saw what looked like four fingers clutching the ledge. Then another hand seized her left wrist and, with lethal force, yanked her through the gap.

The torch fell first and the Spirit followed it, firing uselessly into the dark. She couldn't tell whether he had slipped or jumped, but Rawhead fell with her. Then they were both rolling in a malestrom of limbs and jellied putrescence. The scarf had come loose. She opened her mouth to breathe, only to gulp down the foullest air she had ever tasted.

She fumbled around in the dark for the gun and accidentally placed her hand in what felt like a wet, cold mouth. She cried out and snatched her hand away.

A pale funereal glow defined the edges of the hole in the wall above. Thinking to climb to safety, she started to wade through the corpses, but they shifted and stirred as she moved, sucking her down. The more she struggled, the deeper she sank. When she was buried up to her waist, she felt Rawhead's hand curl around her throat. Just one enormous hand, squeezing the life out of her.

The torch lay close by, shining into a dead man's gaping face. She groped for it, thinking to use it as a weapon. Instead, she touched the illuminated head. The head rocked under her hand. The Spirit realized it was not attached to a body. Clutching the hair, she swung the skull round, smashing it into her enemy's face. Rawhead grunted and momentarily eased his grip. She hurled the head into the darkness he occupied and made another attempt to reach the wall.

This time she succeeded and began to climb, finding hand-holds where there were none. She was halfway up the wall when he grabbed her right foot and dragged her back down into the odorous mass.

She lunged at him, punching wildly, snarling in his face like a crazed animal. Rawhead responded by locking her in a deathly embrace that pinioned her arms and made further resistance impossible. Even then, she still found the strength to butt him in the face. His grip tightened, and he moved forward, forcing her down. Now she was on her back and he was lying on top of her.

It was then that Rawhead kissed her. It was not a kiss of conquest or mockery. It was a tender, searching kiss that asked a simple question. When it was over, Rawhead rolled off her and waited.

The Spirit leaned across and returned the kiss. And then, their brief courtship over, the two murderers consummated their love on a bed of human carrion.

*

It had been the Spirit's idea for Rawhead to play dead.

When the Philosopher had viewed the body and Chef and his men had gone, the Spirit dropped a rope through the gap in the wall. Rawhead threw aside the cold entrails he'd borrowed from Sirus and tore off his maggot-infested clothes. Then, naked, he climbed to safety. He took a long, hot shower to wash away the stench of death. Later, in clean clothes, he took tea with the Spirit in the parlour.

The Spirit stood in the centre of the room. Rawhead was sitting on the sofa. 'Congratulations, you're now officially a corpse,' she announced in her leisurely, unexcitable drawl. 'What are your plans?'

'I'm going to create the greatest gang Manchester has ever seen.'

'Yeah? Who's the frontman?'

'Little Malc.'

When the Spirit had finished laughing, Rawhead said, 'I'm not joking. He's personable. People like him. *I* like him.'

'And he's easy to manipulate.'

'Yeah. Let someone else have the glory. I'll just have the money.'

'Why not take the reins yourself?'

'I've dabbled in public life,' he declared flatly. 'It doesn't suit me.'

She sat down beside him. 'And what's Chef going to think about this? Do you have any idea what you're starting?'

'Yes. I'm starting a full-scale war. You're going to help me.'

'How?'

'You can stay at home and do the cleaning and the ironing.'

She didn't laugh.

'We'll be partners, working side by side. For the time being, you can carry on working for Chef,' said Rawhead. 'It'd help to have someone in the enemy camp.'

'This may surprise you,' she said, 'but I was hoping to retire.'

He shook his head. 'One hundred thousand isn't enough to retire on.'

'I'm getting double that.'

Rawhead shot her a sideways glance. 'I think you're forgetting my share.'

After a moment's pause she nodded. 'But, remember, money can't buy you happiness.'

Rawhead smiled. 'Maybe I'm not looking for happiness.'

17

Love, thou art Absolute sole lord
Of Life & Death.

'A Hymn to the Name and Honour of the Admirable Sainte Teresa',
Richard Crashaw (1612–1649)

Little Malc hadn't been sleeping well. When he did sleep, it was only for an hour at a time. On the night of Rawhead's visit, Malc had returned from the club early. He was in bed by two. By three fifteen he was awake again, so tense that he could hardly breathe. He didn't need pills. He knew what the problem was.

At three thirty Little Malc went downstairs to make himself a drink and there was the problem, sitting in his favourite armchair. Rawhead in a long black coat, looking relaxed and at home. Little Malc turned grey at the sight of him.

'Sorry I haven't been at work,' said Rawhead, 'but I'm back now.'

'How did you get in?'

'Chubb locks are very easy to pick.'

Little Malc just stared at him.

'I know I shouldn't come into your home like this, I'm sorry,' said Rawhead calmly. 'But, for the time being, I can't be seen at the club. And I needed to talk to you.'

Little Malc stood there for a few moments, not daring to move. A short guy in a dressing gown that exposed his hairless chest and his fat pink legs. When the spell broke and Malc walked into the kitchen, Rawhead followed him.

'I'm making some tea,' said Malc. 'Do you want some?'

'Sure.'

Little Malc opened a drawer. When he turned round, there was a large carving knife in his hand. He took a lunge at Rawhead, who grabbed Malc's wrist and twisted it expertly. The knife clattered to the floor. Childishly determined, Little Malc stooped to retrieve it. Rawhead kicked the knife out of reach.

'You've been talking to Chef,' said Rawhead.

'He told me you were dead. You fucking deserve to be,' said Little Malc. 'I know who you are, I know what you've done.'

'What have I done?' said Rawhead. Making him say it out loud.

'You killed my dad. Didn't you? You murdering cunt.'

'No.'

'You are a lying fucking bastard.'

'I never touched your father. I tried, but I could never get near him. He was killed by someone close to him.'

'I know it was . . .' Little Malc tried to say 'you'. He was so nervous that the word mutated into an enormous belch.

'Chef killed your old man,' said Rawhead. 'Everyone in Manchester seems to know that apart from you.'

'You evil twat!' Little Malc flew at Rawhead, fists flailing. Rawhead didn't retaliate, just slapped Little Malc's hands away until he got tired.

'Chef likes setting people on fire. That's what he did to your father.'

'No, he didn't! He didn't!' It was almost a plea.

'I promise you, I absolutely swear, that I'm telling you the truth.'

'Get out. Get out of my house.'

Rawhead unbuttoned his coat. From his belt, he removed a gun with a very long barrel.

'I've got a family,' blurted Little Malc.

'I know,' said Rawhead.

He opened the cylinder to show Little Malc the fat shiny cartridges, then passed him the gun.

'What's this for?'

'I'm putting my life in your hands. That's how much I trust you. If you can't trust me, then you may as well pull the trigger.'

Little Malc meant to do it. He truly did. With a trembling hand, he pointed the cowboy gun at Rawhead's heart and was about to shoot, when he thought how much his wife and his little girls would miss him when he was in prison. Then he wondered if Chef would ever take the kind of risk that Rawhead was taking now. Little Malc knew the answer before he asked himself the question.

Then Little Malc thought of that special way Chef's men had of looking at him, their expressions wavering between pity and scorn. He imagined his dad, screaming as he burned to death. Little Malc put down the gun and started to cry.

Rawhead held him while he sobbed.

'I'm fucked,' wailed Little Malc. 'Everything's fucking well fucked.'

'Listen to me,' said Rawhead. 'You're going to rule this city. Just like your father before you.'

When the tears subsided, Rawhead passed Malc a piece of kitchen towel. Little Malc blew his nose. 'You mean it? You really see me as a leader?'

'It's your destiny,' said Rawhead.

*

Once a month, Chef's men toured the bars and restaurants of Manchester, picking up goodwill. Goodwill was their name for the regular payments received from businesses in the city centre. Generally, people showed goodwill, knowing that if they didn't, they'd end up in a hospital bed, suffering from criminal damage, only to die of criminal neglect.

There was little violence. The Priesthood stayed away from Moss Side and Chinatown, leaving the blacks and the Chinese to be exploited by their own kind. The rest of Manchester was theirs.

Chef didn't like to think of it as fear money. He preferred to think of it as legitimate sponsorship. The city's publicans and restaurateurs were sponsoring his efforts to make Manchester safe at night. This meant maiming any thief, dealer or pimp who wasn't Priesthood-approved. In his own way, Chef did as much to clean up the streets as any policeman.

To Chef's men, picking up goodwill payments was demeaning work. In exchange for a small reduction, many of the city's businesses had been persuaded to contribute by direct debit. This way, the monthly donations went into a Priesthood bank account without the need for unsavoury human contact. But this always left people like Dad Cheeseman who didn't have a bank account and only ever dealt in cash.

So, every month, someone had to tour the town in person.

This month it was Average's turn.

Average was not in a good mood. He'd become a gangster for the thrills. Collecting rent from paupers and old men in bad wigs was not his idea of excitement. Plus the fucking sun was shining, his fucking balls were itching and a gold tooth he'd recently had fitted was beginning to fucking well hurt.

So when Average walked into Dad's place and found a nigger sitting alone at the bar, he was not happy. The nigger looked vaguely familiar. He was acting familiar too, sipping a nice cool beer and behaving like he owned the place.

'Hey, chimp. Where's the fucking zookeeper?'

'In the elephant house, feeding your wife,' said the nigger amiably.

Average was annoyed. Chimps were not supposed to be funnier than white men. It went against nature.

'Aren't there any human beings around I can talk to?' said Average.

The cool nigger just smiled.

'Where's Dad?'

'Dad put me in charge.'

'Then give us the money and I might let you live.'

'Well, there's a slight problem,' said the nigger. Still calm. Still polite. 'Mr Cheeseman isn't happy with the service he's been getting. So he's taken his business elsewhere.'

'Get mourned!'

'It's his right as a consumer. This is a free-market economy. If a man pays for protection, he's entitled to protection. Mr Cheeseman got messed up pretty good by some people you know, and you boys didn't do a thing about it.'

'So fucking what?'

'Also, your boss gave my boss his blessing. He told Malc to go ahead, set up his own outfit, if he could find anyone to back him.'

'Even if he did, what's it fucking got to do with you?' said Average. 'You're a nigger. The niggers rule Moss Side, end of fucking story.'

'Yeah. But I'm a nigger of the future. I work with white guys.'

'Then you're a fucking Uncle Tom.' Average suddenly remembered where he'd seen the guy before. 'I know you. I've seen you at Little Malc's.' He laughed in derision. 'You work on the door, you're a fucking doorknob. Ha! I *knew* I'd fucking seen you.'

'You got me, man. I work for Little Malc. My name's Brando.' Brando extended his hand in friendship.

Average didn't want to play.

'And I'm fucking James Dean. Brando? Ha! That's a fancy name for a fucking nigger doorknob.'

Still laughing, Average tried to walk round the bar to the till. That was when it happened.

If a fighter's good, you don't see the blow coming. All you feel is the impact. That was what happened to Average. He heard a rustle of fabric and felt a whump on his chin that rattled his brains and blurred his vision. It was a straight left jab, but to Average it felt like running headlong into a concrete post. Wrestling with nausea, he was forced to seize the counter to stop himself falling.

The cool nigger was very nice about it. He steered Average onto a bar stool and poured him a nice glass of chilled mineral water. 'Sorry, man. I got my orders, just like anyone else.'

Average sipped the water. He didn't say anything, didn't know what the fuck to say anyway. After a few deep breaths, he got up and started walking.

Seeing that the guy was unsteady, Brando escorted him to the stairs. All the way, you could see Average plotting his counter-attack. It was that obvious. He waited until they were at the top of the stairs, then he grabbed Brando's neck and tried to ram his head into the wall.

Brando slapped Average's hand away and punched him again. Not hard, just hard enough. Average fell down the stairs backwards, hitting his head on every riser until he reached the bottom. It was like a scene from *Laurel and Hardy*. Except when Stan and Olly fell downstairs, they didn't spatter blood on the walls.

*

Early the next morning, the police let Billy go. He arrived home to find Rawhead parked outside his house. Rawhead was sitting in his BMW, reading Billy's latest novel. Billy opened the car door and sat beside him. Rawhead's face was cold and stern.

'Did you tell them anything?' said Rawhead.

'Did I tell who what?'

'Don't shit me, Billy. They took you in for questioning.'

'How do you know?'

'Because the police never tidy up after themselves. Your house is wrecked, they've searched every inch of it. So I'm guessing they put you in a cell while they ripped up your floorboards.'

Billy swallowed nervously. Rawhead remained still, not moving his eyes from Billy's face. 'So what did you tell them?'

'Nothing,' said Billy. 'Not about you, not about me. Absolutely fuck all.'

Rawhead nodded. He could see that Billy was telling the truth.

'I only told them stuff they could check. That Malcolm Priest hired me as a ghostwriter. And that people only started dying after Priest had sacked me.'

'That's good,' said Rawhead. 'That's very good. There may be hope for you yet.'

*

That afternoon Rawhead drove Billy and his daughter to Slippery Stones near Macclesfield Forest. They ambled beside the brook on a mild, sunny afternoon. There was no one else in sight. Rawhead and Maddy threw stones into the water. Billy, suddenly overcome, couldn't stop crying.

Rawhead picked up the child in his left arm. With his free hand he passed Billy a tissue. Billy blew his nose loudly. 'This is really where she's buried? It's beautiful. You couldn't have picked a nicer spot.'

Rawhead nodded. 'But I'm not going to tell you exactly where the grave is. Because you're too much of a blabbermouth. So don't ask me.'

'OK.'

'You're doing the right thing, Billy. Nikki wouldn't have wanted you to go to prison. As long as you continue to keep your mouth shut, you'll be fine.'

'What did you do with the gun?'

'No one will ever find it.'

'I loved that Smith & Wesson.'

'I think you loved your wife more.'

'God, yeah.' Billy tried to smile.

Rawhead wasn't angry with Billy any more. All he felt now was affection.

Maddy had dropped the soft toy she was holding. Rawhead stooped to pick it up and Billy noticed the scar tissue on the back of his hand. The words tumbled out before Billy had time to consider them. 'And to think I tried to kill you.'

For an instant Rawhead tensed and a shadow crossed his barbarous face. Then the danger passed. Pressing the toy into Maddy's hands, he looked directly into Billy's eyes. 'That's all in the past, now.'

Billy shook his head in disbelief. 'You knew what I'd done and you still stood by me? Why?'

Rawhead smiled. The smile contained nothing but warmth.

'I mean, look at me,' said Billy. He was crying again. 'I'm a twat! A walking disaster. Anything good happens to me, I destroy it. What the fuck do you see in me?'

Rawhead glanced down, saw that Billy was wearing his ring. 'Myself,' he answered simply.

*

Chef and the Philosopher went to visit Average in hospital, where he was being treated for concussion and a bruised ego.

They took him a box of chocolates and a glossy car magazine. Average, bandaged around the head and midriff, lay on his bed in a fetid, overcrowded ward.

'This is what happens if you don't take out medical insurance,' joked the Philosopher.

Average didn't laugh. Briefly, in a hoarse and weary voice, he related what had happened. Then he closed his eyes and pretended to be asleep.

Later, walking out to the car park, the Philosopher suggested disciplining Little Malc before things got out of hand. 'We could chop the bastard's legs off. Call it "reasonable chastisement". Do it now, right away, so everyone knows what he's being punished for. I'd happily do it myself.'

Chef unlocked the Rolls and eased himself into the back. 'It's too late for that.'

Chef took out his phone and called the bank, hoping to stop the cheque he'd paid the Spirit. The cheque had already cleared. Chef sighed and lit a cigarette. The Philosopher knew this was a bad sign. Chef only smoked when he was troubled.

'What's the problem?' said the Philosopher.

'Just a feeling.' Chef turned to scrutinize the Philosopher, noticing the lines around his eyes, the faint stubble on his jaw. 'Maybe you should tell me now.'

'Tell you what?'

'Exactly what you saw in that house.'

The Philosopher breathed in and out. 'There was a cellar. You know those mass graves in Iraq and Bosnia?'

Requiring no further explanation, Chef nodded and rolled down his window. He blew smoke out into the crisp, cold air.

'That woman,' said the Philosopher. 'She's the Spirit. Am I right?'

Chef nodded cagily.

'And she really killed all those people by herself?'

'No.' Chef smiled. 'No, that was Rawhead's house. The Spirit killed Rawhead. Any other bodies you saw down there were down to him.'

'Then that guy was something else. I mean, you and me, we've done bad things, right? But nothing on that scale. We're absolute fucking choirboys compared to that.'

'But it's over now. He's dead,' said Chef. 'You said so. You saw the body.'

'I think I did.'

'You *think*?' Chef rolled his eyes furiously. 'Four days ago you were certain.'

'It was that guy who came to the restaurant with Little Malc. So if he was Rawhead, that's who I saw.'

Chef still wasn't happy.

'What's up?' said the Philosopher.

'Like I said, just a feeling. I want you to phone round our friends in Leeds and London. See who they've got going spare. We need new people. They need to be able to shoot. Tell 'em we'll pay top prices for the right men. Can you do that?'

'Sure. Why, though?'

Chef gazed out of the window, his eyes black, his long jaw resolute. 'I think we've got a war on our hands.'

*

The Spirit had a flat at Salford Quays, in comfortable walking distance from Diva and Little Malc. Rawhead drove there to pick her up. It was a Sunday afternoon.

She came to the door in a black dress, smelling of parma violets. She was carrying his copy of *Dracula*. 'Thought you might like this back.'

'I imagined you'd have sold it at Sotheby's by now,' he said.

She looked shocked. 'Sold a priceless masterpiece? Never. Someone rich and stupid might have bought it.'

He passed the book back to her. 'Here. It's yours.'

'Why?'

'It's just a book,' he said. 'It's made of paper. And you're real.'

There was suspicion in the Spirit's dark eyes as she slipped the precious volume into her bag.

They got into the car and sat there. Rawhead had never had a real date in his life. He hardly knew what to say to her. 'I don't even know your name.'

'The Spirit of Darkness,' she said. 'But you can call me Spirit.'

'Pleased to meet you. I'm Rawhead.'

'What's your real name?'

'What's yours?'

She didn't answer. They stared at each other for a long time.

'OK, Spirit,' he said finally. 'Where do you want to go?'

'I'm easy,' she said.

'Somehow, I doubt that,' he answered.

'Go anywhere you like,' she said. 'I really don't care.'

Rawhead took her to meet his landlady.

Mrs Munley was delighted to see them both. Blissfully unaware that she was in the presence of the Spirit of Darkness, Mrs Munley referred to the striking young woman on her sofa as Rawhead's 'young lady'.

'And would your young lady care for a piece of Battenberg, Victor?'

'Her name's Spirit, mum.'

' "Spirit". Oh, very unusual. I suppose it must be one of those modern names.' Mrs Munley almost curtseyed as she passed the Spirit a slice of cake. 'In my day, girls were called Elsie or Doris.'

They took tea together, the old woman and her guests, the two most formidable executioners in the world.

'Victor's kept very quiet about you. How long have you two been courting?' Mrs Munley asked the Spirit.

'Since the dawn of time,' said the Spirit, without irony.

'Oh. Very nice.'

The tall lean man with the shining eyes knew what the Spirit meant. It was as if their relationship had always existed. He looked at her now and felt a strange, sick feeling in the pit of his stomach. Was he blessed or cursed? Rawhead wasn't sure.

All Rawhead knew was that he had found his woman. Now they would love and kill together. The loving had spanned many lifetimes. But the killing had barely begun.

Glossary of Priesthood Slang

altar boy – probationary gang member
Blue Swoon, the – Heaven, the afterlife (see 'swooned')
box – to kill
boxed set – sequence of related hits
car – self-propelled road vehicle, usually with four wheels
chimp – any person of ethnic origin, also used as a verb for
    disrespect, as in 'don't chimp me'.
cracked out – driven insane, usually by drugs
deeply sadden – to beat a victim senseless; also used for near-
    fatal wounding
doorknob – bouncer
dribbler – old-age pensioner
feed – money
goodwill – protection money
Jesus – police officer on the take
juice – anything of high quality, as in 'Rawhead is a juice
    murderer'
mourned – dead, as in 'get mourned', meaning 'drop dead', or
    'he got mourned', meaning 'he died'.
reap – less common variant of 'box'
revved – under the influence of drugs
sadden – to beat someone up (see 'deeply sadden')
sadhouse – prison
scud – semen, also prison officer (see 'seeing Sidney')
seeing Sidney – doing time, based on the belief that all prison
    officers are called Sidney Scud

skew – to extort money, particularly as a loan shark, hence 'on the skew'

skewed out – penniless

sop – acolyte, hanger on

spack(s) – police officer, the police force in general

spacko – anything second rate or dishonourable

stink – prostitute

swoon – to die

Tony – coward posing as a tough guy (after Tony Blair, British Prime Minister)

tool – bodyguard, henchman

tug boy – male addicted to masturbation

weebie – weak or cowardly person

Mob sh. 6/6/09